KILLING ME SOFTLY

First Published in the UK 2013 by Belvedere Publishing

Second edition: 2013

*Any reference to real names and places are purely fictional
and are constructs of the author. Any offence the references
produce is unintentional and in no way reflects the reality of
any locations or people involved.*

A copy of this work is available through the British Library.

ISBN: 978-1-909224-59-9

Belvedere Publishing
Mirador
Wearne Lane
Langport
Somerset
TA10 9HB

KILLING ME SOFTLY

BY

ELIZABETH REVILL

Author's acknowledgements

I would like to dedicate the second edition of this, my very first novel, first released in 1995 to the memory of the late James Norrish who was instrumental in encouraging me to pursue my dream of writing. A wonderful musician, teacher and friend he pushed me to keep writing in my spare time. God bless you, James. I miss you so much.

I must also thank my lovely husband, Andrew Spear who made it possible for me to pursue my writing career full time and puts up with me living on my laptop!

Others who must be remembered from that time are my mum and dad and of course my son, Ben Fielder who always appreciated everything I wrote and Gea Annunziata Austin who impressed on me that it was my destiny to write.

This edition is longer than the first and allowed me to fill out some of the scenes and hopefully make it a better novel.

Major thanks to my new Indie publisher, especially Sarah Luddington, who has been instrumental in supporting me in all my endeavours.

The next one in the series to be republished is the sequel Prayer for the Dying.

Prologue
Worthing: 1987

GIRL BUTCHERED ON PIER - screamed the headline. The handsome young man purchased a Gazette from the newsstand and started to read the main story of the day, describing a shocking murder that had taken place the previous evening on the beach under the pier. Police were heralding the killing as the work of a maniac. He tossed the paper onto the back seat of his car, slid into the driver's seat and started the engine, his gold signet ring flashing in the sunlight.

The car prowled out into the road and headed away from the sea front past the Connaught Theatre, their posters shouting an invitation to 'LEAVE HIM TO HEAVEN', the rock and roll musical that promised a trip down memory lane. He cruised onto the highway that would take him away from the town and its clubs full of women, belonging more, he felt, to Sodom and Gomorrah than a quiet seaside resort.

The car engine hummed comfortably as the motorist changed into top gear. The sunlight flickering through the trees had the effect of a strobe light and the driver shivered momentarily.

He passed a hand over his brow, which was beginning to glisten with beads of sweat, and the action was enough to send his head reeling. Shattered thoughts filled with fragmented, distorted images rushed behind his eyes; a porcelain faced, lifelike doll with her head twisted to one side, a scarf caught by a sea breeze fluttering gently, his mother asleep and the sound of a song crooning in his ears.

"Christ!" He baulked at the pictures and swerved violently across the central white line and back. The tyres screeched alarmingly and an irate driver hooted a warning at him.

It reminded him of something, someone - what? He struggled to remember but the memory was elusive and didn't want to be recalled. He regained his composure and his grip tightened on the wheel. All that remained of his panic attack was a single muscle in his jaw that pulsed violently.

Cathy Parker shook her golden tresses and stood on the pavement in the characteristic pose of a hitchhiker. The red Escort slowed to a standstill and she ran up to the passenger side and exchanged a few words with the motorist.

"Which way are you headed?" she asked. Cathy knew better than to state her destination first. Fatal mistakes could be made that way.

"All the way to Edgware, London, where I'll pick up the Ml to Birmingham. Any use?"

"Will you be joining the Brighton Road and passing through Croydon, Streatham and so on?"

"The same."

"I could do with a lift."

"I could do with the company. Hop in."

Cathy opened the passenger door and climbed in gratefully beside the most impossibly good-looking man she had ever seen. He was dynamic and charming. She was instantly attracted to him.

"Student?"

"Er… yes. History."

"Is the course interesting?"

"It is; well, some parts are a bit dry and crusty but mostly I find it fascinating."

"Which era are you studying?"

"The modern world. Twentieth Century, starting with the First World War going right up to the present day including the origin of the troubles in Northern Ireland."

"You'll have to go back to 1167 to understand that."

"You know about it?"

"A little. I read a bit. It certainly sounds more lively than anything I did at school; Industrial Revolution, Palmerston, Disraeli, the Whigs and the Tories."

"I think I did a similar syllabus for GCSE," smiled the normally reserved Cathy. "The most interesting thing I learned about Disraeli was that he was a ladies man."

"Like Lloyd George?"

"I guess so."

"I didn't know that." He paused, "Tell me, and I know this sounds like a cliché, but what's a nice girl like you doing hitchhiking?"

"It's not something I do regularly. I got separated from my friends and I haven't a bean. No money, no transport," she sighed wistfully, "So, I had to hitch."

The driver's relaxed manner made Cathy feel completely at ease. They chatted like old friends and she was extremely sorry when the car eventually arrived at her destination in Streatham.

Cathy scribbled her phone number on a scrap of paper and gave it to the young man. She stayed on the corner of Leigham Court Road and waved as the vehicle continued on its way.

She threw back her glittering head of hair and stepped lightly into the road. He was a singer. What a fascinating life he had led. She promised herself that she'd look out for his name. Someone with his looks was destined for stardom and fame.

Cathy Parker was lucky. He lost her phone number.

Newcastle three years later

Jodie Stubbs was getting high on a mixture of lager and cider, 'snake-bite' they called it and it was certainly having a deadly effect on her.

She sat at a table in the corner of the smoke filled club with its flashing lights and its music pounding out a disco beat. She counted the glasses in front of her, one, two, three, and four. That's four more than there would have been if that bastard hadn't dumped her. Eighteen months they'd been going out and he'd left her high and dry. Left her for her best friend.

She giggled, "Not so dry, anymore!" But anger soon replaced the sardonic humour, "Some best friend!" The next time she saw her she'd kick her head in.

Jodie was just about to get herself another drink when she felt a pair of eyes burning into her. She looked up and recognised the singer from the cabaret spot who had been on earlier. He was smiling down at her.

"Anyone's seat?" he asked casually.

She shrugged, "Be my guest."

"If you don't mind me saying, you don't look too happy," he observed.

"What's it to you?" she muttered.

"Sympathetic ear perhaps?"

"What do you want to bother for?" she snapped.

"Let's say I could do with some cheering up myself. I'm looking for a soul mate."

"Well, look elsewhere. The last thing I need is another man."

"My, my, you are upset," he said half amused and half chidingly.

"Oh, I'm sorry," she grumbled and immediately relented her irritated tone. "Look, I didn't mean to be rude. I've just been given the big 'E' from the love of my life and I'm feeling sorry for myself."

"Join the club," said the stranger, "My girlfriend's just flown the coop and now I'm drowning my sorrows, three years worth."

The two started to talk.

The next day Jodie Stubbs was dead.

1
Sudden Death

It was dark in George Street, uncomfortably dark. Five of the eight street lamps were out. The others cast an orange shadowy glow that hardly penetrated the gloom. The moon was hidden behind cloud and there were no stars that night, November twenty-fifth.

An old, scraggy, grey tomcat emerged from an alley and paused, its battle scarred body scarcely visible in the feeble light of the lamp, which struggled with the writhing, serpentine mist that crept and slithered along the ground. He gently snuffed the night air of his territory, laid his ears flat against his head and hissed into the blackness before slinking off into the shadows.

Faintly at first, but steadily getting louder, a single pair of footsteps could be heard, punching tiny holes in the silence, as they echoed past an entry adjoining a row of villas. The claret high-heeled shoes occasionally scraped the pavement as they skirted puddles, breaking the monotonous click clack of steel tips on concrete.

The woman halted under the first working lamp and peered at her watch. An errant breeze began to play with the long chiffon scarf draped loosely around her neck. One end flicked lightly across her cheek, settled back on her shoulder and for a moment she froze.

One thirty-five a.m.

It was cold this time of the morning and there was something else. Twice she had stopped and looked behind her since alighting from the bus; twice she had seen nothing.

The hidden cat leapt onto a crumbling stone mosaic patterned wall sending a shower of small stones to the pavement. Her head snapped round. Anxious eyes searched the darkness.

Reluctant to leave the light she stood, hesitating for a moment longer, then shivered, pulled up her collar, shoved her hands deep into her pockets and walked head down, hunching her shoulders against the damp cold.

Another small noise, she stiffened and turned once more. Thinking she detected a movement in a doorway some fifteen yards back, she quickened her pace. A new urgency entered her stride and she stumbled into a half run. She wondered whether she'd feel safer in the centre of the road and was just about to step off the pavement when he struck.

He came swiftly from behind. Three racing steps on the concrete gave her time to draw in the breath for the scream that never came. A hand clamped firmly across her mouth, the thumb and forefinger pinching her nostrils closed. The chiffon scarf became a noose and was drawn tighter and tighter around her throat, biting and burning into her skin. Her feet kicked and scraped futilely on the pavement; weak frantic fingers scrabbled to free herself from his vice like grasp. No air would come. The night went blacker and blacker until the tiny spark of life within her was diminished. She resisted him no more. Her fight to survive was lost. The leather of her claret shoes, like venal blood, scuffed as he dragged the limp form that had been Janet Mason into the entry. Her black patent Mac crackled as they melted into the musty dark.

Feverish and panting, Janet Mason's murderer pulled at her raincoat and ripped it open. Buttons flew from her blouse, the skirt's zip tore and he dragged away the thin lace of her briefs, grunting and mumbling wordlessly.

Six minutes later he was finished, his breathing deep and even. He took out a small pocket torch and switched it on. The click was surprisingly loud in the muffled silence of the alleyway. In his other hand, he held the knife, its cruel steel blade glinting wickedly as he raised it above her soft white flesh. The ritual complete, he gouged the words, 'number one' on the gentle curve of her belly, wiped the blade on the remnants of her blouse and smiled. Then, almost lovingly he crooned a soft lullaby and rearranged her clothes. The remaining button on her blouse was fastened, and her coat closed. Tenderly, he stroked the line of her cheekbone, gently kissed the cooling lips and crept silently into the night, his disappearing figure watched only by the citrine eyes of the cat.

*

Little Tommy Dawkins, for a dare, was to go to the end house where old Mr. Treeves had lived; a cantankerous old man who chased away the children from his entry and his door. This had earned him a reputation among the children of the neighbourhood as an evil old man who consorted with the devil. Mr. Treeves was long gone to an old folk's home but his aura had remained, infecting the house and sending fear into the souls of the local children. Tommy edged warily around the damp, entry wall. His heart beat wildly as he approached the top of the alley and could see the battered dustbins; their lids long vanished for use as shields in a war game taken by the very warriors whose dare Tommy was carrying out. He had to get into the house and take something back with him as proof of his bravery. Then he would have succeeded in the initiation test into the gang.

Tommy sucked the air in through his cheeks. Cautiously, he peered around the top of the entry and into the yard. What he saw there convinced him of every story he'd ever heard about Mr. Treeves. Shuddering and spluttering with shock, he ran as hard as he could, his feet stamping heavily on the concrete and out into the road. He ran wildly on and passed his amazed friends, who shouted after him but he didn't stop until he reached the safety of his own front door.

Thirty minutes later the entry resounded with the noise of Sergeant Pooley and PC Taylor's boots. When they reached the top of the entry the Sergeant hastily radioed for help and a police photographer. The sightless, bulging eyes of Janet Mason stared up at the sky. Her neck was black and bruised and her swollen tongue protruded awkwardly from her mouth. Her clothing appeared undisturbed. She lay on her back, her right arm carelessly flung above her head while her left arm was across her body as if in repose.

*

Detective Chief Inspector Greg Allison and Sergeant Mark Stringer paused over their cups of coffee. The photographs of Janet Mason's murder covered the desk. DCI

Allison reached for a digestive biscuit, dunked it in his coffee and grumbled as some of the sodden crumbs dribbled from his lips onto his tie. He took out his clean white pocket-handkerchief and rubbed at the mess, only making it worse.

"Get down to Hurst and hurry up the PM report," he growled.

"Right, Sir."

Sergeant Stringer drained the last of his coffee and stood up. He glanced across from his notes to the Chief, a large solid man, at least six feet four, thick necked and craggy faced, which now creased in concentration, emphasised his strength of character. His lower jaw slightly overshot his upper giving him something of a bulldog appearance.

"Yes, Mark?" Greg Allison looked questioningly at his sergeant.

"Sir, has anyone notified her parents?"

"Pooley and Taylor, after they'd radioed for help. I shall be going along there myself as soon as I've spoken to the criminal psychologist. I'll need you with me, you've got the address?" Mark nodded as his Chief muttered, "I've a feeling that this is going to be a nasty one," while he reached into his drawer for the comforting Mars Bar that waited for him.

Mark flicked shut his notebook and walked to the door. He hated going to the morgue. Photographs he could cope with, but the smell of death in the city's morgue always turned his stomach. He'd passed out at his first post mortem when he was in training and he was suddenly glad that he'd only had the coffee and had refused the biscuit. He was a smartly dressed young man, clean-shaven and quite handsome with his chiselled chin and full head of fair hair. He steeled himself in preparation for his visit, wishing wholeheartedly that the Chief had sent someone else.

He entered the outer office and Maddie, the Chief's secretary, looked up quizzically, "You off?"

Mark pulled a face, "The morgue."

Maddie raised her eyes and nodded sympathetically, she knew how much Mark hated going there.

"Good luck!"

9

"Thanks, I'll need it!"

*

Mark ran lightly up the well worn, stone steps, taking a last gulp of fresh air before pushing open the heavy, swing doors and proceeding down the corridor leading to Hurst's office. He was breathing heavily, trying to control the nausea rising inside him, as he knocked on the glass panelled door and entered.

Hurst greeted Mark like an old friend and shook him warmly by the hand, "Mark!"

"Johnny - the Chief's sent me for the report on the Janet Mason murder."

"Annie is just typing it up," said Hurst.

"Anything I should know?"

"It's a nasty one. The killer must be some sort of maniac. I've never seen anything like it. She appeared to have been strangled when she was brought in but when we undressed her we discovered the most horrible mutilations. There are words gouged on her stomach." Hurst shuddered as he thought of the pitiful body on the mortuary slab.

"He?" asked Mark.

"Semen was found on her genitals, an excessive amount of force was used. It would require extraordinary strength." Hurst fixed Mark with his eyes, "It's all in the report. Samples of semen, saliva, particles of skin, pubic hair and clothing fibres have been sent to Forensics. We'll get him, he's as good as drawn a picture of himself."

"What did he write?" asked Mark curiously.

Hurst looked grim and hesitated fractionally before answering, "Number one."

Mark felt an icy chill creep over him. The Chief had said that this would be a nasty one. It looked like he was right.

Mark collected the report on his way out, his lungs almost bursting by the time he reached the street. He glanced at his watch, eleven fifteen a.m. He just had time to drop off the report before meeting the Chief at Jackson's Terrace.

He slid into the driving seat of the car, his well-manicured hands tossing the report onto the front passenger seat. His strikingly handsome face, usually open and candid in expression, was now furrowed in a frown; his large, grey eyes set deep in thought.

He pushed the images of Janet Mason's murder to the back of his mind and allowed his thoughts to dwell on his wife, Debbie. She'd been acting strangely this morning, her voice sounded odd when he'd called her to say he'd be late that night. She said she hadn't slept well, but he knew it was more than that. Debbie hardly complained about anything, ever. Maybe that was it. She was bottling things up. He knew she didn't like to worry him unduly and she had been exceptionally tired this week. That was understandable being in her thirty-fourth week of pregnancy. Maybe coping with that and their toddler son Christian was proving too much for her. He'd have to give his mother-in-law, Jean, a ring. Since she'd been widowed, she had been only too happy to give her daughter a hand whenever she needed it, which made her feel wanted and useful again.

There was a loud honk from behind and Mark was made aware that the lights had changed to green. He slipped the car into first gear and moved off, taking the first left to the station.

DCI Allison was lumbering down the steps, his easily recognised gait heading for the car park. Mark tooted and Greg Allison stopped as the car slid into the kerb beside him. Allison lifted up the PM report and squeezed into the passenger seat next to Mark.

"Great! We'll use one car. Is this the report?"

Mark nodded. Allison leafed through the pages and grimaced. The paragraph and accompanying photographs of the mutilations and words that had been carved in Janet Mason's flesh made him whistle long and low through his teeth.

"What sort of a nutter would do this?"

"That's it, Sir," answered Mark, "A nutter."

"Well, if it is," groaned Allison, "It makes our job bloody difficult."

DC! Allison pursed his lips grimly and the car turned into Jackson Terrace. A mother pulled a grubby, three year old with a chocolate stained face out of the gutter and back

11

onto the pavement while she chatted with a neighbour. The two women paused and watched as Allison and Stringer marched up to number three, its door freshly painted red. Mark pressed the bell, which rang out the popular Avon chime.

The curtains that were drawn fluttered briefly. A shuffling step could be heard coming to the door, which opened. A bright eyed, old lady with iron-grey hair ushered them into the house. They followed her down the passage, her slippers slopping off at the heel with each step. She led them into a small sitting room at the back of the house where Janet Mason's mother was sitting, red eyed from weeping.

"Detective Chief Inspector Allison and Sergeant Stringer, Ma'am. Sorry to trouble you at a time like this but we need you to answer some questions," said Allison gently.

"I understand, Inspector. Won't you sit down?" Her voice was weary but sounded well educated, which surprised them. "Put the kettle on, Mum. Tea? Coffee, Inspector?"

"Tea will be fine, thanks," nodded Allison and looked at Stringer who also confirmed his preference for tea.

The old lady shuffled out at her daughter's instructions and the clatter of cups could be heard in the adjacent kitchen.

"What do you want to know?"

"Where did Janet work?"

"Dempseys. She was Mr. Payne's assistant. He's the under manager there. She was doing really well ... She was hoping to be put in charge of Personnel when Mrs. Bowden retired in the spring." Mrs. Mason's voice cracked slightly and she took out a well-wrung handkerchief, wiped her eyes, swallowed hard and then returned the limp rag to her pocket.

"She had a boyfriend?"

"Terry, Terry James. They were going to get engaged on her birthday." She stopped suddenly and bit her trembling lip, "I can't believe she's gone; and like that ... so, so horrible and brutal."

"I know, I know." Allison tried to be as comforting as possible, "Tell me, where does Terry work?"

"Lambert's Garage. He's a mechanic."

"Does he live locally?"

"In Edgbaston, not far really. Just off the Hagley Road in Manor Road North, number twenty-five."

Allison's measured tones continued, "I see. Do you know where Janet was last night?"

"Yes, she and Terry went to the Scala to see a film, then they were going on to Gino's for a pizza. It was their usual Friday night out, see a film and go for a meal. Terry'll be broken hearted. Has anyone told him yet?"

"No," said Allison regretfully, "We'll be going on to see him when we've left here." Allison took a breath and licked his lips, "Mrs. Mason, although it appears that your daughter was murdered by some lunatic, did she have any enemies? Was she worried about anything or did she act strangely at all these last few days?"

Questioning stopped abruptly as the old lady shuffled in with a tray and placed it on the polished teak coffee table. Mark Stringer looked around the room, whilst piping hot tea was poured into Mrs. Mason's best Queen Anne china. The house was tastefully decorated and although the furniture had seen better days, it had once been expensive and in vogue. Obviously the Masons had suffered a loss of income.

Once the courtesies of tea had been exchanged; how many sugars? Did they take milk? Would they like a biscuit? Allison continued his probing and all the while Mark scribbled the answers in his pocket notebook.

"How is Mr. Mason taking all this?"

"Mr. Mason is in hospital. He has cancer. We're waiting for a place at St. Joseph's hospice. He doesn't know about Janet, yet ... I don't know how I'm going to tell him. He's so ill. She's our only child you know?"

There was nothing more to be said, or could be said so the two detectives finished their tea and rose from the chintz-covered suite. They said their goodbyes to the bird eyed grandmother and the soberly dressed Mrs. Mason and made their way to the front door. Neither of them spoke until they were in the car.

"Not what I expected," said Allison as he eased his considerable frame into the seat next to Mark.

"Nor I," agreed Mark.

"I must admit that by the way Janet was dressed, high heels, patent Mac that she was perhaps more of a working class girl. I was expecting her mother to be someone who looked and sounded," he was lost for words, "Different."

"Mmm, it's obvious they must have been well off, once upon a time," said Mark as he started the engine.

"Makes it worse somehow, another tumble on the slippery path of life." Allison sighed and continued, "We'll grab a bite at The Woodman, see the boyfriend, and then move on to Dempseys. Let's see if we turn up anything there."

"Right, Sir." Mark turned the car in the direction of the Square and The Woodman. He squeezed into a place vacated by a silver Renault. After locking the doors they stepped into the public bar.

Cigarette smoke curled up and floated blue in the air over a table where two old men were playing cribbage. One of them touched his cap.

"Morning, Mr. Allison."

"Morning, Dan. How's life treating you?"

"Mustn't grumble, Sir. Mustn't grumble. The wife's a lot better."

"Glad to hear it."

At the mention of the word 'wife', Mark's thoughts turned to Debbie. He flushed guiltily, excused himself from the Chief and went to the phone at the bar. The ten pence coins thudded dully in the box, and he dialled waiting impatiently for someone to answer. He could hear the Chief ordering him a Barbican and a Buck Rabbit. Then his mother-in-law answered in her modulated tone reserved for the phone.

"Jean? It's Mark."

"Hello, Mark, what a pleasure…"

"Can't stop, Jean, I'm in a bit of a hurry."

"Yes?" She didn't probe further.

"I'm worried about Debbie, she's been acting very oddly and we haven't had time to talk. Can you call out and see her; have a chat?"

"Will do. You must be worried?"

"I am. I've a feeling Debs doesn't want to bother me with whatever is concerning her. She knows the pressure

14

I'm under but I'm sure there's something wrong. Can you help?"

"All right, I'll get over there now and do what I can."

"Thanks, Jean." The phone clicked and one of his ten pence pieces was returned. He walked briskly across to the Chief and his waiting drink.

"All right?" queried Allison.

"Yes. Just getting Jean to check on Debs. It's been a worrying time with the baby nearly due."

"Of course, of course." There was an awkward silence between them, which was broken by the arrival of two plates of food. Allison didn't like to become too embroiled in the lives of his men.

Any chance of further conversation was thwarted as the two policemen tucked into their lunch.

"Can I get you anything else, Gents?" asked the barman as the knives and forks were placed on the plates.

"Apple pie and cream for me," said Allison, "It's going to be a long day."

"I'll just have a coffee. Thanks, Ken," said Mark.

"Right you are!" Ken smiled his toothy grin at these two regulars. He didn't mind these coppers. They kept themselves to themselves, didn't intimidate his customers and usually spent a bob or two.

"Drink, Ken?" asked Allison.

"Thank you very much, I'll have thirty p's worth, if I may." He was never greedy; that way his customers asked him again.

Greg Allison was just scraping the last of his cream from his bowl when a short stocky man with thick, unruly hair came into the pub. He glanced swiftly around, spotted Allison and strode purposefully towards him, rubbing his bristly chin as he came.

"Yes, Brand?" Allison hardly had time to wipe his mouth with his napkin. Brand pulled up a chair and sat astride it western style. He pulled at his well-trained eyebrows that bushed out over his eyes.

"Got a hot one for you, Greg. Word has it that Stuart Allen is expecting a shipment, Tuesday."

"Any more info?"

"Julie was dealing Blackjack at the Rainbow as part of our undercover op. Stuart Allen had a meet and chose her table. She paid as close attention as she dared."

"Well?" Allison leaned forward.

"He met up with some Asian fellow, expensively dressed. His dental work included a gold tooth at the front."

"Vencat!" exclaimed Mark.

"Uh? Yeah, well, whoever … Gold tooth handed Allen an envelope and said that the first consignment was to be Tuesday at eleven-thirty."

"That's all?"

"That's all!

"Good work, Brand. Let us know if anything else turns up."

"Will do. Look, I can't stop. I'm off to Kidderminster now, to check on this antique fraud. I'll be in touch."

"Cheers and thanks!" said Allison, genuinely pleased.

Brand moved the chair back and left as speedily as he'd arrived. Mark looked at his Chief, "That's all we need; the drugs case breaking now, just when we've a maniac on the loose."

"Mark, contact Woodward, tell him what we know, get him to increase the watch on Allen and see if we can get a trace on Vencat."

"Tricky customer that one, slippery as a barrel load of eels," muttered Mark.

"Didn't know he was back in the country. See if we can find out how he got in and if he's still here."

"Right, Sir."

"I'll see you back at the station. We'll go to Lambert's Garage together. I want a word with Dan, see if he's got any news for me."

As soon as Mark had left, Allison collected a pint from the bar and moved towards the cribbage table where the air was now thick with smoke. He delivered the pint, forced his body into the chair beside Dan, his nark, and they began to talk.

2
Breaking Down

Tony slammed his fist into the wall; he glared at the crack in the plaster and rubbed his knuckles angrily. His striking features twisted into a grimace as he thought about her. How dare she? How dare she turn him down? Just who did she think she was?

"Tony? Tony? Are you all right?" The thin, nasal voice of his mother with her Birmingham accent, of which he was so desperately ashamed, came through the door.

"Why couldn't she learn to speak properly," he thought petulantly. He couldn't invite anyone home. He'd even had to buy an answer phone and insist on the machine being left on, so that she wouldn't talk to anyone important and put them off.

His mother padded into the kitchen. She was short and squat and wore little woollen ankle socks over her stockinged feet, which were encased in a pair of old fashioned, check, pom-pom bedroom slippers. Her dark, badly permed hair, liberally flecked with grey, poked out from underneath a small, luridly knitted, woollen hat, which resembled the tea cosies she would sit and knit for the church bazaars. Tony suddenly thought of the nursery rhyme, 'I'm a little teapot, short and stout,' and wanted to laugh. He smothered a giggle as he reached for the tea caddy. "Just going to make a cuppa Mum, want one?"

"Yes, please. I'll get the biscuits." She foraged around in a tall cupboard while he flicked on the switch for the kettle. He stared hard at his mother in her plaid, serge skirt that was too tight and too short, showing her bony knees. It surprised him that such a plump woman should have no pads of fat at her knees. Her fawn lambs wool jumper had worn thin in places, showing the heavy corseting underneath that fought to contain all the flab that was struggling to spill out.

A scowl crossed his lightly tanned face as she adjusted a plaque on the wall, which read, 'Jesus is the head of this house, the unseen guest at every meal, our companion when we sit at night, who watches over us while we sleep.'

She narrowed her slit like cobra-hooded eyes, "Don't look so grim. You've everything to thank the Lord for."

He said nothing. A lock of his blue-black hair fell over his forehead, as his hand tightened on the teapot handle, the knuckles on his uninjured hand showing white. His electric blue eyes misted over as he choked back a sob. Tony's mother ran across to him and ran her pudgy hands with palms as dry as parchment over his lean muscular body. Then, she welcomed him into her arms. "Now, don't go upsetting yourself. You've been having those thoughts again. Let Mother cleanse you. We'll wash away your sins." Her face shining with an unnatural light, she led him into the bathroom.

*

Terry James was devastated, his knees buckled when he heard the news. He wiped his square practical hands on an oily rag, ringing it and twisting it, as might a small child beset with grief.

Mark Stringer spoke soothingly and quietly to the young man whose future life had just been so cruelly shattered. Terry's shoulders heaved and he blinked back the hot stinging, salt tears that rose so easily to his eyes and, which threatened to spill over and race down his cheeks.

The shock was so great that Terry James swayed. It seemed for a moment that he might literally pass out. Greg Allison took no chances. He placed his huge hands like meat cleavers on the young man's shoulders then steadied him and sat him in the only chair, which Mark had cleared of old newspapers, invoice books and other debris, in the cluttered garage office.

"I'm sorry to have to ask you this," said Allison, "But we must know where you went and what time you left her, so that we can pinpoint the time of death and establish who was the last person to see her alive."

Terry raked his fingers through his crisply cut, blonde hair. His face had lost the fresh openness that had been present at the introductions and he was looking more haggard

18

and drawn with each question. He dropped the oily rag onto his knee, balled his hand into a fist and smashed it against his other with venom.

"I'll kill the bastard who did it!" A surge of anger momentarily replaced his anguish and grief and he spat out, "Ask your questions!" Allison and Stringer exchanged a glance.

Terry set his lips in a thin line, his chin jutted out and then he said more softly, "Anything to help catch him, anything."

During Mark's careful questioning Terry James confirmed all that Mrs. Mason had said. "Is there any other small detail.... anything else that might place you at the Scala or Gino's?"

Terry James thought for a moment and whispered, "Yes...Yes!" He managed to find more voice and added, "Mario served us at Gino's. He's our favourite waiter. He even shared a glass of wine with us before we left. He will definitely remember us." Terry's voice wavered thinly in the bleak little office as he continued to recount his memories of that fateful evening. "We walked up from the Ringway to Paradise Street and caught the night service from opposite the Hall of Memory. She wouldn't let me see her home and refused to get a cab saying it was an unnecessary expense. We only allowed ourselves one night out a week because we were saving to get married, the rest of the week she'd come to me or I'd go to her house and we'd watch telly.... Oh God!" He groaned and went silent for a moment, then his breath started rising heavily in his chest.

Mark touched his shoulder sympathetically and continued, "What time did you leave her?"

Terry swallowed hard and answered falteringly, "Her bus came first. She caught the number eight to Ladywood. She was going to get off at Monument Road by the baths and walk the rest of the way. That must have been about one fifteen a.m. My bus, the Quinton nine, came along about five minutes after. I got home about one-thirty, my Mum'll tell you. She was waiting up for me," he looked sheepish, "She always does, even though I'm twenty-five." He rubbed his hand over his face, then picked up the oily rag and resumed the tortured wringing and twisting from before.

Allison left Mark to deal with Terry and slipped out of the office to speak to the garage boss. "Everything all right?" asked the pleasant faced, jovial garage owner, Jack Lambert.

He wasn't probing or questioning just naturally curious as to why his mechanic should have a visit from the police.

"No, I'm afraid it's bad," Allison pursed his lips as he prepared to break the news to Terry's boss, "Young Terry's fiancée has been murdered."

"What? Janet?" Jack Lambert's mouth gaped open in astonishment.

"He's taken it very badly…"

"Christ, what do you expect?" Jack Lambert's head was reeling with this information, he couldn't seem to think straight or form any words.

"If you don't mind my saying," said Allison gently, "I don't think he's fit to work in his present condition. He can't possibly concentrate. Handling machinery and so on." He paused and licked his lips, "Not a good idea."

Jack Lambert suddenly seemed to find his voice. His eyes darted back and forth across his yard, "No, no. Of course not. He must have some time off. Give him a chance to get over it. If that's humanly possible."

"That's the ticket, Sir. If you wouldn't mind," Allison prompted, inclining his head towards the office door.

The garage boss acknowledged Allison's meaningful glance and braced himself to face his young mechanic. He took a swift nostril full of air and opened the shabby door. "I've just heard, Mate. I'm so sorry." He stopped; struggling to find the right words of comfort, "There's nothing I can do or say. Words are hopeless at a time like this."

Mark Stringer nodded in silent agreement.

Terry looked at his boss his eyes soulless and miserable.

"Thanks, Jack," his words came out as a strangled sob followed by a sharp intake of breath.

"Look, Tes," continued Jack, "Best you get home. Leave everything as it is. Martin will clear up."

"No, Boss. No! I'd rather be working, keep busy, have my mind on other things."

"Come on, Son. You know I'm right. Take the time off."

"But we're short staffed."

"We'll cope. Get yourself off home."

"Honest, Jack. I'd rather work. If I'm home I'll only brood and think. It'll be worse."

Stringer interrupted, "Mr. Lambert's right, Terry. Better you go home. If you stay at work in your frame of mind mistakes can happen. Catch my drift?"

Eventually, Mark persuaded Terry that it was for the best that he finish work and he collected his coat. His shoulders drooped as he left the premises and he looked a broken man.

Mark nodded to his chief, "Want me to check out Mario and Mrs. James?"

"No, let Pooley and Taylor do that; and get them to check with the bus company, find out who was on that number eight bus and Terry's bus the Quinton nine." Allison thought for a minute and added, "I believe the lad, don't you?"

"For what it's worth, yes I do. He seemed genuine enough."

"Right! Well, we'll get over to Dempsey's see what we can turn up there."

*

Dempsey's was one of those modern buildings that appeared to be made of glass, the sort that Allison abhorred. They made their way into the busy department store, milling with people, intent on Christmas shopping. They took the lift to the fifth floor offices and walked silently on the thick piled carpet to Enquiries.

The girl on reception directed them along the corridor, past Personnel and the Sales department to Mr. Payne's office.

A heavily set man rose to meet them and extended a ready hand when his secretary announced their arrival. His complexion was florid and he was sweating profusely although the building was air conditioned to a comfortable temperature.

"What can I do for you?" Payne asked in his gravelly voice as he gestured them to sit.

"We've come about Miss Mason," Mark began.

"Janet? Yes, she hasn't shown up for work today; most unlike her, she's usually very conscientious about letting me know if she needs time off. I can't understand it. I say, she's not in any trouble is she?"

"I'm afraid I have some bad news, Sir…"

"She's had an accident! Which hospital is she in?"

"No, Sir," Mark said firmly. "I think you'd better sit down." Mark waited until Mr. Payne was seated. The dome of his baldhead was now shining with even more beads of sweat. "I'm afraid she's been murdered."

"Murdered? God, no! Who? Why?"

"That's what we have to find out. We'd like you to think of anyone she talked about or if she mentioned any problems. Anything, anything at all that could help."

Mr. Payne shook his head vigorously so that his chins slapped into his cheek jowls. "Full of life. She had everything going for her and a terrific sense of humour." He broke off and stared out of the window, suddenly dazed.

"Did she mention any friends, Sir?"

"Friends?" he repeated dully, "She mentioned a boyfriend. Other than that… Look, have a word with my secretary, Sue. She and Janet got along really well. She may know more than me. I'm sorry I can't be of more help." He rose again and bid them farewell. "Please feel free to talk to anyone here that you wish. I'll inform our manager, I'm sure he'll wish to us to co-operate in every way." With that he closed the door and made an attempt to apply himself to his daily routine.

Mark found himself returning the questioning gaze of Miss Susan Hardy, who as her lapel pin told him was secretary to Mr. Payne.

"Can I help you?" she asked pointedly.

"Er yes," said Mark momentarily disarmed, "What can you tell me about Janet Mason? I understand you were friends."

"We are."

"Good, then perhaps you can tell me something about her, her likes, dislikes, habits …"

"Just a minute," she interrupted, "What do you mean *were* friends? Has something happened to her?"

"I'm afraid Miss Mason is dead," chipped in Allison, interested to see her reaction.

Mark shot a look at the Chief slightly shaken by his bluntness.

Susan Hardy gasped. "Dead? Oh no! I'm sorry, I didn't know. How awful." She was flustered for a second or two then, asked, "When did it happen?"

"Last night.'

"Was it an accident?"

"No, murder."

Susan Hardy was stunned, as if she didn't quite believe what she had been told, she shook her head thinking she'd misheard, but Mark battered on, "Miss Hardy, we're trying to build up a picture of Miss Mason, anything you can tell us will be a great help."

She nodded, took her fingers off the typewriter keys, where they had been resting, and pushed her chair back.

"She's a great girl and a good friend. Desperately in love with her Terry, looking forward to the wedding and getting her promotion in the spring."

Miss Hardy was a fluent talker and spoke easily about her friend, although she seemed unable to speak of her in the past tense. "She's really popular here, from the lift boy to the director, sometimes too popular."

"Oh, why?"

"Well, some of the guys round here are always asking for dates, even though they know she's unofficially engaged, but Janet's fiercely loyal and has eyes for no one except her Terry."

Sue picked up a pack of cigarettes from the desk and helped herself to a menthol filter tip. She inhaled deeply as if drawing upon a life force and then continued, a stream of grey smoke accompanying her words.

"She got quite cross with Dirk Knowles in catering, he kept pestering her for a date."

"Anyone else?"

"Mr. Clifton in Sales, he asked her out once. Now, he is a dish! I could be tempted myself if he looked my way. Oh, and Barton in personnel, he's been making sheep's eyes at her for weeks."

"How did Janet respond to this attention?"

"Well, she didn't encourage it, if that's what you mean. She always apologised and explained she was getting engaged then, thanked them for thinking of her. She only had a problem with Dirk, he wouldn't take no for an answer. But I can't think he'd do anything to hurt her."

"No, probably not. Still, it gives us something to work on. Thanks for your help."

"Anytime." Suddenly her artificially bright smile, cracked. She tossed her corn blonde hair back from her eyes, which Mark saw were glistening with unshed tears. She stubbed out her cigarette vigorously and murmured almost imperceptibly, "I'll miss her." Then, she resumed typing, quite violently Mark thought.

Allison and Mark left the office. They walked back along the corridor looking at the names on the doors. The third on the right read, 'Personnel', they knocked and entered. They identified themselves to Joyce Bowden, a tall, elegant lady whose age it was difficult to ascertain. Her blue grey hair was swept up into a French pleat. She had a warm expansive personality and spoke in glowing terms of Janet Mason and her talent to get on with people.

"She had an ability to adapt to any situation and was good at helping people with problems, that's why she was replacing me when I retire in April."

"Thank you, Mrs. Bowden. Tell me, is it all right if we speak to Mr...." Mark looked at his notes, "Barton?"

"Certainly, he has the right hand desk in the far corner of the main office, through this door." She extended her cool hand and smiled pleasantly. "Anything further I can do to help just let me know." The door shut crisply behind them.

They spotted Barton in the corner as Mrs. Bowden had described. He was talking on the telephone and nodded agreeably as he gestured them to sit, cutting short his call.

"I'll call you back, Mike. Yes… Sorry about that. What can I do for you?"

"Mr. Barton?"

"Yes?"

"Mr. Barton. DCI Allison and DS Stringer; could you tell us where you were yesterday, Friday the twenty-fifth of November?"

"Why, here at work."

"No, Sir. The evening of the twenty-fifth."

"Evening? Let me think - oh yes, I played snooker at the Strand. I met my mate Des about seven-thirty in the bar, we had a table booked at eight-fifteen for two hours."

"He can verify that?"

"Certainly and so can the club. Look, what's this all about?"

"What time did you leave the club?'

"About ten forty-five."

"Then where did you go?"

"We went to Long John's Pancake House, had a few crepes and a coffee."

"How long were you there?"

"About an hour, then I called City Cabs and went home."

"Where do you live, Mr. Barton?"

"Moseley." Allison and Stringer looked at each other; they both knew it wasn't that far from Janet Mason's by car, just a matter of minutes. "Look, what's all this about?"

"I'm afraid a colleague of yours has been murdered."

"Who?'

"Janet Mason."

"God no! How horrible! Surely you don't think…"

"We don't think anything, Sir. It's merely routine for us to question all her known friends and associates."

"Oh, I see." He looked relieved, "Janet you say? I'm sorry."

"I understand you asked her out?"

"I tried. She was so kind to me after my father died. I wanted to thank her for being so understanding. Just for friendship's sake, but she wouldn't, thought people might talk and didn't want any rumours getting to the ears of her boyfriend. He could be quite possessive you know."

"I see." Mark raised one eyebrow quizzically. They continued talking for another ten minutes or so and Mark wrote down all the relevant addresses and phone numbers. Barton's story would be checked.

*

Tony watched his mother as she slurped her tea. The quick moist lapping noises made him think of a sow feeding at the trough. Her eyes shifted back and forth as she licked her tongue lasciviously from corner to corner of her red omnivorous mouth, before emptying the cup and returning it to its saucer. She sat opposite him, her legs parted, revealing thick, pink, cotton knickers. She attempted a smile. Tony saw her yellowing teeth highlighted by her crimson lips.

"Do you want another?" she whined, and glanced at his still full cup before remonstrating, "You haven't touched the first. Come on drink it up or it'll be cold."

Tony sighed and obediently raised the cup to his lips. The pleasant warmth had an almost soothing effect. He rested his head on the chair back and closed his eyes.

"If you're tired you ought to have a lie down," she droned. "I've told you before; working all day and night, trying to hold down two jobs. It'll wear you out."

"I'm okay, Mum," he said wearily. Tony pulled himself forward and drained the last of his tea from the cup.

"Well, something's bothering you. What is it? Tell your old mum all about it.'

Suddenly, Tony felt himself flush. The room had become suffocatingly hot. He couldn't breathe, and knew he had to get out. He rose abruptly.

"Where are you going?" Her thin reedy tones added to his panic.

His eyes flooded with red and he saw the tail ends of her Isadora scarf. He wanted to reach out and pull them, entwine them around his hands until his knuckles met the skin of her neck.

A dog barked outside. The sudden sound jerked him violently back to reality. One of his headaches was beginning; he could feel the pressure begin to build behind his bloodshot eyes, and an unseen weight seemed to press down relentlessly on the top of his head. His eyelids fluttered momentarily and his face paled in the artificial light. He scratched at the skin on his face, which seemed to crawl with a thousand insects exploring every contour. He tried to cry out but his mother was already at his side, her fat hands holding him, caressing him. He moaned softly, hopelessly as he felt her slab like palms and sausage fingers beginning to palpate his neck and shoulders.

"Come on, Tony love, lie down a while. I'll draw the curtains. You haven't got to be back at work just yet."

The thin line of her mouth started to curve up at the corners as she began slowly to unbutton her cardigan.

*

The two detectives went on through the building, talking with everyone whose name cropped up in connection with Janet. They knocked on Mr. Clifton's door, Head of Sales, but he was out. Mark left his card with the secretary and a message for him to come in and see them at his earliest convenience. They passed along the rest of the corridor and went into the catering department to find Dirk Knowles.

Near the cold meat store they spotted a burly looking man with a black beard and receding hairline. He was severely admonishing a red-faced pimply adolescent who wore the white overalls of the butchery.

"Never, ever take meat out of this store and allow it to defrost, even in part and then refreeze it. For God's sake, Lad, do you want us to be sued? Serve this lot up and we could be landed with a nasty case of salmonella poisoning or worse."

"Sorry, Sir."

"Damned right." He glared at the offending leg of pork, "Get rid of it. Now. And remember only take out the daily quota no matter what Chef says. If he needs any more he'll have to use his microwave to defrost it. Got it?"

"Yes, Sir," said the youth miserably.

"Right!" He watched the lad slouch off before turning his icy eyes on the two men. Mark went ahead with the introductions and Dirk Knowles nodded curtly. He led them

27

into his office, which was cluttered with papers, invoices and boxes.

"Excuse the mess. I'm in the process of moving offices. As you can see, I need more space." He laughed heartily as if he'd just told a clever joke.

Allison and Stringer smiled politely before launching into their long list of routine questions. Dirk Knowles's manner was odd to say the least, abrupt one minute, eager to please the next. It wasn't long before they met with a wall of hostility.

"Just what are you insinuating?"

"Nothing, Sir. We just need to know where you were last night so that we can eliminate you from our enquiries," said Mark.

"Eliminate me from your enquiries!" he exploded, "I suppose that daft, bitch of a secretary of Payne's put you up to this."

"The information did not come from anyone, Sir," interrupted Allison. "We're acting on written information found in a note book belonging to Miss Mason."

Knowles appeared to calm down somewhat at this, although the veins in his neck still pulsed dangerously.

"Sir, it's merely routine. Now, if you could answer our questions."

"All right, all right; let me collect my thoughts, I don't think I was anywhere."

"I see, Sir, at home were you?"

"Yes."

"Alone?"

"Yes."

"Anyone call round? Telephone?"

"No… Yes… Wait a minute, some woman came collecting for the Red Cross."

"What time would that be?"

"About nine-thirty."

"And after that?'

"Nothing, except my sister, Alice, she telephoned around eleven to invite me to one of her dinner parties."

"Right, Sir. Could we have your sister's address?"

"Don't you believe me?"

"Sir, you have to understand, we must check every statement. It's nothing personal." Mark refused to be ruffled by the man's obvious irritation.

Knowles gave them his sister's address and then his own, which was in Bartley Green. The two detectives turned on their heels and left the busy department store. It was nearly five and already dark by the time they reached the station.

There were three messages and a report on Allison's desk. Woodward had seen Allen at lunchtime in Chaplin's Bar and Bistro talking to Peter Sherratt, the manager. He in turn had introduced Allen to some known Brummy criminals. The place had shut at three p.m. but Allen was still inside with these villains. Allison tossed the note over for Mark to read.

"Sherratt? Isn't that the guy who was done for receiving a while back?"

"That's the one."

"Any word on Vencat?"

"Yes, apparently he's taken a trip to a meat importing warehouse in Bristol and is now on his way back to Brum. Well, all that seems safe in other hands for the time being." Allison handed Mark this note too.

"Anything else?' asked Mark.

"Just a report from Pooley to say that the Mario, Gino story appears to check out. Pass on the information we got from Dempsey's to him; that should keep them busy. Oh, and get them to pay Mrs. Mason another visit, ask them to look at Janet's room, see if she **did** keep a diary."

Allison fiddled with the drawer in his desk. He opened it slightly revealing a Mars Bar sitting and waiting to be eaten. He shut it briskly as Mark's voice interrupted his thoughts. And he glanced at the last message in his hand.

"Right, Sir." Mark was just about to leave when the Chief stopped him.

"Mark this one's for you, from Jean. It sounds urgent."

Mark took the note and read it quickly. He made a move to the door, "Is it all right if I go?"

"Sure, there's not much more can be done tonight until we get the report from Forensic; it's all leg work. Pooley and

Taylor can handle that. I'm waiting for the psychological profile. Otherwise, I'll see you in the morning. I hope everything is okay?" He opened his drawer and his hand gripped the tantalising bar, but he didn't remove it.

"I'll let you know, Sir."

"Thanks. Cheerio."

*

Mark sped out of the station. His car screamed out of his parking place and headed for home, as fast as he dared.

Fifteen minutes later, he turned into the avenue, with its trees divested of their foliage, a grim reminder of the winter still ahead. He parked smartly in the drive of his nineteen-thirties semi. Jean opened the door.

"Thank goodness you've come, I've just got back from the hospital."

"The hospital!" Mark almost shouted.

"Look calm down, there's nothing you can do; she's in the best place and she's sleeping now. You can go in later. First, have some tea and I'll put dinner on. Nothing fancy. It's only a casserole. Will that do?"

The front door closed behind them and they walked into the kitchen; the kettle was boiling. Mark sat at the kitchen table and looked anxiously at Jean as she poured the bubbling water into the pot.

"Sorry, Jean; I don't mean to sound ungrateful, just tell me what's happened."

"I came over as soon as you called. Debbie was resting. It seems she had a show and had started bleeding. She knew the best thing for that was bed rest, after her experience with Christian."

Mark nodded. He knew what a difficult pregnancy Christian's had been. She had bled three or four times during the nine months and each time it happened the doctor made her stay in bed.

"Why didn't she just stay in bed? Why is she in hospital?"

Jean passed him a scalding hot mug of tea, which he cradled comfortingly in his hands. "She was alarmed because she hadn't felt the baby move in ten hours."

"Christ no!' Mark's voice faltered. They desperately

30

wanted this baby and were both looking forward to the birth. He half rose out of his chair but Jean made him sit again. "What's happened?" he asked weakly.

Jean urged him to sip his tea and didn't take her eyes off his face all the time she talked to him. "The doctor hadn't got the equipment with him, obviously. They've taken her to the Queen Elizabeth. They couldn't find the foetal heartbeat but that doesn't mean anything. There could be a perfectly simple explanation, the baby might have turned or something, so they shooed me out, told me to see you and to go back at seven p.m. So, no matter what you think or how you feel, get this down you, then we'll go along to the hospital together."

Fortunately, Mark saw the sense in what Jean was saying and tried to eat his meal, but his tortured expression showed his anxieties and in the end he had to push his plate away. "Sorry, Jean. I can't manage it."

"All right; let me clear this lot away and we'll make for the hospital. Go and change. Oh, there are some flowers on the side, for you to take to Debbie. I'll call the sitter." Mark pressed his lips to Jean's hands and silently blessed her. He knew she was one in a million.

*

DCI Allison scrunched up the brown wrapper of his Mars Bar and tossed it into his bin and sighed. He brushed up a crumb of chocolate popping it back into his mouth and sat back in his chair. He was waiting for the psychologist's profile on Janet Mason's killer when the phone rang. "It's Vencat, Chief. He's on the move again."

"Tarnation! Where to this time?"

"I'm not sure, we appear to be on our way to Rhyl. He's stopped off at a Little Chef, for a bite to eat. I'm filling up at a petrol station opposite. I'll keep you informed."

"Do. Stick with him." Allison replaced the receiver firmly in its rest. He sighed deeply; his craggy face deep in thought as he tried to work out what Vencat could be up to. He was just trying to puzzle this out when there was a knock at his door.

"Come in," he called gruffly.

31

A dapper little man of about fifty-five and wearing glasses entered with a serious expression. "I've got that profile for you, Chief," said the criminal psychologist, Colin Brady.

"Mmmm? Oh, thank you," said Allison absently. Then he apologised for his apparent lack of interest, pushed Vencat to the back of his mind and waited for what Colin had to say.

"So, what have you got?"

"We're looking for someone dominated by a wife/ sister/ mother/ girlfriend, someone with a powerful female figure in his life who makes him feel totally inadequate. He will become enraged if his masculinity is questioned. He deflects his anger onto unsuspecting women, trying to dominate, degrade and control them. Resisting attack is likely to make him worse."

"Great! What do we do? Warn women that if this nutter attacks to give in gracefully? The courts would have a field day if we caught him and presented them with a willing victim as a witness for the prosecution."

"Let's hope he doesn't strike again. Although it looks likely that he will. The press haven't picked up on it yet, have they?"

"So far it's only made page ten in the nationals. Sorry, Colin, I didn't mean to interrupt."

"He may have a history of petty sexual offences. Check your files. Anyone with a record for indecent exposure that fulfils the other criteria could well be a suspect."

"Right. Anything else?'

"He could have a strong religious background. Sees himself as punishing his victims. If he falls into this category he is most dangerous. He can probably be both charming and cunning. Likes to think of himself as masterful." Brady tossed this profile on Allison's desk.

"Thanks. I'll get Pooley to check records for sex offenders. We'll match that with what comes back from Forensic, then we should have more to go on."

"He's a lethal customer," warned Brady. "I've sent a memo out to those in my department with clinics and my secretary is contacting all therapists in hospitals and with practices in the Midlands area, in case any of their past or present patients look likely candidates. Who knows, it may turn up a lead before there's another killing."

"Thanks, Brady. That's terrific! We need another attack like a hole in the head."

Brady grinned and pulled up a chair whilst Allison paged for two coffees.

*

Mark anxiously awaited the arrival of the consultant. He sat at Debbie's side holding her hand. He loved her so much and she looked so very tired and so utterly vulnerable.

Jean gently touched his arm as an authoritative figure in a smart suit came towards Debbie's bed. Mark stood up.

"Mr. Stringer?" The consultant extended his hand and introduced himself. "Mr. Greenhalf. I'm afraid we'll have to keep your wife in for a while; we've done some tests and the bleeding is a result of placenta praevia."

"What's that?"

"It means that when your wife goes into labour the placenta will come before the baby, I'm surprised it wasn't spotted before. It can be dangerous but that's not what concerns me."

"The baby, it hasn't moved?"

"No. Now, it might not mean anything but we're worried that we haven't found the foetal heartbeat. It may be that the baby has turned in such a way that the monitor can't pick it up. However, I want your permission to perform a caesarean section."

"Isn't that dangerous?"

"No, not now. The baby's lungs have developed enough for it to be able to breathe unaided and if the baby is in distress, it's the best thing to do."

Debbie turned her eyes to the consultant and said woodenly, "And if it's dead?"

"Well, of course we must consider that too, but I believe it will be less painful to operate now, than to wait and put you through the trauma of labour."

Mark turned to Debbie, took her hands and said quietly, "You can see the sense in that, can't you, Love? You can't go through labour and have nothing at the end of it."

Debbie nodded wearily. "I just feel so helpless and such a failure." Suddenly her eyes widened. She pushed herself up in bed. "It moved!" she said, "Mark! It moved." She started to smile.

Mr. Greenhalf edged Mark aside and gently palpated her abdomen. "You're right, the baby's turning. All the more reason we do the caesarean now." The consultant looked at Debbie and then at Mark.

"Yes," said Debbie. "We want this baby, don't we, Mark?"

"Please, Doctor, whatever it takes."

"Sister, draw the curtains. Get Staff or one of the juniors to prep Mrs. Stringer." Mr. Greenhalf turned towards Debbie and rested his hand on her shoulder, "You do understand what is entailed?"

"I know enough. I'm about to be shaved," Debbie joked. She paused, "I don't want to be asleep for the birth. Is there any way round it? An epidural, maybe?"

"That's perfectly possible," smiled the consultant, "I'll have Sister page the anaesthetist. He'll explain the procedure to you, but there is no reason why you shouldn't be able to witness the birth if that is what you want."

"That is what she wants," affirmed Mark, nodding in agreement with Debbie.

The area around Debbie's bed became a hive of activity as the nurse prepped her and the anaesthetist arrived. He spelled out the statutory warnings associated with the procedure but Debbie still elected for an epidural, as they had discussed. Jean and Mark were sent into the waiting room while Debbie was taken out of the antenatal ward and into the theatre.

Mark was glad of Jean's company. He didn't want to be alone and he was relieved that he was not allowed into the theatre, with his history of squeamishness he didn't think he could cope.

3
Out of Control

Tony was shaking; his excitement was hard to control. On the dance floor, after he'd finished his spot, she'd danced with him. She'd made him feel as if he were the only man in the whole world. She had danced with him readily and easily as soon as he'd asked. Her eyes and body locked onto his as they moved in time to a slow sensual number that aroused in him the deepest feelings of passion and longing.

Annette, her name was Annette. Oh Lord, this was right, wasn't it? It had to be. She appeared made for him. A Barbra Streisand look alike whose bubbly personality and powerful sexuality could make any man hers and she'd chosen him. Tony put her age at approximately thirty-four. His mother had always said a four-year age gap was about right.

He glanced at his watch, five minutes past midnight. She said to meet him in the car park, and that she wouldn't be long. He buttoned up his blue Crombie overcoat and gently fingered the white silk evening scarf at his neck. He watched her as she stepped through the emergency exit at the back of the club, and into the car park, her fun fur draped loosely over her shoulders. Her glossy chestnut hair bounced with life, framing her oval face. From beneath her feathered cut fringe huge blue eyes like a china doll, stared out at the cars searching for his vehicle.

Tony switched on his lights signalling his whereabouts and she shaded her eyes from the glare. Her soft translucent skin seemed to glow in anticipation. She smiled brightly and glided towards him. He opened the car door and she stepped in, her musk perfume pervading his nose and throat and making him want to drown in her arms. He started the engine. Her hand slid across to his knee. This wasn't right! A thousand alarm bells seemed to scream inside his brain. He started to sweat. She slid her hand higher up his leg, finding the mound inside his trousers.

"Ah, he's asleep," she said coquettishly, tracing her finger up and down the bends in his zip. She spread her hands over the inside of his thigh, lingering where leg and groin met, then twisted a circular pattern around the end of the rising protuberance inside his trousers.

He switched off the engine, slipped off his silk scarf and threw it around her neck pulling her to him. His hand like a steel trap closed over hers and forced it behind her back.

"Stop! You're hurting me," she hissed.

Tony's cold smile chilled her to the bone and she started to panic.

"What's the matter you stupid prick? What do you think you're …" Annette didn't finish her sentence. His lips locked onto hers, while with his left hand both ends of the scarf were drawn tighter and tighter. He began to choke the life out of her, his right hand forcing her arm behind her back and continuing, long after the bones had cracked.

He broke off his kiss and looked at her. "Why did you have to do that? Why did you have to say that?"

There was a strange gurgling noise in the back of her throat as he pushed her away from him with distaste. The bitch, try and fool around with his feelings, would she? Well, she wouldn't fool around with them again or anyone else for that matter.

Tony started the car and headed out towards the Clent Hills. No one saw him. No one would remember him anyway. The only people who came to Clent at that time of night were courting couples, who weren't interested in anyone except each other.

He drove into the dark, unlit lanes and did what he had to do. Then, slowly crooning the Roberta Flack hit 'Killing Me Softly'; he wiped his knife on the grass, arranged her body and was gone.

*

Allison had just arrived home and was enjoying a bit of supper with his wife, Mary, when the phone rang. The stark voice on the other end of the line said one thing, "Chief, we've got another." Allison grunted, gave Mary a swift peck on the cheek, struggled back into his overcoat and set off for the morgue. Mary dutifully covered the remnants of his meal with a plate and popped it into the oven to keep warm. She hoped it wouldn't dry up.

*

Allison returned home grim faced. The girl had been identified as Annette Jury. She had a string of convictions for prostitution and had worked as a hostess at Kelly's Wine Bar. Greg Allison set the wheels of this investigation into motion.

He sat at the table as Mary, bleary eyed, in her towelling dressing gown and nightclothes, went to the oven. Greg rubbed his eyes. It had been another very long day, "Sorry, Mary I really don't think I'm able to face the remains of my little bit of supper after seeing the mess they called Annette Jury. The sooner we get this maniac the better."

Mary nodded understandingly. "Not a problem, Greg. Get yourself up to bed and I'll bring you up a night cap."

Greg sighed and lifted his heavy frame out of the chair and mounted the stairs. His mind was running riot. Now, they'd got two linked, unsolved murders on their books; the press would have a field day. Trevor Booth from the Post would come sniffing around. He was like a terrier after a rat, once he got the whiff of a story. Anyway, with all the information they'd feed into the crime computer, as soon as the report came from Forensic, they'd have more to go on once again. Allison was convinced that the killer had as good as left his signature.

He lumbered into the bedroom and prepared for bed, pulling back the covers with a sigh of relief as he clambered in. By the time Mary arrived with a cup of hot cocoa, Allison was fast asleep. She smiled wryly and set the cup on her bedside table. It looked like she would be the one having the nightcap. She slipped off her dressing gown and got into bed beside him. She just prayed he would sleep well.

*

The telephone rang shrilly. Mary Allison quickly fielded the call and turned off the bell. Greg sighed and rolled over. Instantly awake, and ever considerate, Mary slipped out of bed, closed the door softly behind her, and picked up the extension on the landing.

"We've a girl! A beautiful baby girl!" Mark announced.

"That's terrific news. How's Debbie?" said Mary quietly.

"Recovering. The baby's in intensive care being checked over but the doctors think she's okay."

"I'm delighted for you both. I hope you don't mind if I don't wake Greg, he didn't get to bed until three-thirty this morning."

"Why, what's happened?"

"I'm afraid your killer has struck again. Look, I'll get him to call you when he wakes. I'm letting him sleep on."

"Fine. Jean will be at home and she can contact me at the hospital. I want to stay with Debbie as long as I can."

"Of course." Mary replaced the receiver carefully and glanced at the clock, seven forty-five. Mark had been considerate when he had rung believing that Greg would be up having his breakfast. Oh well. She tiptoed downstairs and made herself a cup of tea, then remembered that she'd better switch the telephone bell back on, and replace the receiver just in case any urgent calls needed to come through.

*

Trevor Booth was waiting at the station talking to the desk sergeant. He turned his freckled face affably towards Allison who was lumbering through the door. "Chief, anything I can report on the murders?"

"You'll have to wait until I can prepare a statement," he answered dismissively.

"Oh, come on. Give me a break. I need something worthwhile. Who found the second body? I know a kid discovered the first and I bet the second was a worse little shop of horrors."

"Believe me, Booth, as soon as we've anything to report, you'll be the first to know."

"Look, we know there's been two killings; that they're linked, just give me something as a starter on the rest of the press."

"You have my answer, Booth," said Allison curtly as he walked through past the station hatch and into the offices. Booth swore in exasperation and sat down on the hard bench in police reception and tapped his foot impatiently.

Allison barely had time to reach his office when the phone started ringing. He picked up the receiver smartly, "Allison."

"Sir, it looks like something is really breaking with the Vencat case."

"Well?"

"He's hired a warehouse in Rhyl with a refrigerator store. He's taken a lease for three months starting Monday. He's had another meet with Allen, and the guy running the cold meat store in Bristol has known gang connections."

"My, my, he has been busy."

"That's not all. Two of his men have hired themselves to a private contractor at Bristol docks."

"Well, it looks like things are happening fast. Keep me informed."

"Yes, Sir."

Allison dropped the phone into its cradle just as Mark Stringer, red-eyed from lack of sleep, walked in. "I heard the news, Mark. Congratulations!"

"Thanks, Chief. The baby's still in intensive care but it's just a precaution. When I go to see Debbie later, I expect to see the baby in a cot next to Deb's bed."

"That's good."

"Any developments?" asked Mark. "I heard there's been another."

"Plenty," replied Allison and he filled in the details of the previous evening's events.

Mark sighed, "That was quick! I mean, we knew he could strike again but I didn't expect another so soon."

"No, neither did I, but there again, remember the Yorkshire Ripper, he struck in quick succession, one after the other."

"Mmm."

Just then there was a knock on the door and Pooley entered. "Sir, I think you ought to see this, the crime computer has come up with two similar unsolved crimes. One in Worthing and one in Newcastle upon Tyne."

Allison and Stringer hurried down to Communications and studied the print out from the Home Office computer system, HOMES.

Allison studied the details of the Lisa Shore murder, strangled and mutilated under Worthing pier, two years previously. There were obvious similarities. She had been strangled with her own scarf, left as if asleep and on arrival at the morgue horrible mutilations had been discovered.

The second killing had occurred in the city of Newcastle, the body discovered in an entry attached to a row of condemned houses. She had been strangled by a man's tie, a common chain store brand that had been impossible to trace. She too, had suffered horrific mutilations. Allison had just requested the case notes on these killings when Taylor came in breathless and excited.

"Sir, Anthony Barton's statements don't check out." A gleam came into Allison's eye as Taylor explained, "Everything he claimed in his statement happened, but on the Thursday, not the Friday. I've confirmed this with his neighbours. He wasn't home Friday night. An old lady living opposite couldn't sleep and was sitting in a chair reading when she noticed Barton's car pulling up about three-thirty."

Allison looked at Stringer, "Go and pull him in. Let's find out where he was and why he lied."

Mark nodded, swiftly turned on his heel and left.

Allison returned to his office to prepare a statement for the press. He hated doing this. It was almost impossible to warn the public without appearing to scaremonger. He had eventually come up with something he thought satisfactory when there was a knock on the door. A WPC introduced a dynamic looking man who possessed incredible steel blue eyes, as Mr. Clifton, Head of Sales at Dempsey's. Allison offered him a seat and ordered two coffees. Clifton had an easy manner. He acted cool and confident, looking Allison directly in the eye as he answered each question. He was smartly dressed and Allison noticed the heavy, gold identity bracelet and the ostentatiously expensive gold and diamond signet ring that flashed on his right hand.

Clifton's hand kept flicking up and fingering his tie as he leaned back in the chair. Allison finished his questioning and extended his hand as he rose. Clifton's grip was firm but his palm was moist. Allison resisted the urge to wipe his hand on his jacket. He thanked him for taking the time to come in and closed the door thoughtfully after him as the WPC saw Clifton out.

Allison rose and stared out of the window of his office at the redbrick buildings across the street. The General Hospital was buzzing with life. Two ambulances pulled in with lights flashing. Another emergency, but nothing he had to deal with, he thought, thankfully.

Allison's eyes glazed over as he totally immersed himself in mentally and methodically picking over the facts of Janet Mason's murder. Maybe, just maybe, there was something he'd missed, some small fact, seemingly unimportant but vital to the investigation. He gazed long and hard with unseeing eyes at a nurse in her white cap and blue cape.

A sudden inexplicable feeling of dread crept over him. And he shivered.

The telephone bell jolted him out of his thoughts as he received another report on Vencat. He paged a team of detectives to meet him in the briefing room whilst he notified his superior. "Sir," Allison respectfully addressed the Chief Constable. "Things have progressed with the Vencat case."

"Yes?"

Allison related everything that he knew.

"Take the briefing and call me when you have something to report."

"Yes, Sir."

Allison got off the phone and paged Maddie, "Maddie get everyone together in the briefing room in," he checked his watch, "Ten minutes."

"Sir."

He sat back at his desk and took out his Mars Bar. He just had time to enjoy that before he met his team.

*

When they were all assembled, Allison went over the background of the case. "It seems that Vencat has organised batches of cocaine to be transported inside frozen meat being imported from Argentina. He's set up some sort of packing and trading house in Argentina, which appears to be a legitimate business. When there is a consignment ready, his own men are brought in to pack selected carcasses with high quality packages of cocaine. These are transported with the ordinary meats and shipped to Bristol. He has a couple of his gorillas working on the checking in bay to make sure nothing goes wrong. This is unloaded, repacked and moved to the warehouse in Bristol where the legitimate side of the business is carried out. The cargo with its deadly packages is taken off the lorries and immediately taken to Rhyl where Vencat has his chemists and laboratory ready to cut the pure cocaine and mix it. From there it goes to the different distributors, of which Allen is the main one. We need to keep a constant watch and to follow their progress particularly when the shipment arrives at Rhyl, but without arousing suspicion. Williams and Fry, you've been earmarked for Allen. Don't go in until the money and goods change hands. If all goes well we should get the complete ring. Good luck! Woodward, continue with the briefing."

Allison left Woodward explaining the details of the operation, code named Daytrip and went back to his office where the report from Forensic was sitting on his desk.

The genetic profile from the DNA extracted from the semen revealed a very definite pattern of two genetic characters. Also, blood that wasn't the victim's had been found under Janet's nails. This would be less helpful as it was one of the most common types, 'O' positive. Pubic hair and a loose head-hair with the same DNA characters as found on Janet's clothing showed the killer to have very dark hair. Some dark blue/black wool fibres and carpet fibres had also been found. The report confirmed that Annette Jury and Janet Mason had been killed by the same man. Together with the psychologist's profile, it was estimated that the killer would be a white male, about thirty-eight years of age.

Allison picked up the phone, "Pooley! Send Booth in here, he should be at Reception. Tell him I've got something for him."

Allison tugged thoughtfully on his lower lip while he waited for Booth. He hauled himself out of his chair and went to his office door. He could see Booth turning into the corridor, his freckled face breaking into a grin of earnest enthusiasm as he saw the Chief.

"Maddie, can we have some refreshments in here?" growled Allison to the WPC busy at her typewriter.

Allison and Booth shook hands and went into the office. It wasn't long before they were both sitting at the desk with cups of tea that Maddie had brought them. Allison waited until the door closed before addressing Trevor Booth.

"We need your help. The murders look like serial killings and we need to catch the bastard before he kills anyone else."

"What's in it for me?"

"I'll give you all prepared police statements first, and the right to interview the witnesses who found Annette Jury's body. Fair enough?"

Booth thought for a moment before responding, "Sounds okay to me. What else do you want?"

"Right. Now, obviously I'm not at liberty to divulge certain aspects of the case, we don't want any copycat killings. But, I've been more than fair in presenting you with enough information to write an exclusive on the two murders." He handed Booth a type written sheet, "We need the press to launch an appeal for anyone who was in the vicinity of the Clent Hills last night, travellers en route to or from Birmingham etc. Invite anyone who may or may not have seen anything suspicious to come forward. We know that Annette Jury was killed elsewhere and dumped at the Clent Hills, and that the mutilations were performed on her body about an hour after death."

"Mutilations? What mutilations?" asked Booth.

"That I can't tell you. I said no specific details."

"Was a knife used?"

"That I can tell you. A bread knife of sorts, long blade approximately twenty-two centimetres with a serrated edge."

"Ripper style murders?"

"Similar, equally brutal."

"Motive?"

"We don't know. Sexual gratification and extreme violence is involved. There is no connection between the victims. They appear to have been picked at random."

"Mmm, okay. Look, I'll get on to my other press associates. Do you want me to contact the television news desks? Local radio?"

Allison nodded, "Please. It would save us a job. They can confirm the request if they need to."

"Shall we filter through replies?"

"Any that come your way, please feel free. We've worked together in this way before so you know the form. Oh, and here are the addresses of the witnesses who discovered the second body."

"Right!" Booth gulped down his tea, shook hands with Allison and left, eager to catch the late edition.

Allison called Pooley into his office and explained what he'd organised, "The extension number quoted in the press will be yours, so expect to be busy. You'll get the usual crank calls, of course, but they'll all have to be checked. Is your man back from Mrs. Mason's yet?"

"Not yet, Sir. I'm expecting him to return at any minute."

"Well, when he arrives, get another line through on your desk, he can work with you."

"Yes, Sir."

"And Pooley?"

"Sir?"

"Run a check on previous sex offenders who match our man's description, see if we come up with anything."

"Sir."

Allison sat thoughtfully. He took out the photos of the two victims and stared at them hard as if the pictures themselves held some clue to the murderer's identity that would be yielded up to him if he stared long enough. But nothing came to light.

He rubbed his eyes wearily and replaced the PM reports. The photos remained and something caught his attention and he grabbed the phone and asked for an outside line. He drummed his fingers impatiently on his desk as he waited for his call to be answered.

"Path. Lab," said the lilting voice of Annie James, Hurst's secretary.

"Put me through to Johnny please." Annie recognised the

Inspector's abrasive tones and connected him immediately.

"Johnny, I've just been going over the reports you made and something struck me."

"What's that?"

"The angle of the cuts made by the blade."

"What about them?"

"The wound extending from Janet Mason's right lower abdomen, to beneath her left breast could only have been performed by a left hander. Try the movement in the air."

Hurst did, "You're absolutely right, Greg, a right handed slash would have arced the other way. I should have spotted that; ought to make your job easier too."

"Yes, it should, but that small detail we'll keep to ourselves for a while until you've had time to check the validity of it thoroughly."

"Will do. But it certainly seems likely."

Greg Allison replaced the receiver reflectively, trying to recollect whether he'd met any left handed suspects in the course of his enquiry. He didn't think that he had.

There was a tap at the door. Mark popped his head round, "I've got Barton in interview room two. Do you want to see him?"

"Not just yet. Have you got anything?"

"No, I was waiting for you."

"Just get on with it."

"Sir." Mark left, closing the door quietly behind him.

Allison opened the top drawer in his desk and took out a Mars Bar. He peeled off the top of the wrapper and bit into it, enjoying the smooth texture of the chocolate and soft toffee that hung in strands, which he licked from his lips with the relish of a child. He was just removing the last traces of sticky chocolate from his fingers with his mouth when Pooley knocked and entered.

"Excuse me, Sir. Harmon's back. He found Janet Mason's diary - nothing of any note in there; just birthdays and appointments like."

"Well, it was worth a try. Thanks, Pooley."

"And, Sir, the crime computer's come up with six offenders who fit our man's description."

45

"Fine, now check if any of the six are left handed."

"Left handed, Sir?"

"That's what I said. Then report back."

Pooley closed the door behind him and Allison thought a trip to the men's room was in order, to wash his sticky hands before joining Mark in interview room two.

*

Allison entered the room and dismissed one of the constables. The tape recorder had been switched off and was now reactivated. The interview continued with the interrogating officers identifying themselves and establishing the date, time and Barton's full name."

"Well?" said Allison expectantly.

"He claims he had a rendezvous with a woman," said Mark.

"Good, then he has an alibi that can be backed up."

"Not exactly, he refuses to name the woman."

"Why is that, Mr. Barton?"

"Look, Chief Inspector, I can't divulge her name unless you can assure me that you're not going to contact her."

"Mr. Barton, we have to check your story otherwise how do we know you're telling the truth?"

Barton's spatulate fingers raked through his dark hair. "I've already explained my dilemma to your sergeant here. I was out on Friday night with a lady, a married lady. I can't risk you turning up on her doorstep, checking my story and her husband listening. Why can't you just ask the hotel we stayed at?"

"Because," said Mark with a hint of exasperation in his voice, "It is possible to check into a hotel and to leave without the proprietors or receptionist knowing. It's no guarantee that because you're registered in that hotel that you're actually there."

"I know that," said Barton, using that patient tone usually reserved for explaining something to an obstinate child, "But as I've said before I am not going to be responsible for breaking up a marriage."

"Come, Mr. Barton, aren't you being just a little melodramatic? Can't you tell us who she is and when she is likely to be alone at home or at work, if she works, and I promise you, we will be as discreet as possible? Or, if you prefer she can come here to verify your story."

Barton groaned, "We've been through all this, what's the alternative?"

"Would you submit to a blood test?"

"Anything, but don't make me compromise this lady, please."

Allison gave a nod to the remaining uniformed constable, and Barton was escorted out.

*

At a local secondary school the Assistant Caretaker, Arthur Crabtree was sweeping up the litter scattered by the tuck shop as the last of the stragglers were going back into school after morning break. One student, a physically mature fifteen year old with copper hair pointed at the man and whispered something to her Asian friend, who he knew was called Anne Marie. The two girls sniggered and ran in.

Arthur's mouth set in a hard line and he swept more vigorously

A younger girl sauntered past and Arthur stopped her. He pointed at the girl with the auburn hair running up the school steps, "Hey. That girl there. Do you know her name? And which year she's in?"

The schoolgirl paused and said, "That's Dawn Ashby. She's brilliant at drama and music."

"Is she now?"

"Yes, everyone knows that. She's in year eleven." The girl ran in after the pair and Arthur leant on his broom and looked thoughtful. He set aside his broom and entered the school keeping an eye on the girls who were now just ahead of him.

Dawn and her friend hurried to the gymnasium.

Arthur stopped and watched as the PE mistress came striding out and addressed the two girls, "You're late. Hurry up and get changed now."

Anne Marie ran into the changing room to her locker. Dawn hung back.

"What's the matter, Dawn?"

47

"Please, Miss. I've forgotten my kit."

"Dawn Ashby, that's the fourth time this term!"

"Yes, Miss. Sorry, Miss."

"Once more and it's a detention. Get a kit from Lost Property in my office."

"Yes, Miss."

The gym mistress strode off leaving Dawn looking suitably crestfallen. She noticed the caretaker standing watching and smirking. She turned on him, "What are you staring at? Pathetic old bum!"

Dawn scurried away and didn't see Arthur's smirk turn to cold anger.

*

A few teachers and cleaners passed Arthur as they left the premises that afternoon calling out, "Goodnight, Arthur." Arthur responded in a like manner as he mopped the foyer, running over and over the same spot biding his time until the place was empty and completely devoid of people.

The school clock read 4:45 p.m. Arthur glanced at it and walked to the big wooden doors that led to the yard and car park. He opened it and looked out. His eyes scanned the dark car park, which was revealed as empty as an unpacked suitcase in the muddy school lights.

He slammed the big outer doors and locked them. Next came the heavy iron bolts, which he drew across with a clunk. His keys jangled loudly, as he locked the inner doors, and returned to the foyer.

Arthur looked around stealthily and moved toward the secretary's office. He unlocked and opened the creaky door and entered, closing it softly behind him. He crossed to the filing cabinets and soon found the drawer he wanted, which said 'Year 11'. He quickly rummaged through it until he found Dawn Ashby's file.

He examined it carefully, checked her timetable, and made a mental note of the girl's address before replacing it and leaving as unobtrusively as he had entered.

Arthur finished putting his cleaning utensils away and left by a side door. He made his way to the school gates where a few pupils lingered. Shouts of, "Arf a brain Arthur" reached his ears, which he tried to ignore. He heard them giggling, put his head down and marched to the heavy iron gates. He closed them and then secured the heavy padlock.

More chants followed, "Crabby Crabtree!" He snapped his head up and saw Dawn Ashby with her friends who all laughed and ran off down the road.

Arthur Crabtree smiled humourlessly; he had decided what he would do.

4
Another victim

Dawn Ashby munched her toast as she listened to her mother's incessant chatter. God, how could anyone be so cheerful first thing in the morning? Nothing ever seemed to get her down. She took a sip of her tea. Her mother trilled, "Dawn. Dawn! You're not listening to me."

"Sorry, Mum. What did you say?"

"I asked what your plans were. I'm cleaning for Mrs. Evans this morning, I should be finished around eleven then, I'll do the shopping before going on to work this afternoon. I need to know about food tonight."

"Oh, I've got a free first lesson this morning, then French and double Art. This afternoon we're allowed revision in the library or at home. I'll probably come home."

Dawn brushed back the copper fringe, which stubbornly fell back into her eyes.

"Well, if you're home make sure it's to study, not to play that music of yours full blast and upset all the neighbours."

"Okay, Mumsie, don't worry I'll be good." Dawn stood up and put her arms around her mother's ample waist.

"Don't, you've got marmalade all over your hands, you mucky pup!" laughed her mother.

"What's a little sticky goo between mother and daughter?" teased Dawn.

"You don't do the washing!" said her mother.

"Okay, okay, I surrender! What do you want me to do?" said Dawn.

Mrs. Ashby looked fondly at her daughter and pushed back the rebellious fringe from Dawn's eyes.

"Put a wash on low temperature for me. It's all set, you just have to switch it on."

"And?"

"Two letters on the hall table need posting and there's the money for the gas bill. Will you have time to pay it? It's the wrong end of town for me."

"Consider it done. Wash, letters, gas, got it. See you later." She helped her mother on with her coat and gave her a peck on the cheek.

She may have said more, if she'd realised it would be the last time she'd see her.

*

The appeal for witnesses went out in the press and on local radio news and television stations. Replies began to filter in.

DCI Allison was studying the file on the Lisa Shore murder that had occurred in Worthing. There were definite similarities. Samples of DNA obtained from semen stained clothing were being sent to the lab for cross matching, a difficult process as the DNA had broken down considerably and would require heating numerous times to get enough reproductions for a true coding. Allison was still waiting for the file on the Newcastle murder. He had just taken a bite from his daily Mars Bar when the desk sergeant rang through to tell him that Trevor Booth had arrived.

"Send him through," said Allison, his mouth full of chocolate. He hurriedly chewed his way through the rest of his bar, which spoiled his enjoyment and was just swallowing the last mouthful when Trevor's characteristic 'knock, knock, knock' was heard. "Enter," called Allison.

Trevor walked in red-faced and excited, carrying a sheaf of papers. "Chief, we've had a reasonable response to the appeal, so far. I've compiled a report of names, addresses times etc; most of them are pretty uneventful." He passed Allison a wad of papers, retaining one. "But this one, this looks interesting."

"Cut the dramatics and get on with it," grunted Allison.

"Right." Trevor pulled up a chair. He licked his lips nervously. It was obvious he thought he was on to something. "A courting couple in a field close to the church were quite intimately involved, when a car pulled into the field and stopped about a hundred yards ahead. Their windows were misted up so they couldn't see the make or colour, although the lad, who's something of a car buff said it sounded like an Escort. Anyway, they stopped what they were doing as they thought it might have been the cops on the love patrol and they didn't want to get caught. They opened the window when they heard the other car door open and shut. They couldn't see anything, but they heard the passenger door open and waited for the sound of footsteps approaching their car. There were none. Anyway," Booth was obviously enjoying this; "The cold night air and the threat of the cops had cooled their ardour somewhat so they just sat quietly for a while and waited. When they heard all sorts of grunts and groans, she made a crack about kinky sex, if their neighbours wanted it outside on the wet grass in the cold that was up to them but she did admit it was something of a turn on. That was until they heard some weird noises."

"Weird noises?" asked Allison.

"Clothes being ripped, animal type grunting and that sort of thing. They had just decided that it must an over enthusiastic couple when they heard some singing, a good voice apparently, a man was crooning softly. The girl said it would have been quite romantic if she hadn't felt so uneasy. She didn't know why but she felt unnerved. Shortly after, she wound up the window because she and her boyfriend were getting cold. They think they only heard one door open and close."

"Singing eh?"

"Yes."

"Singing what?"

"The girl thought it was the Roberta Flack number, Killing Me Softly."

Allison raised his eyebrows, "Can the couple remember which field they parked in?"

"Oh, yes. Apparently, it's their regular spot. They can take us there, no problem."

"Right!" Allison leaned across and took the sheet from Trevor and skimmed through the report. Booth was correct. He might have got something. The time tallied, the place looked right. It was something that needed to be followed up.

Booth gave a long, low whistle, "The crooning killer," he looked hopefully at Allison.

"Look Trevor, just sit on this for a while until we check it out, then I assure you, I'll let you use some of it, okay?"

Trevor seemed doubtful then, thrust his hand out to the Chief and grinned his familiar toothy grin, "Right, I'll wait for your say so."

Allison smiled. He and Trevor understood one another.

*

Debbie Stringer gazed lovingly at her new baby daughter, tiny and fragile. This evening, Mark was bringing Christian to meet his new sister. She couldn't wait to see her young son. Poor little chap must be so confused, being babysat, spending one night at his Aunt's and then Granny looking after him, not knowing the whereabouts of his mother.

They had planned it all so differently but at least Christian had been involved in the pregnancy. He'd heard his sister's heartbeat and felt the baby move. Debbie hoped that the present from the baby to Christian would help to alleviate any jealousy. According to all the books she'd read, it was the right thing to do.

She heard a murmur from the cot and struggled to move in an attempt to get out of bed to pick up Catherine. She had never let Christian cry. He'd always been happy and contented and she was going to make sure that Catherine was the same. She looked in the cot to make certain that the baby wasn't just making little noises in her sleep. What she saw there had her immediately reaching for her bell to summon the nurse as she shouted loudly at the top of her voice.

Nurse Lim, a petite Chinese probationer came running, and immediately called for the Sister. Debbie didn't know what to do. Catherine was spasmodically twitching all over, her eyes were rolling in her head and the most peculiar gurgles were coming from her throat.

"Don't panic, Mrs. Stringer," came the Sister's soothing voice as she drew the curtains around the bed. "You won't help your baby by getting hysterical."

Debbie finally found her voice, "What's wrong? What's happening?"

"It's a febrile convulsion."

"What do you mean? A fit?" Debbie was openly crying.

"Nurse Lim, take Mrs. Stringer to the Nurses' Station, make her a cup of hot, sweet tea; get a wheelchair."

"I don't want any tea, I want to stay with my baby."

"It's best if you go." Sister was kind but firm and Debbie found herself being led unwillingly away by the student nurse. She resented the activity that was taking place around her bed, around her baby, but in which she could play no part. Debbie couldn't walk very quickly. She shuffled out into the corridor helped by Nurse Lim, who left her leaning on a rail while she went to find a wheelchair. Debbie looked anguished at the sounds coming from her room, where a number of medical staff were running in and out.

It was to this scene of pandemonium that Mary Allison arrived carrying flowers and a present for the new baby. With relief at seeing a friend, Debbie fell sobbing into a confused Mary Allison's arms.

*

Greg Allison grunted in response to Mark's question. He'd other things on his mind now. Apart from the murders and the Vencat case, a look in his diary had revealed that it was his wedding anniversary, Wednesday. Special celebrations were in order, they'd been married twenty years, and he'd bought nothing, planned nothing and didn't know what to plan or buy anyway.

"Greg?"

The use of his Christian name brought Greg back to the present. Although Mark had permission to be on first name terms, he very rarely used it, except socially. He preferred the old fashioned courtesies at work.

"Sorry, Mark; you were saying?"

"Woodward's left a number, it appears the Customs and Excise men are aware something is up."

"God damn it. Hasn't anyone informed them? The whole operation could be ruined. It's the big fish we want not just the haul and subordinates. Clear it with them and put them in the picture. We'll probably need their help. I'm off to do a little errand of my own. Anyone wants me I'll be back by four."

"Sir."

Allison heaved himself out of his chair, grabbed his raincoat from the stand, and slipped a Mars Bar into his coat pocket and left the office, his bulldog chin jutting forward leading the way to Corporation Street and the shops.

*

Woodward gritted his teeth, he was watching the loading bay from a workman's hut. He kept his eyes fixed on the frozen carcasses as they were unloaded and repacked into refrigerated trucks. This was done efficiently and the men on the docks wasted little time.

Woodward stamped his feet on the cold concrete in the cramped hut that had little protection from the elements. His breath streamed out of his nostrils, cutting through the air like vapour trails. He wasn't alone. He had two men with him for backup in case of impending trouble.

"Do you think it's likely we'll have any bother?" asked one copper called Lane.

The other, Davies, looked across at Woodward, interested in the answer.

"It's doubtful," mused Woodward, "But you never know! Better to play safe."

"What are those two up to?" enquired Davies inclining his head towards the Customs and Excise men who were busy filming the whole proceedings.

"Nothing for you to worry about," Woodward replied, "Customs and Excise are working with us on this one. They want this bust as badly as we do. They're filming the lot. That is their way. Leaves nothing to chance."

"When do we strike?" asked Lane.

"We wait until the trucks have left; then and only then can we pick up the two villains posing as casual labour. This time we mean to get everyone that's involved. The whole rat pack."

"From the bottom to the top?"

"You got it."

The heavy metallic clang of the steel door as it shut on the last lorry to be packed seemed to spur Woodward into action. He signalled his call sign on the radio. "Lorries are packed and ready to go," he murmured. "Alert all cars; stand by to

55

follow trucks. Four just leaving now. All contain suspect meat. They look legitimate enough; they will probably take the direction of the cold meat storage warehouse in Avonmouth."

Woodward waited for acknowledgement before signing off. He wanted to ensure that the way was clear. He allowed a reasonable amount of time to pass in order to permit the genuine workers to disperse to other duties and as a precautionary measure, in case one of the lorries returned unexpectedly.

"Now, Gov?" asked Lane in a whisper.

"No … Hold off. We don't want any muck ups." He let a moment or two pass. "You never know who may come calling."

Customs had finished their reel of film and were loading another. One of the four-man crew glanced across, "Say when you're ready and we'll go for the knock."

Woodward raised a hand for silence. He knew the importance of getting the timing just right. "Okay, one of the bastards is coming out of the office now. The other one's right behind him. They're talking together. Wait! The guy with the beer gut is brandishing a bunch of keys. Looks like he's getting ready to lock up. Carter! Thomas!" He indicated two of the Customs men, "Get out there and approach them from behind. Make sure you cover the side alley by the slipway. Davies, you're with me. Lane, take your car. Block off the gates. Don't let anything in or out. You've got three minutes."

"Sir." Lane instantly obeyed. Woodward only gave him enough time to reach his car then, signalled to the others. It was time to go!

Davies and Woodward moved casually out from the hut and began to approach the two men, still engaged in conversation.

The man with the beer gut was having difficulty locking the huge padlock, which was refusing to close. He had small squinty eyes like an over fat Berkshire boar and the most obscene hands Davis had ever seen. Enormous hands with large spreading fingers and bulbous tips showing an abnormal expanse of nail that seemed to grow right around each finger. His companion, a lean wiry man of athletic build glanced suspiciously at the approaching Woodward and Davies.

"Here, Wilf," he hissed.

"What's up?"

Slim pointed at the coppers, "Who are they?"

"Dunno, see what they want."

"I don't like it, Wilf," snarled Slim. "I'm out of here." He turned to run. Davies took a flying leap and rugby tackled him to the ground, snapping on the handcuffs as Slim's face hit the gravel.

Woodward pinned Wilf against the portakabin door, which rattled loudly attracting the attention of the few workers on the slipway who stopped to watch and enjoy the unexpected entertainment.

"I'm a police officer and I'm arresting you on suspicion of handling illegal substances for general distribution in the UK."

"Piss off!" Wilf spat, "You got nothing on us. Let us go." The huge crab-like hands clawed to be free as Carter and Thomas came through the alley from behind. Carter helped Woodward secure Wilf while Thomas dragged Slim to his feet and showed them both his warrant card. He repeated the familiar words, "You have the right to remain silent. Anything you say will be taken down and may be used in evidence against you."

Both men were led away and unceremoniously shoved into the back of Lane's car.

Woodward couldn't resist a smile. This felt good! He reported in, a note of pride entering his voice, "Mission accomplished ... Yes? ... On it!" He'd received his latest orders and paged his men. "Okay. Lane, Davies? You take them in. You've got all you need. Things have been handled satisfactorily this end. Well done!"

Woodward walked briskly to his car whistling light-heartedly.

The next immediate step was up to Brand.

*

Brand was watching the warehouse from a top window in a derelict building opposite. He could see right down into the yard, which backed on to railway lines. Here, there were several customs men who had been issued with regulation B.R. workmen's' uniforms, right down to the shovels and orange Day-Glo tabards. Apart from the radios, which he knew they had hidden in their donkey jackets, it was impossible to distinguish them from the real thing. They'd managed to get one of their men in at the warehouse as a packer and he was wired for sound.

Customs men were waiting to video the sequence of events at the warehouse, which would be valuable evidence in court. Arrests would be made when the load was on its way to Rhyl, and innocents, of which there were bound to be a few, would be released after interview.

A distorted call sign came through on the radio. It was Woodward. The four trucks had safely left the docks and were on their way. Brand alerted his men and warned the motorcyclist and waiting surveillance vehicle to follow the load without attracting any attention.

Woodward was making his own way to Vencat's laboratory and was leaving Brand and the customs men to deal with things at the Bristol end. Brand didn't have long to wait. He was warned of the convoy's approach. The customs' men set the film rolling as the first truck rumbled into the yard. They watched as the yard became alive with activity. All four lorries pulled up. Six men in overalls began unloading as a gangling man with thinning hair and a moustache appeared to take charge. He directed which carcasses were to go to the warehouse and, which were to be re-loaded onto the third lorry.

"How does he know, which meat to pack?" said Brand aloud. His voice made his partner jump. Things had got very tense while they were watching. Adrenalin was running high.

"Wait! Isn't that Samms?" Their man on the inside had pushed forward.

"I hope whoever's on the tapes is getting all this. What's he doing?"

"It looks like he's trying to find the distinguishing mark on the meat."

"What's he saying? Damn! I wish I could hear."

"We'll know soon enough. Let's just hope they don't rumble him."

The steel doors on the lorry clanged shut. The lanky man with the stilted walk slapped his hand on the back of the container door as a gesture of good luck and the lorry grumbled into life. The guttural splutter of the engine could be heard in Brand's observation room.

He put out a call to the vehicles on mobile surveillance, "Daytrip is underway. I repeat Operation Daytrip is underway. Over and out." Brand made a move towards the stairs. His stride was long and he moved with intent showing that he knew satisfaction would soon be his.

*

The results from Anthony Barton's blood test were sitting on Allison's desk, along with information that none of the suspect sex offenders whose names had come up on the computer were left handed. Mark Stringer stood uncomfortably watching the Chief and awaiting the reaction he knew would come. Greg Allison swore softly, the test had showed conclusively that Anthony Barton was not their man.

"Damn it, Mark, we have so little to go on. Serial killers, who kill at random, as well you know, are the most difficult to trace."

Mark nodded his head sympathetically. He didn't dare speak knowing the Chief's growing sense of frustration.

Allison became tight-lipped; adding to his angst was the knowledge that he would again have to face the barrage of city shoppers since he'd returned empty handed from his trip to town. Allison's mood and temper left a lot to be desired. To cap it all, he thought with exasperation, the newsagent had sold out of Mars Bars and he had been forced to buy some other named chocolate brand that held little comfort for him. Savagely he bit into this as he grimly stirred his tea.

"Beats me," he said aggressively, "How we can know so much about a man and yet we can't find him."

"Come, Sir. We knew it would be difficult. When it's

some maniac, like you said, who kills randomly it takes time. But we'll get him."

"Time is likely to mean more bodies. If we don't get a break soon we'll have the Commissioner breathing down our necks. He's already agitated," growled Allison uncomfortably remembering the telephone conversation he'd endured with his superior twenty minutes earlier. That had done little to sweeten his temper either. "Before you go this evening I want you to chase up the Newcastle police. We've not received their dossier on that killing five years ago. Check Pooley and Harmon's replies to our appeal and contact Colin Brady. See if he's come up with anything, new."

Woodward was heading down the M5 towards the Severn Bridge. He was about four cars back. There was another car detailed to take pursuit from the M4 while Woodward would proceed to Caerlon. Everything had been painstakingly arranged to arouse least suspicion.

The driver of the truck was a thin, weasely little man with lank sandy hair. His companion was just the opposite and had obviously been selected for his muscle.

A glowing cigarette end sparked out of the lorry cab's window and was immediately crushed under the wheels of an overtaking red saloon. Woodward hoped it was an omen that they would crush these drug operatives just as easily. The drug barons, they were the worst, pedalling death in the shape of a dream. His hands tightened their grip on the wheel. He'd never forgotten that pretty, young teenager. Pretty? She was a mess when they'd found her. He remembered her happy laughing face when he'd first seen her with her friends at the Stage Door Cafe, her shower of glossy dark hair, bright green eyes and the sprinkling of freckles on that upturned nose. Then she'd become involved with that Rupert character, who had introduced her to heroin. The downhill slide was quick. She soon became addicted and prostituted herself to feed that addiction. It was then her appearance changed. That lovely thick hair became greasy and unkempt, losing all its lustre. The fresh bloom on her skin withered and faded, replaced by an unhealthy sheen of oiliness and spots. She no longer cared about personal hygiene; her parents abandoned her and although he'd tried his best to help, she wouldn't listen and had regarded him as the enemy not the drug.

He blinked back the tears as he remembered the pitiful state in which they'd found her, comatose in a derelict house, prostrate on a urine soaked mattress. Her wasted, thin arms bruised from the abuse of so many needles. Her veins shot to pieces. Scabs had formed where she had tried to use her legs as another point of entry.

The ambulance arrived but not in time. She was dead on arrival. Woodward bit his lip hard. What a tragic waste of life. If he had caught that Rupert creep he'd have broken his God damned neck. In Woodward's eyes all the pushers, couriers and organisers were equally responsible for Janice's death. They ought to be exterminated like vermin, wiped from the face of the earth.

Woodward, usually unemotional, wiped a stray, lone tear that had escaped from his eye and swallowed hard, trying to suppress the well of emotion rising up inside him with the seemingly physical lump in his throat. He switched on his radio and forced a smile. This was going to be a good bust.

*

Mark sat with Debbie in the office next to the Nurses' Station. Mr. Greenhalf was explaining, "Sometimes after a traumatic delivery, and if the baby has been in distress in the womb, they will suffer a convulsion such as the one you witnessed. Often, it is a one off occurrence, sometimes the child experiences one or two more and they simply grow out of them. Very occasionally it is a sign of something more serious."

"You mean epilepsy?" said Debbie, her voice flat and expressionless.

"In some instances, yes. I can assure you, however, it is usually far more alarming for those witnessing the attack than for the child suffering it."

"How will we know if it's serious?" asked Mark anxiously.

"We will perform one or two tests and keep a close watch on her."

"Is that all you can tell us?" insisted Mark.

"I'm afraid that is all we can tell you for now. It's more important for you both to be calm if it ever happens again. Make sure there is nothing to harm her, no sharp corners in her cot for example. You understand?"

Debbie nodded meekly.

"It's vital that you don't worry and panic. If you want my honest opinion, I believe it is most likely a one off occurrence."

"And if it isn't?" Mark's voice was hard and snapped like a steel trap.

"Well if it isn't, we'll talk further." Mr. Greenhalf stood up as a signal that the interview was concluded. Debbie and Mark went out slowly, Debbie still having to support her stitches from the caesarean section that she knew would take a while to heal.

*

Woodward was travelling on the A470. He'd just passed through Builth Wells. This sort of country always reminded him of Dylan Thomas. He remembered lines from the famous play, Under Milkwood, about Mrs. Ogmore Pritchard, "Very la-di-da. Got a man in Builth Wells." He chuckled to himself; he had an aunt who spoke exactly like one of Thomas's characters. What was it she had said that had amused him so much when she was complaining about her sister-in-law? Oh, yes, "That bloomin' sister in law of mine, she's so bloody house-proud, she even puts paper underneath the cuckoo clock." His Aunty Carol was a natural comedienne and he knew exactly what she meant.

Woodward swerved violently as a white Sierra blazed past, the horn blaring loudly. In his daydreaming the detective had wandered into the middle of the road. He shook his head and concentrated more on his driving. It was dangerous to think too much.

The lorry was there, just four cars ahead of him. He'd taken over from a motorcyclist at Talgarth. The next change over looked like being Newtown. He would then make his way to the warehouse at Rhyl leaving others to cover the rest of the journey. This was going to be the most difficult part of the operation.

*

Allison looked at the pearl necklace he had just purchased from Samuels; perfect pearls, all the same size. Eye catching, gleaming opalescence that would stunningly adorn Mary's neck. He knew she would like them. It had been worth braving the bustle of the shoppers. He smiled with satisfaction as he closed the black satin lined box. He'd even bought some silver foil wrapping paper, and an extravagant black bow and ribbon. Well, there was no time like the present. He started to try and wrap his gift. He cursed under his breath, his fingers becoming clumsier in his attempts to make this gift special. The paper creased awkwardly. He was just about to begin again when there was a knock and Maddie entered. "Sir, I have the file on the Newcastle murder."

"Thanks, Maddie."

She paused and watched his difficulty in trying to wrap the gift, "Shall I do it, Sir?"

"Eh? Oh yes please. I'm all of a dither; fingers and thumbs that's me, at least, when it comes to anything like this. Mary always wraps our presents."

Maddie expertly ironed out the creases in the paper and stopped to look at Allison's gift.

"Oh, Sir! It's beautiful."

Allison flushed with pleasure, "I thought so, let's hope my wife does."

"I'm sure she will, Sir." In less than a minute, Maddie had it wrapped professionally even winding the strands of ribbon around her pen to make them hang like ringlets.

"Thanks, Maddie. I was beginning to wish I'd had it wrapped at the shop but you've done an excellent job, I'm sure it's even better than they could have done."

Maddie smiled, pleased at the praise, "Where are you taking her?"

"I've booked a table at The Celebrity Restaurant next door to the New Rep. We're going to see the Alan Ayckbourne play then have a late supper. She doesn't know, she thinks I'm working. It's all to be a surprise."

He felt embarrassed at the pride he heard in his own voice

when he talked of his anniversary. His feelings ran deep and he found difficulty expressing them even to Mary herself. It was the one time of the year that his actions told their own story and in his own way he was pleased that they did. How Mary put up with an undemonstrative, gruff bear like him, he'd often wondered, but he was glad that she did.

Maddie left his office and the present took pride of place on his desk. He'd lock it away later but now he had to examine the report from Newcastle and see if the computer was right in linking this unsolved case with the two in his territory.

He pored over the details and concluded that Janet Mason and the Newcastle girl, Jodie Stubbs, had striking similarities so there could well be a link. But the Newcastle killing appeared to be a one off. That trail had gone stone cold. Allison couldn't think of anyone interviewed who had reason to be in all these areas. That was going to be a puzzle. Why had there been a killing five years ago, another two years later in Worthing and now suddenly two more in the space of a few days, this time numbered? If this maniac had a blood lust, what had prevented him from killing in the interim period? Prison? Allison's mind ticked over like a computer. He picked up the phone and dialled. "Allison here. Put a trace on all prisoners fitting our killer's profile who were in prison anywhere between December '89 and February '92 and March '92 to November '94. Let me know what you find." He replaced the receiver, it was a long shot and there were probably hundreds.

*

Tony stretched himself in a fitful sleep and woke with a start. The devils were coming to get him he was sure of it. Silently he said a prayer and switched on his bedside lamp. The light was dim. He reached for the cord overhanging his bed and pulled. The light popped softly and he swore.

His mother's voice came reedily through the thin walls, "Tony, Tony are you all right?" She spoke in that nasal twang that he loathed so much.

Immediately, he flushed with guilt at his uncharitable thoughts of his mother whom he knew he should love dearly.

"It's okay, Mum; the bulb's gone in my room that's all."

"I'll come and change it for you. I've got one in the cupboard."

"No, it's okay. You get back to sleep. I'll be all right."

"It's no trouble. It will help keep the demons away. Open your curtains a little, let the street light shine through and turn on your bedside light."

A few minutes later he heard the soft pad of her feet on the landing outside his door. She slithered in, bearing the bulb like the Cross of the Redeemer. Gently humming a hymn, she raised herself onto the bed and stood astride his head on the pillow. Her absurdly short nightdress rose up to her hips exposing her nakedness. She lingered over changing the bulb, stretching and parting her legs more and more until she heard his breath come in short sharp gasps. Then she slowly lowered herself onto his face.

*

The lorry had arrived without mishap. The drivers had no suspicion of the surveillance they had been under since leaving Bristol. Vencat was there! Woodward hissed low and hard between his teeth. The familiar gold tooth flashed in the sunlight as Woodward, through his binoculars, studied this obscene member of humanity, who traded on the weakness of others.

Vencat was grinning broadly as he greeted the two drivers. The weasely man drew out a cigarette and smoked calmly as he watched the two men from the warehouse unloading their cargo of misery.

Woodward knew the chemists were inside ready to start cutting. His mouth was dry. He would dearly love to burst in now but he knew he had to wait. The strain was making him edgy.

The Customs and Excise men were busy filming, gathering more evidence to go against Vencat and his verminous crew. Woodward took a mouthful of the scalding coffee he'd been given. He almost cried out in pain as the hot drink nearly blistered his palate. It certainly took a patch of skin off the roof of his mouth. He suppressed a yelp and spoke into his radio quietly.

"Get ready to move. Wait for my signal."

The truck had been emptied fairly rapidly. It was something they couldn't afford to dawdle over. Now, the weasely man and his companion were shaking Vencat's hand and preparing to leave. He alerted his police vehicles to prepare to tail them so that they could be picked up safely. The video camera was busy recording the passing of an envelope between Vencat, and the lorry driver and his companion. Woodward grinned humourlessly; oh, yes, this bust would taste so sweet to him!

*

Mrs. Ashby was climbing the stairs to the block of flats where she and Dawn lived. She puffed a little as she struggled with her shopping. It was a nuisance that the lift wasn't working. That was the second time this month. Still, she only had to get to the third floor. Evelyn Ashby had finished cleaning for Mrs. Evans, done her shopping and had completed her afternoon's work at the travel agents. She was now on her way to prepare dinner for herself and her teenage, seventeen year old daughter. She hoped Dawn had remembered to put the washing through its cycle. Dawn's music teacher's retirement party was that week and Dawn had said she wanted to wear her pink dress for the occasion. The time was now six thirty.

Mrs. Ashby manoeuvred herself so she could ring the bell with her chin and she waited. She struggled to ring again and called out, "Dawn!"

Dawn didn't answer so Mrs. Ashby put down her bag of groceries with a heavy sigh. She fished around in her handbag for the key. Why did they always have to drop to the bottom of her bag? Mrs. Ashby finally opened the door after wriggling the key in the lock. It needed a squirt of WD 40, she thought, as the mechanism seemed to be playing up.

She was not too surprised that Dawn was not at home. She often stayed until closing time at the library, finding the atmosphere there more conducive to studying than being at home where there were too many distractions and temptations like the telephone and her compact disc player. Dawn could talk on the phone for hours. Mrs. Ashby was always warning her about the extent of their bills; sometimes they were ridiculously high. If she was not hogging the phone then, she would be playing her favourite music selections.

If she wasn't at the library then she was probably around the corner at her friend's Ann Marie. Dawn didn't like to sit around the flat alone, ever since her brother, David, had started at university and her sister Lucy had married. Her Dad had been dead six years now.

Mrs. Ashby took the shopping into the kitchen, making sure the frozen goods went into the freezer first and sighed. She hated shopping. It was such a waste of time. Picking the goods off the shelves, packing them into the trolley, unpacking them all at the checkout, repacking them into bags, getting them home and unpacking them all yet again and putting each item away into the cupboards. It was a real chore.

Mrs. Ashby popped the kettle on while she continued with her tiresome task. She glanced up at the kitchen clock as she poured herself a cup of piping hot tea. It was six-fifty. 'Maybe Dawn was in, if she was listening to her personal stereo, she wouldn't have heard the doorbell and after all, she had been told not to play her music for fear of annoying the neighbours,' mused Mrs. Ashby.

Mrs. Ashby walked down the corridor to Dawn's room. Having had three teenage children, she fully expected the room to be a shambles and made up her mind to speak to her about it as soon as her daughter came home, if, of course, that proved to be the case.

Shuddering slightly at the horrors she expected to find, she gingerly opened the door and found herself facing real horror, a horror far beyond anything she could have imagined.

The room was in chaos and in the middle of it, on her bed lay Dawn. Her school blouse was open to the waist, exposing her adolescent breasts. There were several cuts and stab wounds on her abdomen. Blood had spread darkly and dried onto the sheets. Her short, navy, wool skirt was pushed up around her waist leaving her naked from the navel down. A pair of white, nylon panties was on the floor by her bedside table. Her breasts, stomach and inside her thighs were stained dark brown with dried blood. There was a pillow over her face.

Evelyn Ashby staggered back as if she had been struck. She clutched at her hair and throwing back her head in an agonised gesture of utter despair, gave vent to a primeval cry. Her howl was long and deep from the pit of her stomach like that of a sorrowing she wolf wailing at the death of the moon.

*

In the flat next door Mrs. Nicola Claydon was just enjoying the start of her evening meal. She froze with the fork halfway towards her mouth. The wail she heard was reminiscent of a description of a banshee she had read in some classic tale of horror and although not excessively loud, it was very penetrating and seemed to echo in the room around her.

Mrs. Claydon did not recognise the sound as human and believing that some large abandoned dog was wailing in the corridor outside her flat, she set aside her meal and went to investigate.

As she rushed from her home, the door of the Ashby's flat crashed violently open and Mrs. Ashby came tumbling out in a hysterical state, her eyes wide and distracted and filled with tears. She was weeping and struggling to catch her breath, "Dawn is dead! Dawn is dead!" she shrieked dementedly. Mrs. Ashby collapsed in a heap on the floor of the corridor, shaking and sobbing uncontrollably.

Mrs. Claydon only knew her neighbours slightly, but she knew that Dawn was the daughter and disregarding any personal fear she may have felt at the sight of Evelyn Ashby's stricken face, she moved past the tortured woman and entered the flat, where after looking in two rooms, she found herself staring into Dawn's bedroom and the shocking sight which confronted her.

The glimpse of the pathetic little body was nearly as much of a shock to her as it had been to Mrs. Ashby. She had been expecting some kind of household accident but this was most definitely rape and murder.

Running back to her apartment and with trembling fingers she dialled 999. Response to her call was swift. She hardly had time to hang up the receiver and start to comfort Mrs. Ashby when a patrol car arrived in front of the building, quickly followed by an ambulance.

The ambulance men, complete with stretcher, followed the two policemen swiftly into the room of death but could do nothing. Dawn Ashby was dead and had been so for some time. The paramedics returned to base leaving the two young officers to await Allison's arrival, the police photographer and Forensic.

Mrs. Claydon had by now settled Mrs. Ashby in her sitting room and given her a tot of brandy in an attempt to calm her. Evelyn Ashby was now silent and numb, her eyes opaque and staring. It was to this scene that Allison entered. His usual gruff tone was softened as he thanked Mrs. Claydon.

"One of my WPCs will be with you in a minute. She'll need to take a statement, if you could keep Mrs. Ashby with you whilst the doctor makes his examination, I would appreciate it."

Mrs. Claydon nodded and watched the rain coated DCI leave her flat, for the murder scene next door. Allison breathed deeply and braced himself before entering. He pushed his hands into his coat pockets and his fingers closed around the familiar shape and packaging of his Mars Bar. He would need that later, of that he was certain.

5
Evening Out

The play had been a great success. The cast had been lucky enough to play to a full house and the laughter from the auditorium burst onto the pavement as the theatre doors opened, spilling those who had not paused for a drink at the bar out onto the frosty, night street. Mary Allison tucked her arm into Greg's and looked up at him warmly. Her anniversary had got off to a shaky start with Greg arriving home late. The taxi had run up an extra two pounds in waiting time while Greg had bathed and changed at home. They had only just made the curtain, but now, now all that mattered was the two of them. They crossed the road to the excellent Celebrity Restaurant and were greeted like old friends by the owners and their manageress, Shirley who had already started mixing their pre-dinner cocktails. She smiled broadly at them showing a perfect set of beautiful white teeth.

"What's new in the force tonight? Caught any criminals lately?"

"He's off duty tonight, Shirley, no shop please."

"Right you are. I'll try and keep the outside door closed so he won't hear the sirens at chucking out time."

"Not necessary, Shirley, I'm deaf to everyone except Mary tonight."

Their coats were taken away and hung on the rail. They sat at the bar and studied the menu quietly while they sipped their drinks. "Well, what are you going to have?"

"Mm…. I'm not sure. What are you having?" asked Mary who always liked to know what her partner was having before she made up her own mind.

"I rather fancy steak au poivre with mushrooms, broccoli and sauté potatoes," said Allison.

"I think I'll have the lemon chicken. What are you having to start?"

"I don't know yet."

They sat and discussed the menu fully before ordering and while they were chatting quietly a young man started setting up microphones and a stool in readiness to sing and play some gentle guitar music.

"That's it!" exclaimed Allison.

"That's what?" asked Mary.

"Well, we were wondering why similar crimes could be committed in such different areas. Maybe our killer's a cabaret artiste."

"Or a long distance lorry driver," said Mary.

"Mmm. I had thought he was maybe a prisoner - hence the gaps - but then that still wouldn't explain the time lapse between crimes unless he was a traveller of some sort. Or maybe circumstances forced him to move. Sorry, Darling," he muttered, seeing her face, "I didn't intend talking shop."

"That's all right, just because you've got a night off I know you can't completely divorce yourself from your work. I gave up trying to get you to do that years ago."

"Well, let's put the crooning killer out of our minds for the rest of the evening and enjoy what we have left of the night."

It was then that the champagne cork exploded out of the bottle and Shirley brought glasses over from Val and Ken with their good wishes.

*

He saw her on the dance floor. She noticed he was watching her and she threw him a careless smile that said, 'Speak to me if you dare.' He took another drink, put his glass down on the table and pushed his way through the heaving throng of elbows and knees and stood in front of her. "Would you like to dance?" he asked in a stiff and formal way. His eyes were penetrating and seemed to look right through her. She nodded and smiled mischievously, instantly capturing his heart. This one was different, he knew, this was the one. Her long blonde hair tumbled over her shoulders. Her smile promised a wealth of warmth and love but most of all she seemed genuinely interested in him and everything he had to say.

Tony knew that this one was right.

Woodward glanced at his watch; all was going to plan. A number of lesser villains had been arrested already. Vencat was obviously waiting for a big distributor to arrive and when he did, they could nab Vencat, his chemists and the whole unsavoury band. He had his glasses trained on the warehouse window where he could see the chemists at work, cutting and mixing their deadly packages of death. He grimaced suddenly, Hell! They were even smiling and whistling as they went about their work but not for much longer.

His call sign came through on the radio warning him of the approach of a blue BMW, another motor in Vencat's fleet. It stopped at the side door and a beefy-man, looking uncomfortable in an expensive suit and restricting collar, stepped out of the driver's side and opened the rear passenger door. Old Gold Tooth moved forward to greet Stuart Allen who in turn introduced him to a strangely familiar figure. Vencat nodded curtly at the muscle man, who led the way into the warehouse.

Woodward cursed as they disappeared from view then, heaved a sigh of relief as they came into sight on the chemists' floor. Woodward watched eagerly as he saw Vencat engaged in conversation and smiling broadly, dipping his finger into the white snow like powder held aloft in a small evaporating dish. Vencat invited Allen and Mr. Familiar to do the same. They all nodded appreciatively. Vencat ordered the packing and sat back to wait. More money was exchanged and hands were shaken on the deal. Woodward licked his lips in satisfaction everything was on film, the whole incriminating show!

The coke was parcelled up into twenty-kilo bags. Enough dope to wipe out a city. This was packed into two large Antler suitcases. Vencat ordered Beefcake to take them to the car. He took a further three envelopes out of his coat pocket. He handed one each to the two chemists and the third to a technician who was obviously receiving instructions to share the contents with the rest of the crew. The business of sorting meat resumed and Vencat, Allen and Mr. Familiar moved out after Beefcake to the waiting cars. Vencat left his colleagues with a flash of that gold-toothed smile.

The BMWs were on their way, each taking a different direction and moving safely away from the warehouse. Stage two of 'Daytrip' could be put into action. Woodward ran through the plan in his mind. Customs and Excise would hit the chemists. There was more than enough evidence to put them away for a very long time. And, when the time was right, he and his men would pull Vencat and Beefcake over onto the hard shoulder. He patted the warrant in his pocket; he was going to have the pleasure of putting Vencat and his band away for a good long stretch. Janice's death would be avenged and maybe a number of other tragedies prevented. That would be reward enough for Woodward. The only thing that puzzled him was the third man, someone he knew he'd seen before, and someone of some repute.

The signal came through that the warehouse mob had been picked up and the second BMW had been stopped on the outskirts of Rhyl.

Smiling grimly, Woodward accelerated and pulled out into the overtaking lane and gave chase, a mobile light magnetised to the roof. Three more cars joined as backup.

This was one big fish that wouldn't escape.

*

Arthur Crabtree was half dressed and shaking. He opened the door of his shed and was violently sick outside. He closed the door hurriedly and wiped his hand across his mouth and leaned against the wood, when he heard a shout.

"Arthur! Get in here now or your dinner's going in the bin."

Arthur reopened the door a fraction and struggled to reply, "Just finishing up, dear." He trembled uncontrollably and began to sob as he tried to pull himself together. "God, what have I done?" He retched again but there was nothing more to bring up. He knew he had to regain control of his emotions and put his terrible deed behind him if he was to succeed and find happiness.

He finished dressing and stuffed the rest of his clothes in a carrier bag and left the shed. Dodging the vomit on the path he took the bag and stuffed it into an old tin barrel. He covered it with leaves and other garden waste. With shaking hands he set fire to it. The flames slowly took hold and began to burn the brazier's contents. Now, he had to calm himself. He breathed deeply trying to control the shivering fit that was upon him and he sobbed again.

*

Debbie Stringer held onto her tiny daughter, cradling her with such love that it made Mark catch his breath. He paused for a moment and watched his wife talking fondly to their baby and he felt growing tears of pride, which threatened to spill down his cheek. He cleared his throat. Debbie looked up at him and smiled.

"All ready? Jean's at home waiting. She's made dinner and said she'll be on hand to do anything you want."

"Where's Christian?"

"He's staying with Jean. He's planning some sort of surprise for you and Catherine."

"Right." Debbie slowly rose from the nursing chair and bade farewell to the three mums in that small room. Mark handed Staff a large box of chocolates for the nurses to share, Jean's idea, and picked up Debbie's bag. Together they carefully stepped out into the corridor towards the lifts.

A sister bustled past briskly, "Oh, to be able to walk quickly again and less like a geriatric," called Debbie.

"You will!" laughed the sister. "I've had six." And she strode on purposefully.

Debbie leaned against the wall for support, "It's okay, Mark. It's just these stitches are so damned uncomfortable. Come on let's get home."

"Have they said anymore about Catherine?" Mark asked tentatively.

"Only what Mr. Greenhalf told us. We'll have to watch her, of course, but the tests didn't show anything abnormal, so let's hope."

*

Allison took a large bite of his Mars Bar poking the little bit of chocolate that escaped his mouth back onto his lip and licked it off. He grunted in satisfaction. He turned over the last page of the report on the Vencat bust and Operation Daytrip. At least something had gone right. What a surprise that Birmingham's philanthropic businessman, who did so much for charity, was Vencat's partner in the venture. The man arranged and promoted the big fights. His visits abroad perfectly covered his illicit dealings in drugs. Under the guise of organising matches he could travel abroad freely and without question, especially as he had a whiter than white reputation. If only he could have as much success with the serial killer, just one genuine lead. The evidence they had stockpiled would do the rest. Genetic fingerprinting was indisputable.

Allison sighed and picked up an interim report on the antique fraud that had started in Kidderminster. He leafed through it but he wasn't concentrating. He popped the report back into the in-tray and continued devouring his Mars Bar. He flicked the intercom, "Maddie? Can I have a cup of tea please?" The chocolate had made him thirsty.

He needed to think. There was so much wrong with the Ashby case. He was waiting for the PM results to come through. Why would the killer change his style? He'd always killed outside before. There was a lot Allison disliked about this one. It just didn't seem to fit. He sipped the refreshing hot tea that Maddie brought him and he reached for the phone.

"Harmon? I want you, Pooley and Taylor to double-check everything that has come in on the crooning killer. Even items we've discounted; double-check them all. Get the information fed into the computer, bugger the expense and let's see if anything comes to light."

Allison had no sooner replaced the receiver when it rang impatiently.

It was Hurst, "Hold on to your seat, Chief," Johnny said, "This one's not our man."

"You mean we've got a copy-cat?"

"Looks like it! Terrible mutilations, strangled with her own tights, but no number anywhere, and a different blood type."

Allison groaned. He knew this one hadn't felt right. That's all he needed, another nutter on the loose. "Okay. Thanks, Johnny."

"I'll have the report with you in an hour. Annie is typing it up now."

*

Young schoolteacher, Amy Crosby, sat chatting with her best friend Sheena Latimer. Amy was mooning over a man she had met at a nightclub, earlier in the week, with Sheena, who was trying to warn her to tread carefully as far as Mr. Handsome was concerned.

"He is such a dish. I couldn't believe my luck when he asked me to dance. He stuck close to me all night through."

"I'll say, super glued together. You couldn't have got a fag paper between you. You were that close. You're bound to notice he liked you," said Sheena with a raised eyebrow.

"And I didn't notice you complaining over the drink you shared with the drummer, Rich," accused Amy.

"He was fun," she agreed. "But not my type!"

"Huh! You could have fooled me," laughed Amy.

"I don't know, hon … there's just something too smooth and too charming about him. He seems too good to be true and if that's the case, then warning bells ring!"

"Oh, Sheena!"

"I'm just saying; that's all. Be careful!"

"I'll be okay. I've been married once and I'm not likely to go down that road again, yet. Yes, he's pretty stunning. But, there's more to a man than his looks and… I have to admit there is something I'm not quite sure of…"

"What do you mean?"

"Well, for a start he's so intense." She paused and frowned, "Oh, I don't know, but there is something." She thought some more and Sheena watched her friend's face with a look of concern that Amy immediately noticed. "Don't worry, Sheena. I'm not stupid. Yes, he is gorgeous, but he's older than me, ten years older and oh, I don't know…" Amy tailed off.

"What? What is it?"

"You'll think I'm stupid."

"No, I won't. Tell me."

"Well, it's something I can't put my finger on, not yet, but something's not right, doesn't feel right."

"There you are then, girl. What did I say? Trust your instincts and tread carefully." Sheena squeezed her best friend's hand. Amy smiled and gave her friend a hug. Sheena then asked, "So, where do you fancy going tonight? The Opposite Lock?"

"Yes, I promised Tony I'd meet him there. Do you want to join us?"

"No thanks. But, I'll be there anyway, now, just to keep an eye on you. I'm meeting Steve. He doesn't know it but I'll give him a call."

"Not Rich?"

"No. I told you. That was just a bit of fun for one night, but I will scrounge a drink off you. See you later."

Sheena gave her friend a final wave and Amy shook her head, and mused, 'Sheena was like a mother hen, always looking out for her. But she had nothing to worry about. What could possibly go wrong?'

*

Amy returned home and waltzed into the kitchen. Her mother was busy at the stove preparing dinner. "Mmm. Something smells good." Amy lifted the lid off the big pan bubbling on top of the stove. "Ah stew!" she said appreciatively as the smell of beef, onions, leeks and other vegetables steamed up her nostrils. "Perfect for this time of year, I love it!"

"I know. I've made enough for a few days. It's been simmering slowly all day. Just the thing to keep the chill winds out. Oh, by the way, these arrived for you." Amy's Mum opened the utility room door and brought out a magnificent bouquet of flowers all done up in a green satin ribbon. 'To match your eyes,' the card read, 'Longing to see you tonight. Yours Tony.'

"He seems keen, doesn't he?" It was more of an observation than a criticism and Amy started to tell her mother all about Tony.

*

Tony lay naked, wrapped in the velvet blanket of night. The covers on his bed were tossed back. The room was warm. His door was locked. Not that it mattered if it wasn't, his mother was out at a meeting of the Pentecostal Church and he had three hours before he needed to leave the house.

He saw them in his mind's eye, three of them, beautiful, dark and demonic; three voluptuous wantons who gathered at the foot of his bed. He heard their breathing that grew louder with the excitement at seeing his naked form. He gripped the pillow and pulled it partially over his face. He knew what was coming. He felt the first set of hands, cool, like silk, gently caressing his legs, gently stroking and rubbing, the thumbs rising higher and lingering inside his thighs almost touching his slowly awakening penis, but not quite. The tantalising and teasing had barely begun. Then he felt hot, moist lips and a probing tongue that wriggled and licked in all his hidden places. Unspoken ecstasy rippled over his stomach, the lapping tongue moved across his sides and his chest, again not coming into contact with his genitals. The third mouth pressed, kneaded and licked his nipples, until he was erect and hard. Then the hot breath from their mouths coupled with the heat of their bodies slipped up and down Tony and his ever increasing manhood until phantom hands from imaginings in his own mind, caressed, rubbed and squeezed his searching phallus. A hot tongue ran the length of his thickening member and, without him once touching himself, through the wild fantasies from his own sick mind, hot semen spurted out over his lean, muscular, sweat covered body. He groaned in satisfaction, then he heard faint laughter like the sound of silver bells, as the sirens melded into the shadows, and he was ashamed.

*

Harmon knocked on the Chief's door and waited for the usual gruff instruction to enter. "Sir, I thought you might be interested in seeing these." They were reports that had come in from various psychiatric clinics and although the majority were unhelpful there were a couple of interesting ones that needed to be followed up. One doctor in particular had said that she may be able to help, but was prevented by the code of patient doctor confidentiality. Even so, she had requested an interview with Allison.

Allison browsed through the papers and his eyes rested upon the letter from Dr. Mills. He read it twice before looking once more at Harmon.

"Feed all the useful information into the computer, then file it. Anything that needs following up let me know first and then do it. I'm going to check with Dr. Mills."

Harmon took the sheaf of papers from Allison's outstretched hand. "There is a good week's worth of work there. I would get Pooley and Taylor to work with you. That should help to cut the load," said Allison dismissing Harmon.

Allison dialled the clinic.

"York and Grantham Clinic," a cool, medical, reassuring voice told him.

"Is this the number for Dr. Mills?"

"Yes, Sir. It is." So he had the right number, the anonymous voice asked, "How can I help?"

"Is it possible to speak with her, please?"

"I'll see if she's available."

The switchboard put him through to Rebecca Mills' secretary, who in turn paged the doctor, who answered. "Rebecca Mills."

Her voice was assured and pleasant, enough to inspire confidence in her patients thought Allison. He found himself being excessively polite in his request.

"DCI Allison here."

"Yes?"

"I have received a report that you wished to speak to me and that you may have information vital to our case."

"Ah, yes. This is related to Colin Brady's request regarding the recent murders?"

"Yes, I wondered if you could tell me…"

"I'm afraid I will have to stop you there. I am not prepared to talk on the phone. I'd rather meet face to face. Speak to my secretary, she has my diary and will find a time that's mutually convenient."

Allison was effectively dismissed and transferred back to

the secretary. He made an appointment to see her the following week, Tuesday, two-thirty p.m.

So, she wasn't prepared to talk on the phone. She must have something relevant to report. Allison turned to his overflowing in-tray as he reached for his Mars Bar.

*

Sandra looked out of the window of her tiny bed sitting room. She watched the rain hitting the pavement outside and bouncing up like ball bearings. Her fingers traced the rivulets of water running down her streaked dirty windowpane. She seemed lost, as if absorbed in a world of her own. The wind rattled the ill-fitting glass and gusted under her door where the draught proofing had worn away. She shivered and pulled her already stretched jumper to its limits, to cover her bedroom slippered feet.

It was a dark night with rolling, black clouds that threatened continual lashing rain. Outside reminded her of the set of some old black and white 'B' movie that promised melodrama and murder that she had watched as a child on Saturday afternoons on an old Classic T.V. channel. Sandra turned up the gas fire and returned to the window laying bets on which raindrop would reach the windowsill first. If only she didn't have to go out. The streets were deserted except for the occasional car and those pedestrians who were adequately equipped with umbrella and boots. The wind tugged and pulled at the few remaining leaves on the trees, sending them to their death as they were consigned to a mulching mass to be trodden underfoot. She knew how they felt. Sandra sighed in sorrow at her plight and loneliness.

She rose up from her seat and reached for her grey, drab, worn raincoat hanging on a hook by the door and cursed lightly as her karate gi and a number of other garments slipped off their hangers to the floor. She stared around the seedy room with its peeling, torn wallpaper, a faded design from the fifties. The smell of mustiness mingled with the aroma of fried onions that she'd consumed earlier with a burger for her tea. She reached for the air freshener and liberally sprayed the artificial smell of roses to cover the stale air.

Sandra picked up the letter waiting on the mantelpiece. It was time to post it, to forget her stubborn pride, tell her mother where she was and go home. When that was done, she'd pay one last trip to the arcade, the bright lights, music, and the sound of people, machines and life. Sandra tucked her long, raven hair into a scarf, the two ends of which fluttered onto her shoulder, there to rest until the wind would catch them and play with them. She picked up the letter and her bag and went to the door. With a new lightness in her step, she locked the door behind her and ran down the stairs and out into the rain sodden street.

The leaves that had fallen from the trees had gathered in slippery clumps creating a mulch-like mess. Sandra skirted around the puddles and walked the two blocks to the nearest letterbox. She looked up at the heavens as the sharp shower continued to tamp down. She stopped at the mailbox and withdrew **the** letter, the important letter; the one she hoped would get her life back on track. She pressed the letter to her heart and kissed it. The rain spots on the envelope made the ink on the address run slightly. It looked as if she had been crying when she sent it.

Sandra posted her letter and listened as it fell heavily to join other paper correspondence inside. It was too late to take it back now. She prayed she had done the right thing. By then the rain had lessened to a slight drizzle.

The cacophony of noise from the arcade reached her ears. It didn't look or seem so exciting now. She'd have a chat to Mitch in the change kiosk; play a little on the one-armed bandit and return to pack her few belongings. A surge of emotions flooded through her and she smiled.

She was going home tomorrow!

6
Schemes and Dreams

To the outside world Arthur Crabtree was an inoffensive, mild mannered man, assistant caretaker at Bartley Green High School. But Arthur Crabtree had a dark secret. Locked in his heart was a brooding violence. He harboured murderous thoughts towards his domineering wife, Eileen. Oh, how many times he'd eliminated her from his life, in his dreams, his nightmares and from the blackest recesses of his mind. Many times he'd planned and imagined he'd executed the perfect murder. It was with pleasure, that he felt his fingers around her wrinkled throat, squeezing the life out of her, stilling that complaining whine forever.

He longed to collect the large insurance policy on her life. He knew exactly how he'd spend it. He'd jack the job in for a start; move house and travel, making sure he invested enough to guarantee him a worthwhile income.

His scheming had come to an end. Now, it was time to perform the deed. His tongue darted out and explored his mouth from corner to corner. He rolled his eyes heavenward and coughed. The air rasped heavily in his chest and a silver trail of spittle escaped from his cracked, dry lips. A surge of sickness came from his belly and rose into his throat. Burning, sour acid swam into his mouth as he remembered with distaste his dry run. That had not gone as he had intended and he hadn't enjoyed any of it. He'd needed to kill, to see if he had the stomach for it but he'd made mistakes, mistakes that he would not repeat.

The perfect opportunity had arisen. Two murders and the press were talking about a lunatic on the loose. Such a chance would not occur again.

Arthur had studied the newspaper accounts carefully and tried to build up a picture of the killer and how he worked. He couldn't afford to take a risk that's why he had selected Dawn Ashby so carefully. He knew Dawn slightly; enough to envy her youth, enough to resent her laughter, enough to loathe her copper hair that was so like Eileen's. In his small mind she deserved to die. She'd been one of many who had tittered at the cruel jibes directed at him and had hurled insults herself.

Arthur made it his business to find out more about her, where she lived, her movements and habits. This had all been fairly easy. A glance at the school timetable told him when she'd be free. A second visit to the school office, secretly tapping into the computer, gave him access to her personal details.

Oh yes, it had all been so easy. All that is except the slaughter itself. He clamped a hand to his mouth. Too late, the steaming yellow vomit belched out from him. This was something he had to control. His retching subsided but his hands continued trembling. He glared at them, willing them to stillness. Then, as if to spur him on, he replayed in his mind, like a video, the proposed death of his wife, remembering the details to be corrected, the wearing of surgical gloves, the sitting of the murdered body, the Clent Hills maybe, and the setting up of his alibi. What Arthur Crabtree didn't realise was that he also had a subconscious desire for fame.

*

Tony sat morosely in his chair watching his mother butter the bread. He knew he had to get out. He knew he had to escape this prison. He'd been safe with Sally. Living with her on occasions had been difficult and he'd had to break out from time to time but he'd never hurt anyone. Now the voices had returned and he had been trapped on the sticky gossamer threads that threatened to engulf and cocoon him in the black widow's web of destruction. She had an irresistible hold on him. He was uncontrollably drawn to this disciple of the Lord. The invisible strands that bound him to her were as strong and real as chains and manacles. He shivered slightly. She turned her unblinking, lizard eyes on him and drew back her thin lips, liberally smeared with red, into a gaping grin.

"Why don't you have a bath? You've had a hard day, working at that office and then out on your club nights. Have a night in with mother."

"I can't stay in tonight, Mum. I'm going out."

"Where?" she snapped, "There's nothing on the calendar. You're not singing tonight."

"I've met a girl."

"Not another slut?"

"No, Mum, a nice girl. She's called Amy. I'll bring her to meet you soon."

"I liked Sally. I don't know why you left her."

"It didn't work out that's all. We're still friends."

His mother resumed scraping the butter on the bread. The old chair, with its moquette cover, creaked as Tony rose. Her head slithered round. She raised her forefinger dripping in golden sweetness and snaked her tongue around the running mass of honey, then slowly she pushed her finger into her hot, moist mouth. She smiled and flicked back the ends of her Isadora scarf, which she liked to wear, as he unbuttoned his shirt, dropped it on the floor and mounted the stairs to the bathroom.

*

Allison rubbed his furrowed brow and turned again to the Forensic Report on Annette Jury. Coarse blue nylon fibres had been found on her clothing. They had been identified as coming from a hardwearing carpet made by Flotex manufactured specifically for use in cars. The search was on to discover, which make of car had this carpet fitted. He laid bets it would be an Escort. Fortunately, Flotex, being a relatively new company, kept meticulous records and the search wouldn't take too long.

Allison closed the file and leaned back in his chair, which groaned under the extra strain. He reached into his desk drawer and pulled out his Mars Bar and was just about to unwrap it when his intercom buzzed.

"Trevor Booth's here, Chief. Can you see him?"

"Send him in."

Trevor's freckled face appeared around the door. Allison offered him a chair.

"What can I do for you?" he said, reluctantly replacing the Mars Bar with a sigh.

"It's more what I can do for you," said Trevor. "I've had a good series of stories on the psychological need for some people to confess to murder. And follow up interviews with noted psychologists on this strange behaviour, which has generated a lot of interest, but I've also been sniffing around Kelly's talking to some of their girls."

"And?"

"The head girl or 'mother' as they call her, is Marie; she's the one with all the jewellery and she reckons Annette had a date."

"Go on."

"Apparently, Annette was in the Ladies chatting to one of the other hostesses, Zelda, saying that there wasn't much doing at the bar that night and she'd hooked someone who took her fancy. She was going to give him a freebie because he was quite a dish. Apparently, he didn't realise what she was and that amused her."

"I see. That is interesting. The girls all clammed up when our boys interviewed them. They saw nothing, heard nothing, and said nothing. At least that was the message that came back to me."

"Well, I reckon another visit is in order and maybe a little blackmail."

"What do you mean?"

"Well, Marie is working to fund her own jewellery business and rumour has it that she's not entirely 'snow white' in her dealings. It seems that she's taken possession of some diamonds from a rather dubious source, which she is in the process of resetting for her own firm. A little information like that in your favour might persuade her to speak."

"And Zelda?"

"Try some sort of line with gambling, she's a compulsive; prostitutes herself to feed the addiction, always waiting for the big win."

"And what do you want in return?"

"I'm coming to that," he licked his lips nervously and leaned forward, "My intuition tells me that the Ashby killing doesn't tie in with the others. I want the real facts and permission to do a little ferreting myself. Plus, I want to be the first to hear if anything new breaks on the case. Do we have a deal?"

Allison massaged his chin thoughtfully and nodded, "I'll give you what you need on Dawn Ashby. Who knows, you may just turn up something. The rest, I can't promise. What do you need to know?"

Trevor Booth grinned, pushed his specs back on his nose and took out his notebook.

*

Arthur Crabtree unplugged the hole in the games storeroom and fixed his eye to the peephole that looked into the towel room next door to the gym and watched.

He'd seen Luke Saunders disappear in there, after evening rehearsals of the school play, with his pretty year ten girlfriend, Karen. They'd trapped the door handle with a chair so that no one could get in and pulled out an old gym mat, which they covered with some school towels.

Most of the students were unaware it existed. The heat in that room was incredible. Situated next to the boiler room and away from prying eyes it was the perfect place to go for a quick smoke or a little bit of nookie.

Arthur Crabtree would make sure they were not disturbed, he needed something of Luke's.

He gazed in fascination as Luke opened Karen's school blouse and released her pert, firm breasts with nipples like rosebuds, erect and pointing cheekily upwards. Passionately, Luke fixed his hot, velvet lips on one and drew her down onto the makeshift bed. His other hand pushed up her skirt and eased down her thin panties revealing an expanse of silky flesh and a rising mound of rich chestnut pubic hair.

Tremulously and with a maturity far removed from the usual clumsy fumbling associated with adolescence Luke took the proverbial packet of three from his back pocket. Arthur's pupils dilated as he watched the foreplay, fun and teasing that went on, until protected by a sensitive gossamer coat Luke thrust deeply into her.

Arthur silently rejoiced. Oh, the wisdom of education today and the warnings of AIDS doled out to schoolchildren. Now, all he had to do was see where the little rubber packet would be deposited!

*

"Hya Mitch! How are you doing?"

"Fine, darlin'. Fancy a chip?" He offered Sandra a taste from a vinegar soaked bag of chips. The tantalising smell wafted up her nostrils, she took one, blew on it and popped it gratefully into her mouth.

The flashing lights and tawdry tinkle of coins in the machines that blipped, hummed and burped, jangled a welcome to lost souls who had nowhere else to go.

A combination of harsh, loud, jarring sounds accompanied the blinking coloured bulbs that lit up the sign that read 'Arcade'. It attracted truants, runaways, gamblers and Tony.

Sandra fished in her pocket. She took out two single pound coins and changed them for ten pence pieces. She gave Mitch a perfunctory smile. He responded with a broad wink before returning to his chips.

Sandra squeezed past a youth of about fifteen, with greasy hair and a wind chapped face, his eyes frantic, as he hammered the nudge button with agitated skill.

Sandra settled for a good old-fashioned fruit machine and let the ten pence fall in the slot. She pulled the chromium-plated arm that shone silver under the glare of the lamps. It jerked back with a satisfying clunk. The fruits spun round and locked into position, bar, bell, lemon. She tried another coin.

Two steel blue eyes looked up at the movement across the aisles. His gaze was drawn to the long ends of her scarf flapping intermittently in the gusting wind breezing through the draughty palace of fun.

Tony's hand, moist with sweat, slipped off the wheel controlling the game 'Out run' and he watched her, his inner thoughts and problems forgotten.

Tony had a need to gamble. Only by immersing himself in a game of chance could he find release from his troubled mind, silence the voices that shrieked inside his head, and quiet and soothe that nagging spirit that threatened to rage and run riot in his brain. His eyes, now solidly fixed on the ends of her scarf, underwent a subtle change. Anyone who saw the look in them, at that moment, could not fail to be filled with fear. It was like setting the fuse on a time bomb. He watched and waited. The explosion would come later.

*

"I've already told the police everything I know." Marie protested.

"I'm sorry, Miss, we're just going over our statements and re-checking one or two things. Please bear with me," repeated Mark.

Marie snorted in exasperation and proceeded to examine her left hand that displayed a heavy twenty-two carat gold ring encrusted with numerous sapphires surrounding a single diamond of over three carats.

"On the night in question…."

"On the night in question," Marie interrupted, irritated.

"On the night in question," insisted Mark, "We understand that you heard Annette talking about a date she'd arranged?"

Marie shook her head impatiently and turned to go, "I don't have to listen to this."

Mark caught her wrist and swung her around, "That's an exquisite diamond you have there. I hear you've an eye for a good stone," he remarked pointedly.

Marie stopped and drew in her breath. A middle-aged man in a grey pinstripe suit with crinkly grey hair and brown horn rimmed spectacles stepped forward from the bar. "Is this person bothering you, Marie?"

"No, Barney. It's okay," she placed out a restraining arm, preventing Barney from accosting Mark. Reluctantly, Barney went back to his drink at the bar.

"All right, Mr. Stringer, what do you want to know?" Marie muttered ungraciously.

"Now we're getting somewhere," mumbled Mark and they sat at a small alcove table together.

"Let's start at the beginning shall we?"

Marie sighed heavily making her reluctance and annoyance felt, "It was a quiet night. Not many punters in, you know, looking for … looking for company."

"Go on."

"Annette arrived at her usual time around ten. She sat at

the bar. I remember Barney bought her a drink. He's good like that." She stopped and flicked her hair away from her face.

"And?"

Marie sighed in exasperation but continued, "She took a seat close to the dance floor and scanned the room. It was her usual style. She had that knack of choosing her client rather than the other way round. We always said, show her a man, any man and she could make him hers. She was clever like that."

Mark nodded. Now he'd got her talking he didn't want to stop her flow.

"I didn't see who she picked, I was busy myself." She paused," But I know her routine. She would stroke the stem of her wine glass, looking down and then raise her eyes and fix them on her target, look down shyly and look up again and engage eyes. Then she would moisten her lips and if she was feeling really intense she'd run her tongue around her lips as if... well, you know."

"Would anyone else have noticed?"

"Barney, maybe. Or one of the other girls."

"They won't talk to me."

"They will if I tell them to. We don't want to lose anymore of them. Try Zelda, Annette spoke to her in the Ladies room."

"Where is she?"

"Marie looked at her watch, "She should be in any time, now. Come on, I'll introduce you to Barney."

Mark closed his notebook and followed Marie to the bar. Introductions were made and Barney and Mark began to talk.

*

Arthur Crabtreee was delighted. Everything was going according to plan. He zipped up his waterproof all in ones, secured his helmet, started his Honda one-two-five, and set off home.

Tomorrow was Eileen's night for bingo. Tomorrow he would have his chance. A strange fluttering started inside him. He licked his lips nervously as he went over each detail in his mind. The video would be set to record the evening's viewings and subsequently wiped. He'd got the car safely stashed away in a lock up a few streets away. No one knew he'd bought it. He'd got it from a private ad in the paper, paying cash, after first disguising himself and using a false name. He'd have no problem selling it and was certain the way he'd arranged things that he couldn't be traced. He'd drive the car into the house garage when it was safe. He'd ensure Eileen had a couple of Mogadon crushed up in her regular, evening hot chocolate. He'd pop out for his can of four from the off license at the corner shop, as he always did on bingo nights and chat to the two ladies who ran it. Then, while Eileen slept, he would prepare the bathroom, and strip himself naked, wearing only the surgical gloves.

There was bound to be a lot of blood. He could clean this up afterwards relatively easily. His phone calls had to be timed just perfectly, one to his daughter, Pam and then to the 0898 number that he had been ringing regularly on bingo nights. He'd leave the phone hanging on, until he was safely back, and then ring Pam again under some pretext. At the right time, he'd put in a call to the police when Eileen hadn't returned home.

With his limited intelligence, he was sure it would work.

*

Sandra chinked the money in her hand. She'd done well tonight, and that was rare. She usually went home broke but this time she was up! It had to be a good sign. Her luck was changing. She thought she'd stop while she was ahead. After all, the extra cash would come in useful when she travelled home.

She stopped for a few last words with Mitch. Neither of them noticed the cold, ice blue eyes locked on her, watching the ends of that temptingly attractive scarf that danced in the wind calling to him.

Sandra leaned across the booth and gave Mitch a peck on the cheek. "Thanks for being a friend and listening to me all those times I went off on one."

He shook her warmly by the hand, "No problem, Sandra. I shall miss you and our chats; after all you're not the only one who off loaded. You listened to me, too, and gave me some good advice."

"But it was you who persuaded me to have the courage to mail my letter."

"That was nothing. You're doing the right thing. I'm sure your parents will welcome you with open arms."

So, with a skip in her step and a final wave, she moved out of the arcade and into the street.

*

The sky ripped open with a jagged lightning knife bleeding its white fire momentarily in the inky blackness. The street was lit clearly for a second and then plunged back into shadows as the rumble of thunder thudded dully overhead. As black storm clouds rolled bruising the midnight blue sky to an angry purple Tony determined that it was time to leave. His eyes watched the figure of Sandra as she retreated into the night. He collected his winnings from the slot machine he'd been playing and watched as the figure of the girl melded and morphed into someone else.

Tony pulled up his coat collar and with the stealth of a cat eager for its prey he stepped out into the night.

Mitch watched him vanish into the gloom and yawned. His chips finished, he took a bite of his freshly polished apple and browsed through the pages of his auto magazine and cast a desultory eye over the small ad's page.

No one else saw anything. The boy with the greasy hair was searching his pockets for more change. The other visitors to the arcade were engrossed in their machines.

*

There was another fork of fire and an ear splitting crash as the storm rumbled overhead. It was as if a battle from Hell had spilled out onto the earth bringing with it all the forces of evil. Tony watched and followed his prey.

Sandra thrust her head down and ran through the rain.

Tony stoically and determinedly paced behind her.

Sandra raced on down the road, making a dash for the fish and chip shop. She ran inside and waited her turn behind three other customers. Tony saw her laugh with the Italian who served her. His eyes narrowed cruelly.

She stood in the doorway, hungrily munching her sausage and chips, waiting for the rain to subside. Tony went into the telephone box on the opposite corner and studied her reflection in the scratched mirror. Her image changed each time her scarf fluttered. He picked up the phone and dialled a disc and listened to the tinny music coursing down the line from the top twenty.

*

Sandra took a last swig from her can of coke and threw her rubbish into the already overflowing litterbin that scattered its debris into the street and she set off in the light drizzle that remained from the storm. She headed for her seedy, dingy, little bed sitting room.

As she walked up the hill she suddenly became aware of her isolation. It made her wary. There were few cars. The roads were mostly deserted. She quickened her pace as she turned into Vernon Road. She could see the street lamp shining outside the flats three quarters of the way down the road. Her foot kicked against an old can, which rattled and clunked. The sound seemed absurdly loud. There was a sudden gust of wind, which flicked her scarf up like a butterfly's wings only to resettle again on her shoulder. Sandra stiffened and tensed. She was sure she heard someone behind her.

She hated this street. It was dark and forbidding. Several of the houses had incredibly high hedges, nearly as tall as the houses themselves. How or why anyone would let their hedges grow so tall, she didn't know unless they did it for nefarious purposes and utter privacy. The place unnerved her and for some reason that feeling was stronger tonight than usual. But she was determined not to let her ghoulish fantasies get the better of her.

She often convinced herself that there was someone lying in wait for her, ready to pounce. But tonight, she dismissed the idea as silly, the fruits of an over active imagination enhanced by the storm. Sandra stood on the kerb then, hesitated. The rain had collected in large pools where the drains had become blocked by a mess of soggy, dead leaves.

She walked along the edge of the pavement. Her trainers

made little noise except for the occasional splash when they hit a puddle. Her feet were wet, cold and uncomfortable. She was even looking forward to sitting in front of the meagre gas fire in her miserable attic room.

The can rattled, caught by the wind maybe, or…? She turned to see and came face to face with Tony. His face was a frenzied mask of hate. He reached out and grabbed her arm.

Instinct and years of karate training took over. Keeping her elbows in tight to her body, she yanked hard and sharply raised her knee. Surprise registered in those demonic eyes as he was jerked forward, thrown off balance and winded. Sandra swung her arm back and fore and suddenly twisted it out of his jailer's grip. He lunged at her and she neatly side-stepped his attack whilst delivering a perfect gyakazuki to his kidney. Without thinking, she swept his feet from under him and as he fell she brought her knuckles down onto the bridge of his nose. The bones made a sickening crunch as the uraken made contact.

Tony's mind was racing. This wasn't supposed to happen. He rolled over, blood streaming from his nose. The pain spurred him onto greater anger and he recovered sufficiently to reach in his pocket for the knife. The knife he so lovingly used to mutilate and degrade.

He was finding it difficult to breathe. He opened his mouth and gasped for air. Rage and hate gave him extra strength and before Sandra had a chance to turn and run, he was back on his feet. They faced each other.

Sandra glanced at his blood-smeared face and his almost inhuman eyes, now devoid of any emotion. They were cold and dead like the black abyss from a nightmare.

Quickly, she dropped her eyes to his chest. That would give her the best indication of when and how he would attack next. For a moment they seemed suspended in time. A million thoughts tumbled through her head. Tanto dori, the knife defence, she hadn't learned it although she had trained regularly in Wado ryu karate and achieved the grade of purple belt, she had left home before grading for her brown belt.

She struggled to remember what her Sensei had said and

the demonstrations she had seen. Tony sensed an advantage and charged at her. Sandra attempted a mawashageri, but she was not quick enough. He caught her leg and pulled her towards him, slashing her thigh in the process. Her supporting leg slipped on the muddy pavement. She went down, knocking her head on the concrete. Dazed and confused she cried out and he was upon her.

A shout and some laughter came from the bottom of the road. Tony looked up. It was no good; he would have to finish her now, here, like this. The ritual knife was raised and plunged deep into her chest. He was rewarded with the sight of bright, red blood that frothed and bubbled out of the wound; a perfect sacrifice to quench his voices. A humourless smile tugged at the corner of his mouth as he stood over her. He lifted his heel and drinking in the pale look that he saw as his mother's face, superimposed over Sandra's unconscious visage, he gave a grunt of satisfaction and savagely brought his foot down on her throat. Thinking he had crushed her windpipe, he rose up to flee into the night.

The two young men who had turned into the road saw the scuffle near the corner. They started to run when they saw the glint of blue steel come hurtling down onto the still figure on the floor.

"Hey, you! Stop!"

The men began to run. Tony paused momentarily, then his wits returned and he raced off and disappeared into night's brooding shadows. Crazed by a bloodlust, and excited by the perpetuating fountain of crimson blood he'd drawn from his victim, but with his ritual incomplete, Tony went marauding into the night.

The men reached Sandra, and luckily for her, they were both student doctors who checked her vital signs, "She's still alive. Quickly, get an ambulance."

The other hammered on the nearest door. Nothing. He sprinted to the next, which had lights on downstairs. He pounded hard onto the wood and eventually the door opened and an elderly man squinted out suspiciously, "Yes?"

"Call an ambulance now. There's been a knife attack in the street. Hurry, please."

The old man hurried to his hall telephone and dialled nine, nine, nine.

*

Natalie Blakeney flicked her long, auburn hair out of her eyes as she squinted harder at the nail she was filing. Bloody nails, just when she'd got them all the right length she'd broken one trying to prise the lid off an aspirin bottle. Now, she was in a bad mood as well as having a headache. The phone rang. She picked it up. All she heard was the click of the receiver and the dialling tone.

"Creep!" she screamed into the mouthpiece before slamming it down. That was the fourth odd call she'd had this week, almost as if someone was watching her.

She pulled her flimsy robe around her and popped her camel coat over the top and went downstairs with a saucer of milk for her cat. 'Fluffy shouldn't be out on a night like this, she'd get pneumonia or whatever cats get,' she thought.

Natalie called from the doorstep at the top of her voice, "Fluffy! Here, Fluffy, Fluffy, Fluffy!" But the wind took her words away and rendered them useless in the wildness of the night. She was just about to go in when she saw a faint movement in the bushes at the end of the short drive. Thinking it was her wandering cat returned, she ventured further out into the drive, calling and making encouraging noises to draw Fluff out from her shelter and into the house. "Here, Puss. Come on, Fluffy." Natalie was getting soaked and swore softly under her breath as she moved deeper into the shrubbery at the front of the garden toward the street.

A scream of terror hit the air and died to a whisper on the wind.

*

Allison had just opened his front door. He was wet through and in a filthy temper, which matched the night around him. He was in the process of removing his dripping raincoat when the phone rang.

"Chief, we've got number four, on a patch of waste ground by the new flats in Moseley," sighed DS Stringer.

"What do you mean, number four?" snapped Allison.

"That's what it says; either Dawn Ashby was his…"

"That's impossible!"

"Or we're missing a body."

Allison groaned as he heaved himself back into his sodden coat, reached for his hat and amid Mary's protests stepped back out into the raging night.

7
Survivor

Allison closed his eyes in satisfaction as he lingered over the taste of the smooth chocolate and melting toffee. He sighed dreamily and for a while the rigours of work and his streaming cold, a result of his previous night's investigations, were forgotten. That is until the interruption of the telephone.

"Sir?" It was Mark, calling from Dudley Road Hospital.

"Well?" grunted Allison, his moment of reverie lost.

"The young lady they brought in last night has been identified as Sandra Thornton, a runaway. She's in intensive care."

"Have you interviewed her yet?"

"No. We won't be able to either. She's in a coma. The doctors don't know whether she'll pull through. She's lost a lot of blood. It's touch and go."

"Get a uniform on duty there round the clock. And get hold of those two student doctors who found her. We need to go through their statements again. Have her parents been informed?"

"They're on their way. They received a letter from her this morning. She had just written to them. Ironic isn't it? She was going home."

"Listen, I don't want the news of this to get out; if it was our man, and it may not be, let him think he's succeeded. We won't have anything concrete until Forensic come through. I'll go and see Trevor. He can help us in this"

"Right."

*

He'd tried to tell his mother he was leaving but she wouldn't listen. She played on his sympathies, and on his logic, manipulating him, controlling him, and bending him to her will.

He rose suddenly from the table with its plum velveteen cover, sending the chair flying. He caught his thigh on the sharp corner of the table and winced.

His mother's unblinking eyes settled accusingly on him, "The Lord sees and hears everything. That's his punishment to you."

"Oh, Mum! I'm being punished enough. I've told you."

"You haven't told me everything," she whimpered in lament.

"I know you've tried to explain things to me, but I can't cope. Like Dad, I just can't cope."

"Leave your father out of this."

"I can't, Mum. I have the same disease. I gamble."

Tony's mother raised her eyes in supplication and hurriedly crossed herself, a remnant from her Catholic days. "You don't. You're not like him. He didn't treat his Fluffy like that."

"Fluffy! I've always thought that was a stupid name for you."

"Don't sully his memory. That was his special name for me.

Something clicked in Tony's mind. He had a sudden vision of a woman in a camel coat with scarlet nails, calling his mother. He fought to retain the memory but it dissolved and now, his mother was sitting him down, stroking his arm with her parched, dry hands.

"I've told you. I understand. I know about the devils that come to you and I know the way to get rid of them," droned her reedy voice.

"How do you know?"

"It's not as strange as you think. I used to have disturbing thoughts. Blasphemous, you might say. I was so in love with Jesus that I sometimes used to imagine him as a man. An earthly man with physical needs, desires and wants. Jesus would come to me and I would satisfy him."

"What?"

"Oh, I know. I felt ashamed as you do. I felt unworthy and evil and the minister of the church showed me the way. He cleansed me as I cleanse you."

"But it's wrong, Mum. I feel it's wrong."

"You've never questioned me before."

"I know, but perhaps it's time that I did."

"It's that girl, Amy. She's filling your head with nonsense."

At the mention of Amy, Tony's face clouded with sadness and for a moment his eyes lost their haunted look, only to be replaced by blind anger. He did something he had never done before. He struck his mother.

She let out a scream and her hand went up to her stinging cheek. She looked deep into her son's troubled eyes and a thin quavery voice launched into her rendition of 'Rock of Ages'.

Tony threw his arms around her ample middle and sobbed like a baby, crying out in his sorrow to be forgiven. "I'm sorry, Mum. I'm so sorry. Forgive me please."

She disentangled his arms from around her and pointed to the stairs. There was only one way she was prepared to forgive him, this he knew. Meekly, he ascended each step slowly and with trepidation while she bared her stained yellowing teeth broadly, in anticipation of what was to come.

*

DCI Allison marched into his office without a word. Maddie raised her eyes at Mark Stringer who was chatting to her. "He doesn't seem in a very good mood. Maybe, I'd better get him a coffee."

"Better make it two. I've got some important news for him," said Mark, and he knocked lightly on the door before entering.

"Sir, the report from Flotex is through."

Allison looked up. He didn't speak. He was nursing a head cold and his nose was red and sore.

"Apparently, they've identified it as a carpet that was used in the Rover two thousand series during nineteen ninety but they have discontinued its use."

"I'd have laid bets it was going to be an Escort. So, where does that leave us?"

"All Rover two thousands made during eighty-nine and ninety were fitted with it, so we're looking for a car from that year currently in the area. That shouldn't be too hard."

Allison's face furrowed into creases as he perused that fact, "What happened to all the off-cuts?"

"Pardon?"

"Think about it, Mark. They're not going to use all the carpet. There must be some left somewhere and I want to know what happened to it. We'll need to examine every car registered and I want a check on all workers at Flotex who had anything to do with that carpeting. No possibility must be ignored." Allison sneezed loudly, "And double check the carpet fibres with current samples, we have to be sure," he managed to grunt before being beset by a fit of sneezing. He took out an enormous clean white handkerchief and blew his nose hard sounding like a worn out kazoo.

Maddie knocked and came in with the coffees as Allison sat stone-faced. He nodded curtly leaving Mark to thank her.

*

Tony came out of the bath, his body glistening with water droplets. He was wrapped only in a short, skimpy, white towel. He could never find the big bath sheets he'd put in the airing cupboard, although he'd bought many. He was convinced his mother cut them down to make smaller ones. He had hoped to catch her in the act and challenge her and wondered what she'd say.

He tentatively opened the door; praying to himself that she wouldn't be there. She was waiting for him on the landing. She had the bottle of baby oil in her hands. As he brushed past her she flicked up the towel under the pretence of looking at his bruise.

She tutted, "That looks sore. It needs some tincture of flower of arnica on it, I think. It will bring out the bruising and fade it quickly," she said and before he could protest, the little protection he had from her prying eyes was whisked away. His worthless piece of towel dropped to the floor. She stooped to pick it up. He stood motionless, like a small child.

Still crouching under the guise of rescuing his towel, she poured some of the oil on to her hands and slowly started to rise; stopping when her face was level with the top of his thighs. Her hands now slippery with oil glided up his legs. Tony flinched and groaned.

Tony's mother parted her lips and sighed as she

100

investigated his most private parts. He was helpless to resist and he knew what was expected of him.

*

Sandra Thornton's parents had kept a constant vigil by her bed. Her mother talked constantly and soothingly to her, telling her news of all the family and her friends. "I hope you can hear me, Sandra. I'm told this is what you need to hear and you must know that all is well at home. All arguments have been forgotten. In fact, I can't even remember what we quarrelled about. It was obviously something very trivial. Anyway, it doesn't matter. You must know Dad and I love you so much, we just want you home, back where you belong. Our life has been dreadful without you. We have missed you so very much. You must fight this and come back to us. I promise you nothing else is important. Just your health and being back with us where you belong. No more rows, no more problems, just getting you home. I love you, Sandra. You must know that. Deep in the recesses of your heart, you must know that. You are my little girl. Please, please get well, my darling daughter."

The constant blip of the cardiac monitor registering Sandra's heart beat and the hum of the machines in the room told of the seriousness of her condition. Outside on the door sat a uniformed constable waiting patiently, ever hopeful of her recovery.

Mrs. Thornton bowed her head in anguish and sobbed. Her husband tenderly put his arms around his wife's shoulders. "She's got to pull through. She's got to," she murmured. "My mouth is so dry. Here I am chattering inanely like an idiot. I didn't realise it would be so hard. She must get well."

"All we can do is be patient and wait,' said Mr. Thornton wisely. "I assume if it hadn't been for her self defence skills that she would be dead by now." Mr. Thornton pulled his wife up and ushered her out, "Come on love, go and get a cuppa. It's my turn now.'

Mrs. Thornton reluctantly allowed herself to be led away from her daughter's bedside and Mr. Thornton retook the position by the bed. He switched on a recorder and played

101

some of Sandra's favourite music. The strains of harmonious sleepiness that was lulling, soothing guitar music started to filter through to Sandra Thornton's brain. Her eyelids fluttered once, but Mr. Thornton with his head bowed didn't see.

*

Mark Stringer pushed through a crowd of young coppers off to the canteen for lunch. He was excited and it showed. He made his way to the Chief's office; this couldn't wait.

Maddie looked up expectantly, "Chief's out, Mark. Gone to get some Lemsips for his cold. He shouldn't be long."

"Great!" he said with exasperation, "Just what I need."

Maddie pursed her lips in a bemused fashion and Mark continued, "Some news has come through from Flotex that he ought to see. I'll leave it on his desk. Tell him I've gone to Dempsey's. When he's read that he'll understand why," with that he opened Allison's door and tossed a sheaf of papers on his desk and then dashed out.

He added to Maddie, "Tell him to look at them. They're important."

Maddie barely had time to nod her agreement before Sergeant Stringer was gone.

Mark's pulse was racing, he was sure he was on to something. It couldn't be just coincidence. It just couldn't. In his trade he didn't believe in such things.

He took one of the station's cars and headed through the heavy Christmas traffic for the big department store. He passed Rackham's with its bright lights and tinsel offering a welcome to all who entered and soon was in view of the glass monstrosity they called Dempsey's.

Once in the lift, he made directly for the offices and Miss Susan Hardy. She was at her desk, with her typewriter clacking. She looked up as he approached her.

"Yes?" she looked questioningly at him and then a sudden flood of recognition washed over her face. "Wait a minute … You … you're from the police."

Mark nodded. He took a deep breath to calm himself and keep his voice even.

She spoke first, "How can I help?"

"Before you started as Mr. Payne's secretary, where did you work?"

Susan pulled a face as if thinking, which she didn't need to do and promptly responded, "After I finished at college, I took a temporary position with a company in Oxford. I stayed there for about eighteen months but I missed home too much, so when this job was advertised in the company magazine, I applied for it and here I am. Why?"

"What was the name of the company?" He hardly dared wait for her answer.

"It was fairly new, I think they settled on the name Flotex."

Mark's delight was difficult to contain, "I knew it!" he exclaimed, "I knew there couldn't be two Miss Susan Hardys."

He cracked his fist into his hand and grinned at the bemused Miss Hardy who coolly raised her eyebrows as she glanced down the passageway and said, "Isn't that your boss?"

Striding down the corridor towards them was Allison, his nose buried in an enormous white handkerchief.

"You got my message then?" said Mark.

"Yes, pity you didn't wait," he snorted. "I was only a few minutes. Well? Is it the same Susan Hardy?"

"I think that's already been established. Look, what is all this about?" she demanded icily.

"I'm sorry, please bear with us. We asked Flotex for a list of their workers in the carpet industry and they sent us a complete list of staff and personnel. If they hadn't been so thorough and obliging we might never have known."

"I hate to be the damp squib but what has all this to do with me?"

"We're trying to trace off-cuts from carpet manufactured exclusively for the Rover two thousand series in nineteen eighty-nine and nineteen ninety. Did you by any chance have any come into your possession? It could help us to find Janet's murderer," said Mark in a rush.

"Oh, I had half a roll of some really tough cord. My boyfriend at the time said it was surplus to requirements."

"What happened to it?" probed Allison gently.

"Well, let's see," she thought hard for a moment, "I used some as foot wipes, gave some to my Dad and brother for their cars. I used a piece of it to line the boot of my car and the rest I gave away."

"Who to?'

"I can't remember. I bought a wad of it in here, told people to help themselves.... that it was useful as car mats and car boot liners." She screwed up her face, "Sorry, I can't be of more help."

"Tell me, do you still have the same carpet lining in your boot?" pressed Allison.

"Yes. I do."

"Then could we take some samples away for tests?" queried Mark.

"Certainly, be my guest." She reached for her bag under the desk and pulled out her car keys. "I'll come down with you to the staff car park. Take what you need."

"We also need to find out who else has some of the carpet."

"Can't you question the staff again?" she asked.

"Not yet," said Allison, "There may be a better way."

8
Whirlwind

Amy frowned. Things were happening too fast. She couldn't keep pace. She was being swept off her feet. Wooed as if by an old fashioned suitor.

Flowers arrived daily. Presents, trinkets all given with love and tenderness. She had never met such a 'gentleman' before, but alarm bells were ringing loud and clear inside her head and now, Tony had left his mother's house and moved into a cramped bed-sit just to be near her. She knew he was angling to live with her in the flat above her Mum and Dad's; a little bit of independence they had given to her when her marriage had broken up.

Did she want this? She thought not, but she was being railroaded into a position that would be difficult to get out of without arousing his anger. She'd experienced it once and didn't want it to happen again.

She thought back to the evening in the pub when he had really frightened her. His voice had been cold with anger when she had suggested putting a ten pence piece in the one-armed bandit. He demanded that she leave the machine alone. Amy unused to being ordered around by anyone had cheerily ignored his order. She shivered now as she remembered the wrath this act had incurred.

His icy tone had flared into red-hot temper, the violence, of which had terrified her. She had never seen him like that. The transformation that had taken place in his face, and his expression, had showed a side of him that she did not believe existed and secretly she worried. She was getting in too deep, too quickly. She remembered Sheena's warning. Sheena had met him several times and had never taken to him and didn't trust him. But somehow or other he played on her sensitivity, carefully manipulating her, using his own form of emotional blackmail.

"Come on, Pidge. I said I'm sorry. Don't look at me like that. I'm tired that's all. Look at all I have done to be with you. I have left a comfortable home with my mother to live in a pokey bed-sit just to be near you. You should know, I was going to get back with my ex, Sally; she had an enormous house, even asked me to be a partner in her business. I was just about to move back in with her ... But then I met you. I fell for you, deeply fell in love with you, and all the money in the world wouldn't take me from your side, now. No one else matters."

He constantly reminded Amy of all he had done for her. He had managed to convince her of things that weren't even true.

"In fact, you could say I left Sally for you," he told her. "As soon as I saw you I knew you were the right one for me. I didn't want to hurt Sally but it wasn't fair for me to stay with her just because of what she gave me or could give me... I needed you.

He laid it on with a trowel. Sally it seemed had everything, money, a luxurious house, membership to exclusive clubs, and her own business. And she'd pampered Tony; she'd given him everything and anything he'd wanted, but he'd given it all up for her.

Morally, she felt responsible. It was she who had enthused so much about his singing and told him that he should concentrate on this as his career. She remembered ruefully, what she had said to him. "Give up your day job. Get yourself an agent. You're good! Really good! Honestly, you could make it. But it won't all come to you on a plate; you've got to work at it." Her words came rushing back to her.

She now screamed in frustration. She hadn't expected him to give up his day job at Dempsey's, instantly, just like that. Sheena had warned her that the relationship was progressing too quickly. And Sheena wasn't keen on him. She had made that clear enough. Amy knew that. But, she didn't know why Sheena felt that way. Tony had suggested it was jealousy.

Amy rubbed her forehead and her hand strayed to her throat. He made her feel guilty. Somehow, psychologically, he was putting pressure on her. She was making decisions about his life for him and she didn't like it. But ... He was a dish! He was interesting, gentle and normally very kind. She was seriously attracted to him.

The battle raged inside her head. She continued to think and remember, going over events in her mind in an attempt to focus and sort out her feelings.

She felt strongly that Tony needed looking after. Especially after what had happened the other night. Some drunk had smashed him in the face after one of his gigs. She felt it was partly her fault. Amy had been dragging her heels, by not attending every event, trying to cool his ardour but without much success. Her absence seemed to make him keener than ever. She truly believed that if she'd been there with him that night it wouldn't have happened. He wouldn't have stayed so late and he wouldn't have had the fight. Amy could see that he needed her.

Amy finally came to a decision; Tony's decision. She knew she would have to speak to her father. How she would broach the subject she didn't know?

Tony had said, "Come on, Piidge. All fathers love their daughters. He would do anything for you. You can twist him around your little finger. I know if you were mine you could ask me anything and I'd never refuse."

"It's difficult, Tony. I have never lived with anyone before and I was a virgin when I got married. My father is a fan of respectability and doing things the right way. He doesn't like immodesty or living in sin as he calls it."

"Well, if it's too hard an ask…" his voice trailed off.

Amy was being well and truly forced to make a decision that she wasn't ready for, nor was she certain that it was the correct thing to do, at least not for her. Things seemed to be gambolling along and it seems currently, she was not assertive enough to turn him down. Privately, she worried but Tony played her like a seasoned professional bludgeoning her doubts into submission. She was getting in way over her head.

*

Allison scratched his head thoughtfully and sneezed suddenly, splattering his desk with tiny droplets of water. He sniffed, feeling very sorry for himself, and reached for the mentholyptus sweets he'd been forced to buy for his sore throat.

A quick look at his overflowing in-tray showed him that he needed to set to and clear the backlog of administration. He hated paperwork, but it had to be done. He ploughed his way through a pile, signing this and that; referring case notes to the charge of subordinate officers to type up when he came across a hurriedly scribbled note. He was just about to screw it up and consign it to the bin when he saw the name Bowden. Bowden? That was the woman in charge of Personnel at Dempsey's. He read the note carefully. It seemed Mrs. Bowden had some information that may be relevant to the case. She had left a number. Allison picked up the phone and dialled.

"Joyce Bowden, Personnel, please."

"One moment. Who shall I say is calling?"

"DCI Allison here. I had a message saying she might have some useful information that could help with our case?"

"I'll see if she's available."

*

Tony was supremely content and confident. He leaned back in the rocking chair, now *his* chair and smiled. His heavy, expensive, gold identity bracelet covered the faint scratches left by Janet Mason's scrabbling fingers. He struggled to recall how he had got them but he couldn't even remember, he couldn't remember any of it. Some spiteful cat, he'd told Amy and she'd believed him. She had no reason not to, not yet.

Amy studied his face and he put out a hand to her. "Come and sit with me."

"I can't," she giggled. "We'll break the chair." But she went all the same. He pulled her close to him enveloping her with his love and she snuggled into him like a baby.

All of Amy's doubts were slowly vanishing, subdued by his constant attention and courtesy. This had to be the most loving man she had ever met. Now she understood why so many women went for older men. They made you feel like one in a million.

There was a shout up the stairs. "Amy! Tony! Dinner will

be ready in ten minutes." Amy's Mum had invited them both for dinner.

A moment of sadness gripped his heart. This is what a real family was. This is what he should have had, not being an only child suffocated by a mother who ruled his and his father's life. He swallowed hard and Amy noticed the change on his face.

"Tony, whatever's wrong?"

He smiled that little boy smile that touched her so deeply, "Nothing. I was just thinking."

"Tell me," she persisted.

"I was just thinking how much I envy you."

"Me?" Amy gasped in surprise, "Why?"

"I'll tell you, sometime."

"Why? Don't you trust me? I've told you, your problems are my problems. I want to share everything with you." He looked deeply into her eyes. "That's what was wrong in my first marriage. We didn't talk enough; we didn't share our grievances, fears, hopes and dreams. If we had, we might still have been together."

"Then I wouldn't have met you. And that doesn't bear thinking about." He studied her face hard. This beautiful creature had rescued him from misery and the web of evil that had pervaded his life. She looked so understanding, so sympathetic; so he thought he would tell her about his father.

He cleared his throat, "I don't know if I can tell you this; I don't know how you'll react."

"What do you mean?" quizzed Amy.

"I don't want you despising me."

"How could I possibly despise you?" asked Amy amazed. She looked at his handsome face now forlorn and full of sorrow.

Tony's voice became plaintive, "You could hear things about me you don't want to hear. Things that will make you feel differently about me."

"Don't be silly. I cannot think that there is anything you could say that would change my feelings for you."

"I wish I could believe you."

"You can."

Tony looked deeply into her loving eyes that were filled with concern. He felt calmer than he had for a long while, for months. Perhaps, after all, an even greater peace would be his if he did explain his feelings a little more.

"I expect you know that I'm an only child," he began hesitatingly. "Never had a real home life, not like yours, with parents who love you properly as parents should." Tony swallowed painfully when he imagined what Amy's life must have been like and then, compared it with his own lonely, early years. "I never really knew my father. He committed suicide when I was sixteen."

"I'm sorry. I had no idea."

"No, why would you?" he said abruptly and stopped. His eyes filmed over and he stared into the corners of the room, the shadows of which changed shape, filled the recesses and spread along the floor. He gasped as if trying to find the courage to speak.

"Go on."

Tony blinked and continued in his cultured tones, "I was doing really well at my studies then. I went to a good grammar school. My marks and reports were excellent. I could have made something of myself. I was school chess champion, captain of the cricket team; I even tried out for Villa and played for the schoolboy team and then my life was shattered. Not all at once, but in small fragments, tiny shards, sharp edged, cutting as they went in, chipping away at my heart until all that was left was a mechanical pump. I'd forgotten how to love, Amy. Until I met you." His eyes were artificially bright.

Amy smiled sympathetically and Tony's words continued to flow. It seemed that now he had begun he couldn't stop. "Dad was a singer, not seriously, just part time; a bit like me. He played working men's clubs and so on. A voice like Frank Sinatra, Mum said. I never heard him sing that was forbidden. Don't ask me why. It always seemed crazy to me. But she and Dad were happy, after a fashion, until Mum became involved with an evangelist who promised to save her soul, make her reborn.

He paused and dropped his earnest eyes that had studied her face so intensely. He had been watching for any glimmer of distaste or any sign that Amy had felt disgust; but Amy's expression didn't change. She had returned his gaze steadily without blinking. He raised his lids once more and his eyes continued to search her face. "I remember it as if it was yesterday. She changed. She changed so much."

He shook his head sorrowfully as if it still hurt him to recall those painful days. "Sundays were the worst. I wasn't allowed out. I was forced to sit at my desk and learn passages from the Bible." He laughed humourlessly, "Even now I can recite in order, all the books of the Bible. Even now, I can quote from the scriptures, a verse of wisdom for every eventuality, a word of comfort, or a word of damnation. And every day I was reminded of the Hell that would be upon me if I denied the Lord."

Amy's stomach started to churn; her heart began to pound disturbingly. She fought to control her unease, to keep her facial expression calm and unchanged. She needn't have worried, years of teaching and facing all kinds of unexpected situations had trained her well.

"My friends would be outside playing, laughing, having fun. I had to stay in and learn the Bible. 'Blessed are the pure in heart for they shall see God.' She thrust her beliefs at us more and more. Dad did all he could to escape. He chain smoked, he drank too much, and he gambled. With him everything became an obsession. He sought refuge in his gambling until, hopelessly addicted, he could cope no more. One day he took his own life."

"How awful," said Amy. The sound of her own voice made her jump.

Tony's cultured tones had dropped in pitch and became soft and confiding. "He hanged himself. Mum found him." Tony snorted through his nose in derision, "Do you know what she said after he had taken the most important decision of his life?" Amy shook her head. No words would come. "I'd bought steak for tea. What a pity, I'd bought steak for tea..." His words petered out and his head fell on his chest. Amy tilted his chin with her fingertips. His eyes lifted to her face and he continued, "Then there was just Mum and me. We'd 'got each other' she said."

"Well, now you've got me," murmured Amy.

She gently stroked his face; a single tear ran down her cheek. Tony kissed it away. "I didn't mean to upset you."

"That's all right," she paused and her tone grew softer, "Now, I understand why you hate gambling so much; why you were so angry when I put money in the fruit machine at the pub."

"I over reacted," he apologised. "I shouldn't have said and done what I did."

"The wall won't forget in a hurry," she laughed "I ought to put a circle around the dent and label it Tony Creole, December Twelfth 1994."

"Using my stage name are we?"

"Yes," she said firmly, "Because you're going to be a star!"

"I wish I could be as certain as you."

"You are, and together we'll make it happen, you'll see. You'll be famous!"

*

Trevor Booth smiled at the Chief. He was right where he wanted to be; in the middle of an investigation that made him privy to information denied to the rest of the press. He'd been allowed special access to Mr. and Mrs. Thornton, who had agreed to the use of an interview in any eventuality.

"Chief! Thanks. That really does give me the final scoop. I shall have such a wealth of stories it's sure to help me move up the ladder."

Allison grunted sagely, "Well, what we want to do, Trevor, is to let the killer think that he's succeeded. We don't want him coming after her. If she recovers she could be the only one who can identify the bastard. And Lord knows we don't want any more killings. Enough blood has been spilled."

Trevor inclined his head in agreement, "Tell you what, I'll put out a press release announcing the death of Sandra Thornton. I understand her parents are only too happy to comply, not wishing their daughter to become the target of some nut who feels threatened by her survival," offered Trevor.

Allison growled back in his usual gruff manner, "That's the ticket ... Was there something else?" he asked, noticing Trevor's typical 'I know something else' expression.

"Well, I have turned up a few interesting facts that may or may not prove useful and I would like your permission to follow my own line of enquiry."

"Tell me what you've got and I'll let you know," said Allison in a non-committal tone.

"Right." He took a deep breath, "I've been poking around the school that Dawn Ashby attended."

"Yes?" Allison looked interested and leaned forward on his desk.

"I spent some time chatting to Dawn's friends. These chats have revealed a close chum, Anne Marie, who had one very interesting titbit to offer. The assistant caretaker, 'Arf a brain Arfur', as the pupils call him had given Dawn the creeps, apparently. She'd often said that she felt he was watching her. Here, I've written it all down." Trevor passed this report to Allison who leafed through it cursorily. "What I'd really like is to do a little ferreting myself, see what else I can learn. Of course, I would pass everything onto you."

"Of course," said Allison sardonically. Allison leaned back in his chair and puffed loudly as he thought. He knew his department was over stretched. "All right, then. Go ahead. I suppose it could be useful. Do a little watching or ferreting."

Trevor's delight was more than apparent and he grinned from ear to ear.

"Just one stipulation."

"Yes?"

"First, we'll schedule a visit from the uniformed branch to this man. I don't think that would go amiss," Allison decided. "Stalwarts, Pooley and Taylor will be put on the job. We'll see what they can discover. They will first pay a call on the school caretaker either at the school or his home. And if Anne Marie and the other students and staff clam up, as well they might, or if they refuse to corroborate your findings it

113

will make things easier for you. You already have their confidence so they may be prepared to say even more to you." He shook his head vehemently, "It's a strange old world where coppers are despised and investigative reporters have the haloes."

*

Trevor Booth left the Chief's office with a spring in his step and walked into a milling throng of police and CID all billing and cooing over Mark Stringer's baby daughter, Catherine. Trevor briefly joined in the congratulations and said a few words to a blushing Debbie Stringer. He shook Mark's hand and went out into the street.

It was already getting dark. The dusky clouds with hues of pink were rolling across the sky signifying the death of the sun and the awakening of the twilight hours. The wind tugged at his coat and Trevor pulled it around him more firmly, buttoning it right up to the neck, in an attempt to keep out the prying fingers of the wind and cold. He shivered suddenly and looked round. The station windows bright with artificial light, and the celebration party, told him that it would be a while before coppers Pooley and Taylor would be off to visit 'Crabby Crabtree', another of the caretaker's nicknames, and he convinced himself that there was no harm in him having a look in that direction himself. Trevor started to whistle and speeded up his step, reaching his car just as the first drops of rain began to fall.

*

Before Allison went out to join the group gathered around Mark's baby, he called Joyce Bowden at Dempsey's again. She'd been unable to take his call the last time he rang, as some emergency had cropped up and she still hadn't got back to him.

Greg drummed his fingers impatiently while he waited to be put through. "Joyce Bowden?"

"Yes, sorry, Inspector. You are on my list of people to call."

"You have something to tell me?"

"Yes, it may or may not be important."

"I'll be the judge of that, go ahead."

114

"Well, you were asking about the off cuts of carpet that Susan Hardy brought into the office."

"Yes?"

"I had a piece to line my boot after I spilled petrol on the old liner and had to throw it away."

"Go on."

"I sold that car with the off cut to a gentleman in Handsworth."

"Thank you. Do you have the name and address of the man?"

"I do. It was fairly recently. Hold on a moment it's in the drawer."

She relayed the name and address and Allison jotted it down, "Thank you, Mrs. Bowden. We'll check it out. Was there anything else?"

"No, no, but if I think of anything else, I'll let you know."

The news wasn't that exciting but it may be a useful lead. Greg thanked her all the same.

9
Killing Spree

Arthur Crabtree could scarcely contain his excitement. Tonight was the night. He had planned it all so very perfectly, no one would know, no one would suspect. He sat in his armchair and attempted to read the paper. His wife, Eileen was still dusting and cleaning the surfaces around him; surfaces that were already gleaming and didn't need anymore cleaning.

He folded the paper he'd been reading fervently and rose. The headline read 'KILLER LOOSE ON CITY STREETS'. He tucked it under his arm as Eileen immediately came across and plumped up the cushion where he'd been sitting. She pointed at the cup and saucer on the floor by his seat, and in her whining voice instructed him, "Take that out with you."

He meekly picked them up and walked to the door.

"I suppose you're going out to that shed of yours. God knows what you do in there at all hours of the day and night. Proper little pigpen it is. Don't go washing that up. I'll deal with it. They need more than a rinse under the cold tap."

Arthur stopped momentarily before entering the kitchen but remained silent. Eileen shrieked after him, "And mind you wipe your feet when you come in. I don't want muck all over my kitchen floor. As if I've got nothing better to do than run around after you all day. Are you listening?"

Her answer was the slamming of the kitchen door that led to the back yard and his shed. Eileen sniffed disapprovingly and sprayed the room with an air-freshener and deodoriser.

Arthur walked down his garden path from the back door to his shed. He carefully undid the padlock that would keep prying eyes out and disappeared inside. He switched on the single light bulb that swing in the centre; the light illuminated his meagre workbench space and the walls, which were adorned with clippings of the murders in Birmingham and certain facts in the reports had been ringed in red ink. He knew he would have to get rid of this evidence after the deed. He didn't want the chance of suspicion to fall on him.

He tugged at a large black bag, which was hidden in the corner, placed it on his battered workbench and opened it. It contained a motley assortment of knives and small handsaws. He lifted each one up in turn as if it was some sort of ritual before he placed the blades on his grinder and sharpened them. Sparks flew and the smell of steel filings pervaded the air and his nostrils, and he sneezed.

Satisfied they were acutely sharp and fit for purpose he replaced them in the holdall but he kept hold of one particularly wicked looking blade and tested it on a ripe tomato, which cut like butter. He wiped the blade, raised his eyes to heaven in supplication and smiled.

Now content that he had the correct tools at his disposal he felt a celebration was in order. He opened a small fridge, which contained a few cans of beer and some chocolate bars before turning his attention to a small box below the freezer compartment. He opened it and the misty smoke of liquid nitrogen billowed up and he withdrew a little tray. On the tray were a number of used condoms. He smiled in gratification before placing them at the back of his bench to defrost. He grabbed a can of beer, pulled the tab and took a swig before switching on his radio, which was playing some rap and pop song, Gangster's Paradise. Quite appropriate really, he would be in paradise once Eileen had gone from his life.

He opened his sandwich box and removed one left over from lunch and took a bite as his face creased in concentration. Arthur's eyes gleamed artfully as he reached in his pocket and took out a box of Mogadon sleeping tablets. He studied the box, carefully, reading the instructions and dosage directions. He was almost shaking with excitement and anticipation. Tonight couldn't come quickly enough.

*

Arthur was prostrate on the floor by the television and video recorder setting the machine to record the evening's viewing. Eileen scowled when she saw her husband prone on

117

the carpet and sniffed disapprovingly. "What rubbish are you recording now?"

"It's for later on, in case I fall asleep. I hate missing the ends of things. Are you out tonight?" was his well-rehearsed answer.

"It's my bingo night. You know that. And don't go leaving beer cans all over the place like you usually do.

"No, Dear. Sorry, Dear."

Eileen crossed to the settee and unnecessarily plumped up the cushions. Arthur's fists clenched and unclenched tightly in anger. He scrambled up and a look of alarm crossed his face when he saw Eileen pick up a large manila envelope from his seat and peer inside. He hadn't intended her to see that and he silently cursed himself for not hiding it away earlier.

"What are our insurance papers doing out?" she complained in her whining, pinched tone.

Slightly unnerved and thinking on his feet he replied, "Just making sure they're all in order."

"Why wouldn't they be?"

"We've a bond maturing soon," he said evasively. "Then, we can enjoy a bit more money."

"Don't think you'll fritter it away on rubbish."

"No, Dear."

"Make sure they're put back in their rightful place," she ordered.

She turned sour-faced and a whiff of lavender filled his nose, as she left the room. Arthur picked up the envelope and pulled out the top document. It was a Life Insurance Policy on Eileen for two hundred and fifty thousand pounds. He sighed happily. Soon that money would be his, but he wouldn't make the mistake of collecting it too quickly. He would wait and play the grief stricken husband; the policy would be an afterthought, a long afterthought. He wasn't in any hurry to cash it. There would be less suspicion that way.

*

Tony sat with Amy watching the evening news, but he wasn't listening properly, his mind was elsewhere. The shadows in the recesses of the room seemed to change shape

118

and spread across the floor. This was something he was not prepared to see.

Amy looked at him, concerned. "What's wrong?"

Tony stifled a small cry, "It's nothing, not really."

"What? You can tell me. We share everything, don't we?"

Tony nodded. The lie rose easily to his lips, "I was just thinking about Dad and how he died."

"It must have been awful."

"It was. My life was in bits. Not all at once, but in confused jigsaw pieces, tiny parts, which didn't link, which confused. I was a mess. All this chipped away at my heart until I was numb. I've already told you that I'd forgotten how to love, really love, until I met you." Amy smiled sympathetically and Tony's words continued to flow. "Dad was a great singer, you know. He should have taken it up seriously, instead of part time."

"I thought you said you hadn't heard him sing."

"I hadn't but I heard other people talk about his voice, not only Mum, but the people next door they all agreed he had a voice like Frank Sinatra in his early days before the cigarettes got to his throat. She and dad were happy, they were, until she became involved with an evangelist." He sounded as if he was trying to convince himself. "That man… He promised to save her soul and that's when it started. I was seven. She changed. She changed so much. Every day I was reminded of the hell that would be upon me if I denied the Lord. Dad did all he could to escape. He smoked, one after the other, drank and gambled. Everything became an obsession; until he couldn't cope anymore… you know the rest… I don't want to keep repeating myself."

"Yes, but if it helps you to talk, then talk. It will do you good, help you to focus and accept the past. That's all it is, Tony. It's the past and you've kept things bottled up inside you for far too long. You need an outlet, someone to listen and that's me. I'm a good listener."

"I know," he said softly. "I know…"

*

Eileen Crabtree sat watching the evening news, while Arthur read the paper. Her bag, coat and hat rested on the

119

settee ready to go out. Arthur looked across slyly at her and spoke especially nicely to her, "Time for a cuppa. Do you want one?"

Eileen was immediately suspicious and demanded, "Why? What have you done?"

"Nothing. I just thought with you going out to Bingo and it being a cold night, it would do you good, warm you up. Why not have a hot chocolate? You know how you like it."

Eileen sniffed imperiously, "Very well. But don't go making a mess. I've just cleaned up."

Arthur retreated into the kitchen meekly with an odd smile on his face. He whistled as he filled the kettle and switched it on. Milk was poured in the pan and set to boil. He just prayed she wouldn't march out and oversee what he was doing.

He took a number of Mogadon from the packet in his jacket and crushed them up with a spoon to a fine powder. The hot chocolate was prepared in a mug and he added the crushed sleeping tablets and mixed it all up, before making himself a cup of tea.

Being well trained he placed the cups on a tray and wiped down the worktop and tossed the J cloth holding the tablet residue into the washing machine. He sniffed the hot chocolate and, satisfied it smelled all right, he took a teaspoon and tasted a mouthful of the chocolate, swished it around his mouth and spat it into the sink then vigorously rinsed his mouth with water. Satisfied he lifted the tray and made his way to the sitting room.

"Here we are, Dear. A lovely mug of hot chocolate."

"Why aren't you having one?"

"I just fancied a cup of tea, that's all." He smiled at Eileen and took a slurp.

Eileen received the mug as if she was doing him a huge favour by accepting it. Arthur sat and sipped his tea. He watched her covertly out of the corner of his eye. He willed her to drink it down but Eileen was taking her time.

"Better finish that up, Dear. It will set you up for the journey to Bingo. It's cold out tonight and my gosh, look at the time!"

Eileen took another sip, "It's too hot. You know I can't drink things too hot. I'll have to leave it."

"No!" Arthur almost shouted. Eileen looked across at him bewildered. "I'll add a tot of cold milk and then it will be fine." He dashed to the kitchen to fetch some milk and Eileen held out her cup for him to add a splash. "There. Now you can drink it."

Eileen looked at him as he stood over her, "Anyone would think you were trying to poison me," she laughed humourlessly.

Arthur joined in, "Ha, ha! Just trying to show you how I value you," he said.

Eileen grunted. Arthur watched her and she swallowed down the last of her hot chocolate. He whisked the mug away from her and swilled it out in the kitchen sink before placing it in the dishwasher. When he returned to the sitting room, Eileen was sitting in the chair in her hat and coat. She looked uncomfortably hot.

"Are you all right, Dear?"

"I think I'm coming down with something. I feel a bit woozy."

"Do you want me to get you a drink of water and an aspirin?"

Eileen shook her head, as if to clear it, and blinked, "Please…"

Arthur went out and searched the cupboard for the tablets and poured a glass of water. He went back in and saw Eileen had fallen asleep and slipped down in the chair, her head lolled on her chest, and he smiled.

*

Trevor Booth sat in his car and started the engine. He studied the petrol gauge, "Bugger!" he said aloud. The red light was on and he needed to get fuel before he could drive to Bartley Green, which was a fair distance away from the town centre. He turned on his wipers as the rain began to tamp down like ball bearings, bouncing off the bonnet of the car with accelerated speed. People could drown in this much rain, he thought. The wipers were working overtime, over and back, over and back in a repetitive rhythm that was almost hypnotic, so Trevor decided to sit and wait for the downpour to finish before setting off. What he had expected to be a short job was now going to take much longer.

He decided he'd grab a bite to eat on the way, but for now he took out his notebook and began to jot down the questions he would ask Arthur Crabtree when he finally met him.

Several minutes later, the rain no longer blinded him and Trevor pulled out of his parking space and into the oppressive wet night. He headed for the nearest garage on route to the Garden House Hotel on the Hagley Road where he could park safely and grab himself something to eat. He realised he'd skipped lunch and was now absolutely famished. He'd get fed and then he could think more clearly.

It could be a long night.

*

Eileen was now laid out cold and slumped on the floor. Arthur pulled off her hat, which was at a strange angle and reminded him of a comic character in an old black and white movie he'd seen as a child. Old Mother Riley came to mind, but he couldn't be certain. It was a long time ago.

Arthur caught hold of her arms and began to drag her out of the room to the hallway and foot of the stairs. He looked up at the flight of stairs, which stretched before him and sighed before attempting to haul her up them.

He tugged at her and heaved her up each step as if he was hauling a carcase of meat. Her head bumped on each step as he moved. He stopped, wondering whether the activity would rouse her but he needn't have worried and he rather enjoyed the bump, bump, bump of her head on each step.

Arthur's breathing was heavy by the time he reached the top of the stairs. He dragged Eileen across the carpet and into the bedroom where he struggled to pull her onto the bed. He switched on the electric blanket to keep her body warm and calmly picked up the phone on the bedside table and dialled.

"...Hello, Trudy?... Dad... Yes, Mum's out. Bingo night... I look forward to our little chats, too. ...Yes, no interruptions..." He continued chatting to his daughter for a further five minutes, "Yes, love you, too." He replaced the receiver when a thought occurred to him, 'the back door and her hat!'

Arthur ran down the stairs, dashed into the kitchen and bolted the back door. He dived into the passage and secured the front door, too. He didn't want any disturbances. Arthur took her hat and placed it prominently on the hall table where he could see it when he removed her to her final resting place. She never went out without her hat.

He paused and thought a moment, then snapped his fingers, returned to the kitchen and removed his packets of now defrosted sperm, which he'd taken from his shed, and hidden in the fridge and he placed it safely on the counter top before he opened the broom closet. Arthur took out a bag from which, he removed a small hacksaw and a serrated knife and grinning ghoulishly he placed these on the tray with the semen, walked to the hall and began to mount the stairs.

*

Booth had finished an ample plateful of steak and ale pie and patted his tummy in satisfaction. He paid his bill and made his way out into the car park and into the continuing driving rain. He hurried inside his vehicle and moved out onto the busy Hagley Road. With his windscreen wipers still working at break neck speed he made his way back to Five Ways, circled the roundabout and began to travel toward Harborne. The traffic was heavier than expected and Booth was forced to sit in a stop start traffic queue, which was frustrating for him and all other drivers.

The wipers continued to beat out a regular rhythm and he found himself tapping the steering wheel in time to their constant click, squeak, click and squeak. The car in front of him stalled and impatient motorists hooted at the hapless driver from behind.

Booth cursed, "Shut it! He can't help it. We all want to get going again."

The car in front spluttered back into life and the line of cars proceeded along the flooding streets. A VW pulled out of a side turning and skidded to a stop scraping the wing of another vehicle, which unable to stop had aquaplaned across the road.

"Great! That's all I need." Booth was thinking aloud. He even thought of turning around and heading home but his dogged persistence that he always demonstrated, when he was on a job, won through and he gripped the steering wheel hard and continued moving forward.

The rain was, at last, starting to ease. Not so the traffic but Booth knew that once through Harborne he would encounter less cars.

He would get to Arthur Crabtree's house within half an hour.

*

Arthur Crabtree was effervescently jubilant. He raised the freshly sharpened bread knife aloft. He wildly jabbed the air, brandishing it like a cutthroat pirate from days gone by.

He was naked, except for an old psychedelic cravat, a relic from his mod days in the sixties, tied around his head karate style, and a pair of fine surgical gloves.

Arthur Crabtree gave a whoop and did a frenzied dance reminiscent of Hitler's jig when he heard France had fallen.

Eileen was still unconscious, and now lying partially clothed in the bath.

He had a sudden thought. Why didn't he think of it before? Damn and blast! It was sod's law! There were bound to be traces of the drug in her blood when they did the autopsy. How could he get around this? Arthur decided he would have to sit by the bath, watch and wait. And when he saw signs of her coming to, mistakenly believing that the drug would then be out of her system, he would strangle her. The prospect of having her wake to this fate, to see the recognition of her murderer reflected in her eyes, filled him with a peculiar excitement.

A sick knot twisted in his stomach like some writhing serpent. What if he couldn't go through with it? What if she overcame him? What if? What if?

These fleeting anxieties he chased out of his head and Arthur Crabtree made up his mind. He would have to proceed. He carefully closed the bathroom door and sat on the toilet seat and stared at Eileen's face. The packets from Luke Saunders' amorous adventures were sitting on the

124

toiletry shelf. He raised the knife and plunged it into Eileen's chest. There! He'd done it and he started to hum as he went about his gory work.

*

Trevor turned into Jiggins Lane and kerb crawled his way up the road, checking the numbers as he looked for the right house. Pretty soon he spotted it and parked his car. No one saw him arrive. Not a curtain twitched, not a soul moved. The rain had eased slightly but the keen wind sent icy chills through every opening in his coat. Trevor walked up the path. There had to be someone home. The lights downstairs were blazing and he could hear gales of canned laughter from some inane quiz programme on the television. He rang the bell and waited.

*

Upstairs in the bathroom, Arthur froze. A bell? Who the hell was it? Arthur hadn't expected any interruptions. The lights and TV were on, all part of his alibi. Maybe if he waited they'd go away. He could be in the bath... A visitor wouldn't know that he wasn't. But, what if they didn't go? He could call out, shout he was bathing... ask them to come back later.

Curiosity overcame him. He wiped the carving knife on the shower curtain and hurriedly scrubbed his hands. Safe now to emerge from this bloody tomb, he tiptoed out onto the landing and peeped out of the window, safe in the knowledge that he couldn't be seen.

Trevor Booth was staring up.

Arthur felt a cold stab of fear. Could he be seen after all? Sweating profusely from his exertions and fright, Arthur didn't know what to do.

He watched the figure below as Trevor shrugged his shoulders and rang again. The noise was shrilly discordant in Arthur's ears. He ventured nearer and looked again. He hadn't a clue who this carrot-haired fellow was. Maybe, he would be safe after all. Being in something of a dither he slipped back into the shadows on the landing, his breath puffing in short wheezing rasps. He heard a rattle as Trevor tried the back gate. Arthur knew it was locked. He was

125

unaware that their black plastic dustbin was conveniently placed by the back gate. He had no idea that Trevor had clambered onto it, hopped over the fence and into the yard.

Arthur ventured once more to the window. He sighed deeply with relief. The stranger had gone. The threat was no more. He waited until his breathing had returned to normal and then went to continue with his grisly task. Arthur had just completed syringing Luke's semen into Eileen's vagina and over her belly when he heard a crash. The sound made him jump and he stabbed himself with the needle. Cursing at yet another interruption, he stepped out of his chamber of horrors and gingerly moved towards the stairwell.

Slowly, he inched his way down the stairs, all caution now forgotten. Blood drops ran in rivulets down his naked flesh and gruesomely plopped onto the floor, damning him to a guilty verdict and life imprisonment.

*

Outside Trevor strained to see in through the kitchen window. He cursed as he sent a spade and a garden rake that had been resting against the wall, crashing to the ground. A narrow band of light shone onto the black and white Ajaxed tiles. The thin beam of light gradually grew wider. So slow was the gradual increase that at first Trevor thought he was imagining things. The kitchen door crept open still further.

With shock and revulsion Trevor found himself staring at some ghoulish escapee from a Hammer Horror film set. He was staring at the demented eyes of a madman bathed in blood, bearing a huge knife dripping with shreds of flesh.

Trevor had seen enough. He ducked down out of sight and waited until he heard the scuttling footsteps return into the hall.

Fighting for breath and to quell the surge of sickness rising within him, he scrambled back over the gate and retreated to his car, which lurched off down the road in a series of kangaroo jumps to the nearest phone booth. Outside the phone booth his stomach relinquished his earlier meal of steak and ale pie into the gutter. Colin wiped his mouth and with a shaking hand he picked up the phone.

Five minutes later sirens were heard in Jiggins Lane.

10
Continued Investigation

"It seems that Annette Jury had three regulars; an old bloke, Barney Reubin, who often bought her time at the club; the club's DJ and resident pianist, Steve Jenkins as apparently they had an on-going thing; and there was some businessman, who comes to Brum twice a month from the Smoke who always saw Annette. None of them were at the club the night she was killed." Mark Stringer drew up a studded leatherette chair with a padded seat and sat opposite Greg Allison. He continued, "Apparently, Annette was a real comic book character, an ex-stripper turned pro. She enjoyed her work, although she originally went into business to provide for her little boy. Sometimes, if someone took her fancy, she'd entertain them for their company."

"Have we got any leads on the date?"

"She danced with a few that night. Some camera man in with a crowd from Central TV; the singer doing the second spot; and a group of soldiers on leave."

"Find them and see them. We want statements. Have we got any names for them?"

"Cameraman's someone called Johnny. He pops in most weeks nicknamed 'Ace'. There were two singers on that night, Tony something-or-other and Paul Berry. Neither of them had appeared there before. Marie is checking the books to see if their names and telephone numbers are in the events diary or if they were booked through an agent. No one could help on the soldiers, it seems it was a local lad on leave with some mates."

"Get someone onto it and run the names you have got through the computer."

Mark acknowledged, "Sir."

Allison continued, "Okay, Mark, run it all by me again, let's see what we've got. It helps me to concentrate my mind and work things through."

Stringer repeated his findings from his interview with

Marie and Allison listened again. He rubbed his chin and took a breath as if he was about to speak and then paused.

"It's one hell of a mess," he complained, still tugging at his chin. "What have we got? Four murders, a savage, brutal attack, which may or may not be our man, and an idiot caretaker who's done his wife in, copy cat style, and who's probably responsible for the Ashby killing. We're still waiting for Forensic to confirm that. And to top it all, I've just heard that Crabtree has confessed to the lot."

"Crabtree?" exclaimed Mark.

"That's right! Taylor says he certainly knows a lot about the murders. But he hasn't come up with one detail that convinces me he was responsible. Anything found at the house?"

"The arresting officer's report said there were collections of press cuttings on the murders with sections highlighted in red."

"A whole collection on each one?"

"Yes, why? What are you thinking?"

"He's such a small man. It's difficult to imagine that he'd have the strength to destroy the life in Janet Mason, but I suppose anything is possible."

"I reckon he did his wife in, hoping to make it look like our man."

"Yes, you said. What about Dawn Ashby?"

"Practice run?"

"Possibly."

"Okay, Mark let's see what comes back from the blood test. Get on to Hurst, see if we can tie Crabtree to the Ashby murder with something conclusive."

"He can't be our man, Chief. He's not even left handed."

"No, that would be too much to hope for."

"So, what do we do?"

"Wait. Sit and wait. Let's see if this interview with the psychologist, Rebecca Mills gives us anything more to go on."

"Yes. And if Miss Thornton recovers, hopefully, she can tell us about her attacker."

"Heard anything from the hospital?"

"Not yet. We've got a man there. He'll contact us if there's any news."

*

Things were happening at the hospital. The parents' steadfast watch at Sandra's side was paying off. She had stirred twice and her eyelids had fluttered. Her favourite music was being played; her Mum and Dad talked to her, constantly reminding her of their love and of the happy times they had spent together.

Now, her Sensei, whom she loved and respected, had travelled from Bristol to see her. He replayed a video of the last competition in which she'd competed, commenting on the moves and mistakes of herself and her friends. He talked about the club and the changes that had just been brought into the syllabus. This they had been awaiting for the last two years. He urged encouragingly, "Come on, Sandra! Technically, there's no one better at your grade. You can do it! You can go all the way to First Dan. I've always said the biggest fight you can have is with yourself. That's the battle that's on now. Prove me right. Prove you're a winner! The Grand Master comes over to tour Britain in the New Year, you don't want to miss that."

As he finished speaking Sandra's crystal blue eyes blinked open. Her parents hugged. Euphoria hit the unit. Sandra awoke feeling disorientated. Her first conscious observation was that of clinical white walls, a pale blue curtain that was ripped on its hangings at the end of a metal runner and a strong smell of carbolic mixed with disinfectant, and something else that she couldn't quite recognise. She thought at first that it was a scene from some horrific nightmare with plastic tubes connected to her arms and nose; her face, neck and body bandaged, fluids dripping in and out of her and the overwhelming feeling that she was unable to breathe and was suffocating. Her breath bubbled out of her like someone with severe bronchial problems.

Increasingly, she began to feel that it was all real; that the faces watching her were real, faces she recognised were not from her dreams; nurses in their cool crisp manner were efficiently taking her pulse, sticking syringes into her; and

129

they, too, were all real along with the blipping sounds of the monitoring equipment and the harsh brightness of the fluorescent lights; the doctor was staring down at her and the awful dawning of what had happened and why she was here was upon her.

The clamp on the stand at her bedside holding the plasma glinted in the light like the flash of a sharp blade; a blade with a serrated edge. She screamed at the top of her voice and scrambled wildly from her bed tearing out a tube and sending a fountain of blood from her arm, spraying the walls and her parents. Their shocked blood spattered faces were frozen in alarm. Sandra crashed into a trolley and pulled over the stand holding the plasma bottle onto the floor. She sprawled there weakly, sobbing pitifully as her life force pulsed out of her.

A nurse leapt into action and stooped down. She pinched the vein shut and replaced the tube back into her arm while someone else gave Sandra a calming injection of pethadine. "Relax, Miss Thornton. It's going to be all right. You're not in any danger. You're safe now. Everything is okay."

These were the last few words she heard before the drug took hold and she melted away leaving her thoughts and fears behind, jettisoning them until another time. She relaxed and the shriek of lines that contorted her face as she relived her nightmare vanished to a calm and serene look. Sandra's parents once over their initial shock clung to each other in relief.

Their daughter was out of her coma.

*

At two-thirty on the dot, a week after the original appointment had been cancelled, due to pressures of work, Maddie introduced a coolly elegant woman in a crisp navy linen suit, teamed with a freshly starched lemon blouse. She was a lady of indeterminate age with a wonderful head of Titian hair that belonged more to Botticelli's Venus than to a practising psychiatrist.

Allison gestured Rebecca Mills to sit. She crossed her legs neatly at the ankles and directed her intelligent grey-eyed gaze into Allison's eyes, and caught him in his admiring glance. He flushed like a guilty schoolboy and was momentarily stuck for words. Finally, he cleared his throat and stuttered out a request for two coffees, embarrassed by the unnerving effect that this woman induced.

After the arrival of the drinks and the polite trivia associated with such ceremonies was over, Allison broached the subject of the meeting. He cleared his throat, "You said you may be able to help us Dr. Mills?"

"I also said that I wouldn't breech any confidentiality, so no names."

Rebecca Mills had a voice that was mesmerising. Her melodic tones were pleasing to the ear and Allison found himself displaying a silly smile on his face. He endeavoured to shake it off. "I understand. So, how can you help?"

"This visit is really to put **my** mind at rest. You see, when I read the memo and your killer's profile, one of my clients immediately sprang to mind and then when I went through the entirety of my files I found a couple of others that could possibly fit the bill."

"I see. Go on." Allison's' tone was measured and his usual gruffness had evaporated.

"What I need is some information or detail that might help me eliminate them from suspicion, for my own peace of mind."

He frowned, "I'm not sure that's possible."

"Then I shouldn't have come," she rose to leave, "I'm certain I'm making a big mistake anyway. I'm almost sure that none of my patients could have committed such terrible acts of violence."

Allison stopped her with a wave of his hand; he tossed her a file of police photographs of the slayings, "Take a look at these and then say you're not prepared to help."

She sat back down and examined the photos. Allison studied her face carefully. Her expression didn't change. She shut the folder with a sigh. "Appalling mutilations, I really think that if anyone in my care did…" she, too, was struggling for the right words, "That," she shuddered.

Allison noticed that some of her outwardly cool confidence had disintegrated. He leaned forward in his seat. "Then?"

131

She continued, "Then I would know. I'm convinced I'd know about it."

"But what if you're wrong? Do you want more women to die this way?'

She moistened her lips, "I can't tell you anything."

"If I tell you our man is left handed, would that be of any use?'

She thought for a second, "That cuts it down to two."

"Who?"

"I said no names," she said firmly and uncrossed her ankles neatly, tucked them under the chair and sat back, searching Allison's' face. It was clearly a method of hers to extract the most she could from her patients. He felt like a naughty child being reprimanded by a teacher and he didn't like the feeling.

"Then I really don't know why you came." Allison was getting exasperated with this woman, both for unsettling him and for being so obtuse.

"Mr. Allison, my only wish is to see if I can be of assistance. I am currently treating a young man in his thirties who has extreme difficulty relating to women. He can only successfully make love to prostitutes or women he doesn't know. If he forms any sort of relationship he cannot perform the act. He had an extremely repressed childhood, was totally dominated by his mother. Hated her to the point of wishing her dead. When she did die he couldn't forgive himself, thought somehow his imaginings had made it happen, and felt responsible. He has suffered from blackouts and on one occasion came to my practice cut and bruised, in a dreadful state with no recollection of how he'd received these injuries. The next day in the paper, I read of the Thornton girl attack."

"Go on," pressed Allison, his eyes lighting with fervour thinking that he may at last be getting somewhere.

"I was concerned enough to contact you."

"So, let us check him out."

"No! I cannot breach patient confidentiality. I'll do that in my own way. I'll know."

"And then?"

"In that instance I will have to go to the board. Like you, I don't want any more killings. Women are already running scared in Birmingham."

Allison shifted position in his seat and the chair creaked punctuating the pause between them. "You said there was someone else," he said eventually.

"Mmm, not very likely."

Allison waited. Rebecca Mills scrutinised the Chief's expression hard before finally speaking. "Another patient comes into my care intermittently. He was sixteen when I first treated him. He had a complete mental breakdown after the death of his father. He believed that if he'd stood up to his mother and her religious fanaticism that he could have prevented his father's suicide. He acted irrationally and had a history of exposing himself from his bedroom window to an elderly widow, who lived next door. He ensured he always hid his face behind the curtain, whilst displaying the rest of his naked body to her. It was never reported to the police. He stopped his activities when she complained to his mother," she paused and studied her fingernails thoughtfully.

Allison said nothing.

"He's had a couple of unsettled periods in his life and I have witnessed some incidents where his anger and hostility has frightened me. But he's in a stable relationship now. He can't be your man."

Allison sat still and silently as he waited for her to continue. It seemed silence drew more from her than questioning.

"Mr. Allison, I've said more than I should. Let me make routine appointments with them both. I'll check them out myself and if I feel there is any cause for concern I'll persuade them to talk to you."

"And if they won't?"

"As I said, I will have to refer to my governing body."

She stood up gracefully and smoothed down her skirt. Allison's former hesitancy was forgotten. She no longer attracted him. He was not impressed. He shook her hand and smiled cursorily as she left the office.

The door clicked gently, behind her. Immediately, Allison

was on the phone, "Get a twenty-four hour watch on Dr. Mills' practice. I want to know who goes in and out. And when," he snarled.

Greg Allison pushed back his chair and perused the scene outside his window before feeling in his pocket for his habitual Mars Bar.

*

Amy's face furrowed disapprovingly. Her life was becoming hopelessly entwined with Tony's and she was beginning not to mind. Slowly but surely, Tony's immense charm and charisma was battering those clamouring, alarm bells into silence, leaving only an occasional ching. They had been living together for three weeks now, but they still hadn't made love. Tony wanted to take things slowly and she hadn't pushed it. They slept together and the amount of tender loving that went on was much more satisfying than many full-bloodied relationships she had enjoyed.

She sipped her coffee wistfully and gazed across the room at him, sitting relaxed in her grandmother's rocking chair with the stray cat they'd adopted on his lap. He looked as if he belonged there. That haunted look she had sometimes glimpsed on his face, if only fleetingly, had vanished.

He was intent on the Big Match, but intuitively felt her eyes on him and he glanced across, "What's the matter, Pidge?'

'Nothing, I was just thinking.'

"What?" his eyes flicked back to the screen.

'When am I going to meet your Mum?'

"Soon."

"You said that last week."

"So I did."

"And?'

"And you will. I promise. Why?'

"It's just …" Amy was stuck for words for a moment. She couldn't say that she felt this woman whom she'd never met, was a threat to their happiness and that she'd noticed an almost imperceptible change come into Tony's eyes and voice when she spoke of her.

"It's just…" he pressed.

"Well, you've met my Mum and Dad and I've heard so much about your Mum, I'd like to meet her."

A sullen scowl blackened his handsome features, as he said through pursed lips, "You'll meet her."

"Tony, what is it?'

His lower lip trembled and he swallowed hard. Full of concern Amy jumped up from the couch and sat at his feet. He ran his fingers through her soft tresses and she gently brushed his lips with her fingertips.

He murmured, "You'll hate me if I tell you. You won't understand."

"Of course I will. I want to share everything with you. I've said it before; your problems are my problems. What is the point of being together if you can't trust me?"

He looked at her sympathetic green eyes now searching his anxiously, and he tried to find the right words. "I don't want you to think any the less of me."

Amy smiled soothingly, "I love you. How could anything you tell me possibly make any difference?" Amy knew as soon as she said those words that she meant it with all her heart.

"My mum, she's a good old stick. She's had it tough trying to bring me up on her own after… after Dad died." He stopped and fingered the heavy, gold identity bracelet at his wrist. The ginger cat on his lap grumbled softly as his rest was disturbed. "I'm ashamed of myself."

"What do you mean?'

He hesitated, "It's… She's not the best educated, not like you and your family. I suppose she never had the chance. I know it shouldn't make a difference but it does. It always has. Her social skills and idea of etiquette are zero. I hate to say it, but I am embarrassed by her… Truly." Tony continued to explain. "I hate the way she speaks. She has the most appalling nasal twang and Brummy accent. Her grammar's none too good either. Oh, I know it's wrong but I really don't like my friends meeting her in case…"

"In case?"

"In case they think less of me. I don't want to be laughed at."

"Why you snob!" laughed Amy with relief, "Of course I wouldn't think any the less of you. What do you take me for? Friends should like you for you, not your Mum. If they criticise her to you, then they're not real friends."

"She doesn't live in a very salubrious area. It's a bit rough."

"So what?"

"She keeps it nice. She has the best swept path in the street; she scrubs the front door step so you could eat off it and her letterbox shines. They say cleanliness is next to Godliness." He paused again as if trying to redeem himself. "I offered her a chance to move but she didn't want to. She likes keeping the memory of Dad alive. She says she couldn't do that anywhere else."

Tony smiled and his whole face shone with light and love. He kissed her lightly on the lips. "Okay, I suppose it is about time the two women in my life met. I'll do something about it," and he returned his gaze to the Aston Villa match on the box.

Amy stood up and straightened her bathrobe, "Just going for a bath. Won't be long."

A pair of amber eyes stared unblinkingly after her, then, as Tony caressed its head the cat folded his paws underneath him and closed those knowing eyes.

That night Tony and Amy made love. It was over very quickly but she found his shyness endearing and surprising in a man of his years. He held her close and whispered, "Did I make you happy?"

She sighed and not wishing to hurt his ego, murmured, "Yes", and returned his hug.

Tony fell asleep like a baby in her arms. But Amy lay awake in the dark fingering the tiny scratches that remained on the underside of his wrist.

11
Meeting Mother

Tony smiled stiffly and formally. He was obviously not at ease.

The table had been laid with a starched, white, cotton cloth and the best bone handled cutlery taken from its wrappings for the occasion. Tony's mother had once been a silver service waitress so, not a thing was out of place.

Amy stared wide-eyed in wonder around the room. She thought it was clean but old fashioned. The dark, heavy furniture and thick beige wallpaper with its raised maroon pile pattern would have been better suited to an Indian restaurant.

The sculptured face of Jesus stared back across the room at her from above the fireplace, whilst Christ on the cross was over the door to the stairs. The wall by the dated hi-fi hosted a picture of the last supper and a glass on the frilled windowsill was overflowing with palm crucifixes. On the sideboard, on the coffee table, in every conceivable place Christ watched.

Amy felt uncomfortable. She smiled cheerily at Tony's mother, trying to suppress her revulsion. This resulted in her chattering inconsequentially about the weather or anything else that came to mind, anything to fill the void present in the room. Unnervingly, she could not rid herself of the warning feeling that crept through her bones, at times the hairs on her arm stood up and a shiver would run through her. The heavy oppressive atmosphere there made her feel nauseous. She struggled to keep her face impassive and quell the rising sickness. She looked up at Tony's mother's face and attempted a smile.

"Do you read the Bible, Amy?" the thin nasal voice asked as a plate of roast chicken was placed in front of her.

"R.E. was my second teaching subject," she answered brightly.

The pendulum clock ticked slowly on the mantelpiece

punctuating the long awkward pauses in the difficult conversation.

Amy picked at her chicken. It was undercooked and red. She felt her already sick stomach turn. She diverted her attention to the vegetables, and determined to listen rather than speak.

Tony talked proudly about Amy's achievements, and his mother's serpentine head nodded as she listened. "Amy passed out top of her class at college. She took charge of part of the Duke of Edinburgh's Award. She even took a party of students away and was presented to Prince Edward."

His mother sniffed and forced a brittle smile to her face, "How wonderful. You must tell us all about it."

"Not much to tell, really. He didn't say too much."

"Still it's an honour. Royalty, eh?"

Amy looked down modestly and was relieved when his mother scuttled out into the kitchen, Amy whispered apologetically to Tony, "I can't eat this. It's not cooked."

"It's her eyes, she doesn't see so well. Just eat what you can," he mouthed back at her.

"Mum! Amy's not very hungry," Tony called, "It's my fault. She ate before we came. I forgot to tell her we were eating here," he lied glibly.

"But Tony, I told you I'd be cooking," she moaned.

"I'm sorry," said Amy, "I feel awful."

"Don't worry. Leave what you can't eat," added Tony and gave her a wink, which seemed remarkably out of place in that room.

Tony's mother returned to the table reverently bearing a hand carved wooden box filled with tiny paper scrolls.

"Go on, take one," he urged.

"What are they?"

"They're quotations from the Bible. If you pick carefully they should tell you something about your life."

"Like fortune cookies."

"Not like fortune cookies. These are the Lord's words," Tony's mother said sourly, her eyes glittering dangerously.

The unlikely trio dipped their hands in the box and each took a scroll. Amy unrolled hers and looked at it.

"Go on, read it aloud," Tony's mother urged.

Amy swallowed hard and spoke hesitantly. "It says: *Behold 1 know your thoughts and your schemes to wrong me. Job twenty-one, verse twenty-seven.*"

Tony's mother looked across slyly with her hooded eyes and drew back her lips slowly in the semblance of a smile.

*

Allison slapped his hand on the desk in exasperation, "It doesn't pan out."

"Sir?'

"I don't understand it. If these fibres from Susan Hardy's Flotex carpet were the same as the fibres picked up by Forensic then we'd have proof that someone at Dempsey's was involved in the murder of Annette Jury and Janet Mason."

"Why? What's wrong?"

"Colour, Mark, colour!" snapped Allison, "Our fibres are blue black. The samples taken from Miss Hardy's car boot are most definitely blue. The structure is the same. It's a Flotex carpet but the colour is wrong. Damn!" Allison was by now, nearly apoplectic with frustration.

"So, it really was just a coincidence?"

"Not in my book, Mark. Get all the statements from Dempsey's double-checked."

"They've been double-checked."

"Check them again, we've got to be missing something."

Allison viciously ripped the wrapping on his Mars Bar. Investigations were not progressing at the speed the Chief Constable and Commissioner would have liked. Allison was still smarting from the phone call received some fifteen minutes earlier where he was dressed down with the lack of progress in the case.

He took a mouthful of his Mars Bar and chewed vigorously, not savouring the treat as he usually did.

Crabtree's DNA coding matched none of the samples taken from the victims. There was nothing to identify him with Dawn Ashby. Even though he had been covered with his wife's blood on arrest, the DNA samples of semen did not belong to Crabtree. Allison was confused. He felt in his gut that the little man was responsible for the Ashby girl's death. But, he had nothing that would stand up in court apart from hearsay and circumstantial evidence. Of course, it was possible that some maniac had butchered Eileen Crabtree and the discovery of her body had tipped 'arf a brain Arthur over the edge into the lunatic state in which he'd been found, but Allison doubted it. Crabtree had waived his right to a solicitor and was now insisting that he was a multiple murderer. To cap it all, the little man with the Reginald Christie glasses, worn deliberately in emanation of his hero, was ambidextrous. That blew the left-handed theory clean out of the window. Allison hadn't thought of that.

*

It was late. The lights were out. Tony turned to look at Amy, her head next to his; her blonde hair showering the pillow; her breathing deep and even. The moonlight filtered through the gap in the curtains sending its silver beams shafting to the carpet in a milky pool of light. Tony's eyes widened as a shadow in the corner stretched and grew up the wall, slowly taking form. He gasped. It couldn't be! It wasn't happening. First the tumble of raven hair, the sensuous red mouth and the tempting white flesh. The Delilah of his dreams was coming for him. She shouldn't. She couldn't! He was with Amy. In a relationship he was safe; he knew that. Then why had she come?

Tony suppressed a cry. He bit hard on his hand. He sat up suddenly taking the bedcovers with him. Amy turned and murmured in her sleep. Tony's body was trembling. He retrieved the duvet and tucked it back around her. She nestled into his side and sighed sweetly.

Tony started to panic. He shouted, "No! Leave me alone!"

In an instant Amy was awake. The bedside light was on and she cradled Tony in her arms. "What's wrong? You called out in your sleep."

His eyes lingered on the disappearing shadow in the corner of the room that was now melting into nothingness. He shook his head.

"You must have been dreaming. Are you okay?"

"Yes. I'm fine … I just had a bit of a shock. That's all."

Amy brushed her hair sleepily from her eyes, "Want to tell me about it?"

Tony's cunning tongue took over. He couldn't tell her what he'd seen, not yet. She didn't know him well enough, yet. "It was Dad. I dreamt about Dad."

"Oh, I'm sorry," she whispered.

"No, no, don't be … You see, I haven't told you the complete truth."

Amy leaned up on her elbow, "What are you talking about?"

"It's my fault Dad died."

"What do you mean?"

"If I'd stood up to Mum with Dad, he'd never have taken his own life. I didn't. I let her rule us."

"Sweetheart, you were sixteen. You can't blame yourself. Come on now, let's get back to sleep," she lay back down, drew him into her arms and kissed him gently, smoothing his hair like a child.

Tony lay there, still and rigid until Amy was sleeping once more. Then, like a thief in the night he stole from her bed and crept out of the room. He tiptoed along the dark landing, through the passageway to the lounge at the end of the corridor. He took his briefcase from under the bookcase and unlocked it. He reached for a pen, and from under a false panel in the case he selected a hardcore pornographic magazine. Then he set to, drawing, altering, and writing.

The full bosomed beauty in the centrefold had darts drawn into her breast whilst a pair of scissors snipped dangerously close to the nipples; knives pierced her genital area, blades entered her mouth.

He defaced and degraded these women still further. They sat on knives, masturbated with guns, and sprouted ink blood drops from this biro torture.

Some three quarters of an hour later he felt a great deal better. He tossed the magazine back in the case and returned to bed.

Amy stirred and he slid down beside her. She lovingly put

141

her arm across his stomach and for a while, his desires satiated, Tony slept.

*

Mark exploded into Allison's office flourishing a sheaf of papers. "Sir, Sir!" His excited voice demanded immediate attention. Allison put down his pen and waited.

"You were right. The Flotex **is** the same carpet. It's not two different samples."

Allison was interested, "How do you know?"

"Apparently, it was a slip up at the lab. If the fibres are lit from the top when they're under the microscope, the colour shows blue. If they're lit from underneath the same fibres look blue black. The same fibres but the way they're lit, alters the colour."

Allison's eyes gleamed, now he really did have a reason to turn Dempsey's upside down.

Allison collated the files from Dempsey's, scribbling the odd note here and there. For the main part he could see no discrepancies, no line of investigation ignored or unchecked. He read again Susan Hardy's statement and the names of all those who had any involvement with Janet Mason. He proceeded to examine all the individual statements, as the names arose. It was quite possible that as the checking hadn't been done by one person and that some little thing had been forgotten, or some small detail omitted.

He noticed that most of the roll of Flotex carpet had been accounted for and further questioning on this point had revealed nothing new. Even the gent in Handsworth that Joyce Bowden had informed them about had proved to be a dead end. This was disappointing.

He was just about to consign the statements from Dempsey's back to his filing cabinet when he did a little mental calculation. There was one missing, one that hadn't been checked and rechecked and accepted. Allison foraged through his in-tray and the other papers on his desk. No, he was definitely missing one statement. How could that happen in an investigation as important as this?

He flicked on the intercom, "Maddie, as soon as Mark arrives back from his jaunt, send him in."

"Yes, Sir."

Allison sighed and leaned back in his chair. A Mars Bar would be just reward for his efforts this morning.

*

Amy was not easily shocked, but all the same she had been somewhat disturbed when she arrived home early from a shopping trip with her mother. She had gone out reasonably early and had left Tony in bed. She didn't expect him to be still in bed when she returned.

A great deal of confusion seemed to come from the bedroom as she started up the stairs. As she pushed open the door she came face to face with Tony, naked and glowering at her. She had no idea what was wrong. He grabbed an armful of covers and something black that she couldn't quite see and flounced angrily out of the room.

"Sorry Tony, I didn't mean to wake you. I didn't realise you'd still be asleep," she apologised.

Amy thought it best to leave him alone. He was so unpredictable sometimes. She heard the sound of the loo flushing and the bath being run. She went to make a coffee.

Tony emerged about fifteen minutes later, fragrant, damp and full of remorse. "I'm sorry, Pidge. I didn't mean to snap. You know what it's like. I'm not a morning person and working into the early hours at the clubs I'm not at my best in the morning. Sorry."

Amy smiled, and muttered, "It's all right, Tony, really."

Tony took her hands, "Leave all that shopping and come with me."

"What?" she laughed. "I can't. I've got things to do."

"Things that can wait. Come on. Come with me," he coaxed and cajoled, and laughingly led her into the bedroom. He pulled her down on the bed and she started to giggle. He kissed the corners of her mouth and stared longingly into her eyes.

A few minutes later they became deeply involved in the most exciting foreplay, Amy was teetering on the brink of an explosion deep inside her when Tony reached for something black that he had hidden under the bed. His tongue probed down inside her ear, as he panted out his request. "I want to

143

do something. Will you let me photograph you, darling? Will you?"

Amy stopped, her passion and desire forgotten.

"Please?" he implored.

Amy didn't know why, but it seemed easier to say, 'yes' than to refuse and she came face to face with a Polaroid camera.

"I want to take some pictures of you," he whispered. "They'll only be for my eyes." He already knew what she'd be thinking.

So, Amy let a few innocent shots be taken of her. She played up to the camera with some innocent cheeky poses, but she didn't expect when their lovemaking resumed that he would capture her oral love play on film.

"NO!" she exclaimed. "Give me that." She snatched futilely at the camera with its incriminating photograph. Tony laughed and turned the whole thing into a game. He teased her with the picture putting it within reach and then snatching it away, until they were both laughing on the bed.

"Please, Tony, please don't keep it," she pleaded, "If anyone finds it they'll know it's me. I couldn't bear for it to get into the wrong hands. I've never had a photo taken like that before. I don't see why you need it. You've got me here with you, you can see me anytime."

He turned to her, "Stop worrying. You are so beautiful. I just want something to remind me of you, if ever you're not around. I promise you it's for my eyes only."

Amy stopped arguing. She went very quiet and made up her mind that she'd let the matter drop, for now. But at the first opportunity, she would seek out those pictures and destroy them.

The following morning, when Tony was bathing, Amy started to hunt for the pictures' hiding place. It was a somewhat stunned Amy who uncovered a stash of photographs of Tony's genitalia, pictured from all angles and some taken reflectively in a mirror. All with his face hidden.

Amy didn't know quite what to do, whether to say anything. If she did, then he would know that she had been rummaging through his things. She put them back in their

144

hiding place, guiltily and bit her lip. What was she getting herself into?

If she'd known for whom the photographs were intended she'd have been even more horrified.

*

Allison sighed, there was now no doubt. All the statements from Dempsey's checked out. His hunch had to be wrong and yet he felt in his gut that something was amiss. Knowles', Barton and Clifton's blood tests, had all proved conclusively that they were innocent. The fact that Clifton's alibi had not been followed up immediately was now of little importance and could be deemed as just another snarl-up in police administration. He spoke gruffly to Mark, "There has to be a connection I can feel it, but I can't damn well prove it. What's come in from Kelly's Wine Bar?"

"The leads from Marie went nowhere. We sent men in, as you asked, to frequent the place for over a week, to see what they could hear."

"And?"

"Nothing. The club had no written records of the bookings the night of Annette's death. The diary didn't reveal an agent's name or who was performing. It was all on hearsay. I checked with all the Cabaret Artistes' Agencies that I could find in the Midlands directory and made a list of names of those who had worked there. I've left Harmon checking through them."

"What about the mother hen, Marie, or whatever she's called?"

"Well, although Marie has promised to contact me if anything else came to light, I've heard nothing, yet."

"Don't hold your breath." Allison somehow knew that she wouldn't be in touch. He thumped the desk in exasperation, "All that we can hope for is that the Thornton girl will recover sufficiently to give the police artist a good description of her attacker. By God, Mark she was lucky. I'm certain that Sandra Thornton was the one who got away. We must hope she recovers sooner rather than later."

"At least, there's been no more deaths," offered Mark, trying to placate his boss.

"No. Three months have passed and there are no more bodies. But I don't like it, Mark. I don't like it at all. Of course I'm glad for the public's sake but I'm unconvinced that we've got the killer in custody."

"Sir."

"Look, why don't you help Harmon. I need to think."

Mark took his leave of the Chief and Allison sat back in his chair. His face was furrowed in deep concentration as he silently went over more facts.

*

Crabtree was being kept on remand for his wife's murder and Brady the psychologist had held a number of sessions with him. He'd been trying to glean some sort of insight into this man's mind that now, had sadly tipped over the brink. He reported back to Allison, "The man is mad, totally insane. I've performed all the usual tests and I believe you can't trust what he says."

"What's the next move?"

"I'll keep working with him but I'm convinced he harbours a secret desire for fame. This is at the root of his confessions. He has been oppressed for so long in such a miserable marriage where he felt belittled and demeaned that he had appallingly low self-esteem. Now that this attention has come his way it has made him feel important and oddly, for the first time in his life, he feels valued."

"Keep trying. We must try and get him to open up sufficiently that he will renege on his confessions. We have to get to the truth."

"I think you'll have more luck if Trevor Booth talks to him. Crabtree has become quite close to him. He's told me this himself. He's more likely to reveal his secrets to the reporter than me."

"Booth is due in, shortly. If you care to wait, you can sit in when he comes to speak to me. Between the two of you we should be able to work out how to get him to co-operate."

"Yes, okay, Chief. Strangely, even after his initial shock in Jiggins Lane Trevor Booth has become so involved with the little man that I know he's experiencing more success than me. An element of trust has grown up between them."

Allison made a mental note to have Booth in his office again on a more regular basis, just to talk through his findings.

As if on cue, Maddie paged through that Booth was in the building and soon they heard the characteristic knock, knock, knock on the door.

Trevor opened it, "Oh, sorry, Chief. I didn't realise you were busy. Maddie told me to come through."

Allison waved him in, "No, no, Trevor. Come in and sit down. We need to pool our information. What's the state of play with Crabtree?"

Trevor moistened his lips, "You know I've been writing articles for the Post hinged on certain personality type's need to confess?"

"Yes," grunted Allison. "I've been reading them. "Very good," he admitted grudgingly.

"I'm aiming to write a book on Crabtree, his life and revelations."

"I assume this is all with the small man's agreement and blessing?" said Brady.

"Yes, of course."

"I know that Crabtree is sharing information with you that he hasn't imparted to Brady or us. But, in your judgement would it stand up in court? I am not asking you to break your reporter's code of confidentiality."

"What are you asking then?"

"I am hoping that you would be able impress on Crabtree the importance of sharing his knowledge. Try to persuade him somehow, to share this information with the police. He must be made to see that we don't want any more deaths and his confession to all the crimes means a serial killer is going free and will be free to kill again."

"What's in it for him?"

"We can say that he co-operated fully with the enquiry… Come on, Booth you're a clever chap. I'm sure you can achieve this."

Booth thought for a moment, "All right, I'll see what I can do. I'm not promising anything mind."

"That's all I ask," said Allison gently. "But now, now I

147

need to ring the hospital again and get the latest on the Thornton girl. I want you, Colin to work with her. We'll get a police sketch artist there as soon as possible."

Colin Brady nodded. Booth made his excuses and left Allison and Brady to discuss the case still further.

*

The good news was that Sandra Thornton was recovering. The tragedy, which had so dramatically rocked the family, had brought them all much closer together. Disagreements forgotten; they were rebuilding positively the bonds that would negate any future dissent.

Her surface wounds had now healed. All that was left to remind her of the savage attack was a livid, purple scar that coiled like a serpent, where he'd twisted the knife, under her left breast. Her voice, although husky, was improving daily. Her attacker had not done as much damage to her windpipe and voice box as he had supposed. Now she was growing stronger she was feeling more like her old self.

The detectives were keen to question her and her memory had been sketchy to begin with; she could only remember a pair of coldly calculating eyes, intense pain and the colour red; but gradually her sessions with Brady and the continued gentle questioning by the police were triggering flashes of memory. Bit by bit, they were piecing together the events of that fateful evening. Brady was convinced that after a few more sessions the jigsaw would be complete and Sandra would be ready for the police artist. She was allowed to leave hospital but was not to return home until she had helped create a picture of her attacker.

She and the family were placed in police rented accommodation until she would be allowed back to the family home many miles away.

The brutal assault had left Sandra jumping in alarm at the smallest movement or sound. And going out after dark was a complete impossibility. But, the family were convinced that with patience, love and understanding she would eventually become her bubbly energetic self, again. All Sandra could do was hope.

"I'm sorry, I can't be more helpful," she said to Brady.

"Don't worry. You're doing fine. We know a lot more about him than we did. We know he is definitely dark haired, blue eyed, around five foot eleven in height, and of a muscular, athletic build. You will soon be ready for the police artist."

"Do you think so?"

"Yes. I want one last session with you. I'll take you back to the time of the attack and if you feel confident in reliving it. I can progress onto helping you regain your confidence and help you to put it all behind you."

"Can you do that?"

"It's my job."

"I'm not sure I'm ready for this but I just can't bear living with this constant fear that he's out there. I'm scared of my own shadow. The smallest noise or any quick, sudden movement and my heart pounds, and I break out in a sweat. I'm hopeless; I can't go out after dark. My social life will be nil. Roll on summer," she smiled apologetically.

"What you are feeling, I promise you, it's all perfectly normal. We will try and get these panic attacks under control. Do you trust me?"

Sandra nodded, "Yes, you've been more than kind."

"Then, let's go ahead," he nodded his head and Sandra found herself nodding, too. "Same time tomorrow?"

Sandra sighed heavily and agreed, "Same time tomorrow."

*

"Why can't we just make love?" Amy asked.

"It's not that easy, Pidge,"

"Why?"

"You know my back-ground. You know my mother. I've got so much guilt locked up inside me."

"I know. I know you find it difficult that you feel it's dirty. But doesn't it make that guilt worse when we play games?"

"No, because, you see, you are not you, and I am not me, so it's all right. I find it hard to make love to someone I care about. I know it sounds stupid. One night stands have never been a problem for me. Making love to someone I don't know is easy, but when love, real love, enters a relationship I have all sorts of difficulties, please bear with me, Pidge. I'll get over it. With you, I know I will, because you are the sweetest girl in the world."

Amy smiled and suppressed the tiny niggling doubt that was creeping up to nag her. The more she tried to understand Tony, the more she realised she didn't know him, at all. She was discovering just how complex his mind was; and the more she learnt the more she blamed his mother.

Amy was not a prude but she was becoming more and more alarmed by the love games that she was being coerced into playing. It seemed that whenever she and Tony went to bed, they could never *just* make love.

Certainly the teasing and foreplay almost always culminated in her extreme satisfaction making the act itself redundant, but she still had a desire for what she called a normal relationship.

Most of the time she was required to be either, a prostitute, or masseuse, sometimes a schoolteacher, at others a French maid, occasionally a schoolgirl, or serving wench. The repertoire was endless, and many of these games she admitted that she enjoyed herself. But, she didn't like it when she played a girl who said 'no' and who ended up being raped. It went against all her principles and she asked for that game to be taken off the list.

All Tony's sexual fantasies were acted out with love and tenderness, otherwise Amy would never have consented but she did dislike his need for pornography. She'd tried to share it with him, to laugh about it and to persuade him that she didn't mind. But mind she did and as she encouraged Tony to share his secrets and desires with her, her worries grew. Outwardly her face didn't change, when he confessed some incident from the past but inside, her stomach knotted, twisted, and in her heart she felt there was something very sick about this man. In her own mind she knew she would have to seek some sort of escape. But how? He was living with her. How could she get away?

*

Trevor Booth strolled nonchalantly along the corridor to Allison's office whistling cheerily. He stopped at the big man's door, knocked and waited for the gruff order to enter.

"Chief, I know how he did it, and what's more he's prepared for me to tell you."

"Who are we talking about?"

"Crabtree. I've got him to talk and he's revealed his whole plan. From start to finish; the thought that his own daughter could be a victim of a killer persuaded him to share all the gory details."

Allison grunted affably, "Good. Good. Now come on, Trevor. Talk"

Trevor Booth licked his lips and related the events that led to Dawn Ashby's murder and that of Eileen Crabtree. Allison didn't interrupt. He nodded and jotted down the odd note. It was good to know he had been right in his assessment and thinking. Crabtree was a copy cat and the Ashby girl had been a practice run."

*

Debbie Stringer was having a tough time at home. Mark's load was considerably heavier at the moment and he wasn't on hand to help when she needed it, and even with her mother's aid she was finding it difficult to cope. Catherine was a beautiful baby but had not been very well of late and had taken to bouts of crying. No matter what Debbie did, nothing seemed to pacify her. She rocked her and talked to her. She sang to her and fed her but the small bundle of fury just went redder and redder in the face and screamed even more.

Christian was being more demanding too, and although she didn't mean to, Debbie knew she was neglecting Christian's needs for those of Catherine.

Debbie was at her wit's end. Her mum, Jean, couldn't get there until three that afternoon. It was one of the days that she worked. Debbie thought she was going to go mad. She was feeling headachy and feverish. She hadn't even found time to dress. She was becoming someone who lived in her pyjamas day and night.

She thrust Catherine down into the carrycot on the coffee table. At this Catherine screamed even louder. Debbie went into the kitchen to make a cup of tea. She took Christian with her and sat him safely in his high chair at the breakfast bar and made him a drink of Ribena, closing her ears to the din coming from the living room. He pointed with his chubby little hand towards the sound, "Cathwyn cwy," he said solemnly.

"Yes, and I can't stand it any more," she murmured. She knew she'd have to talk to someone or go mad. She couldn't ring Mark. He'd already taken more than enough time off to be with her. She looked at her watch. It was four more hours before Jean would arrive. In desperation she called Mary Allison.

"I didn't know who else to call," she cried, "I'm so sorry to bother you."

"Ssh! It's all right. I know what it's like I've had three. Take a long deep breath and relax. I'll be over as soon as I can."

Debbie thanked her gratefully and sipped her tea. Catherine was still screaming heartrendingly in the lounge and now Christian was becoming distressed.

Debbie lifted the toddler out of his chair and cuddled him, tears streaming down her face.

"I'm sorry, Darling. Mummy is so very tired and I'm not feeling too good. Poor Mummy! And I don't know what's wrong with Catherine either."

Christian returned his mother's hug. He popped his dimpled fist into his mouth and stared at her with big wide eyes. Debbie smiled down at him and kissed him. It was amazing the soothing effect that he had on her. He ran to get his Postman Pat van and sat happily, on the kitchen floor sorting his different coloured shapes that fitted into the back of the van.

Debbie went back into the living room and picked up Catherine, who was still sobbing hard. She walked around the room with her, singing softly and gradually the wails subsided and an exhausted Debbie could at last sit down and feed Catherine, who promptly went to sleep at her breast.

Some fifteen minutes later the doorbell rang. Mary had arrived.

Debbie opened the door quietly to admit her; Catherine was still in Debbie's arms asleep.

Mary removed her coat, rolled up her sleeves and took charge.

She took one look at Debbie, gently removed the baby, who stirred lightly, and placed her in the cot on the table in the dining room. She put her fingers to her lips, ordered her to put her feet up in the sitting room, where Christian was playing and went to make her a drink.

She soon returned with a mug in each hand and passed one to Debbie.

"How long have you been like this? And how long has Catherine been so grizzly?"

"I don't know, about a week, I suppose."

"And your breasts are they hard or enflamed?"

"They are a bit sore."

"Hm. I suspect, no, I'm almost sure that you have a touch of milk fever or mastitis. It's exhausting you and upsetting the baby. You stay here and rest. Close your eyes if you can."

"I should get dressed."

"You need to rest. You can change later."

"So, what do I do? Milk fever you said?"

"And mastitis. You must try and feed Catherine as often as possible to empty the milk from your breasts. It will get easier. You may need antibiotics. Jean can organise a doctor's visit when she gets here. In the meantime rest is the best thing. So feet up and relax. I'll see to everything else."

True to her word, Mary Allison, whisked through the house, dusting and cleaning, making beds and tidying up. She used an old Eubank carpet sweeper instead of the vacuum cleaner, as she didn't want to disturb the baby. Debbie slept and Mary played quietly with Christian until Jean arrived.

12
Confessions

Amy was happy. Things were working out after all. It seemed her policy of persuading Tony to confide in her all his fears and terrors, were bringing him renewed confidence.

She didn't realise that his confessions were just the tip of the iceberg; that he was becoming more and more reliant on her; that he was sapping her strength, leeching onto it to survive; and that this continued vampirism would eventually make her inter-changeable with his mother and how dangerous that would be.

Tony was finally making love to her, without any external stimulus, without any games. He was making love to *her*. Her own passion and desire was forgotten, so delighted was she with the very simplicity of the act that she watched his face, drinking in every sigh, every roll of his eyes, every movement of his mouth, every flutter of his lids; and just as he climaxed she thrust hard against him, giving him extra pleasure by tensing and releasing her internal muscles rapidly in succession.

He gave a strange little cry such as she'd never heard before and appeared to look deep into her eyes and yet seemed not to see her.

Amy waited until his juddering had subsided and kissed him gently, "Darling, that was fantastic." Tears of joy shone in her eyes, "Tell me, what were you thinking of just then?"

"I can't tell you," he murmured.

"Of course you can. We share everything don't we?"

Whatever he'd shared with her in the past, including his confession of aberrant behaviour in his teens against the widow next door, Amy was not prepared for his next words.

"I was thinking about my mother." Amy was stunned, thinking that she hadn't heard his tremulous whisper, he repeated it, "I imagined that I was making love to my mother."

This time, Amy had no words. She fought to disguise her

utter shock and revulsion at this latest confession. She hoped her distaste was not evident. Now, she was deeply worried and if she admitted it, she was also a little frightened.

*

Allison had, had a hunch, he sent out a request to the DVLA for registered owners of Ford Escorts in and around the West Midlands. As was expected the computer printout was immense. There were reams of papers and hundreds of thousands of names. He took a cursory look through them and then passed the list onto Pooley and Taylor to check each entry against any names that had come up during the investigation.

They divided the work between them and Taylor drew the short straw, whilst Pooley would stay snug and warm at the station to deal with the phone enquiries, Taylor was sent out into the cold to check a couple of the recognised names on the list. His first stop was in Sparkbrook.

*

The doorbell rang shrilly. Taylor let his eyes examine the front of the house that stood out from the others in this run down area. The dwellings on either side were shabby and uncared for, but this one had sparkling clean windows, a neatly swept path devoid of weeds, a step that was so well scrubbed it looked as if someone could eat their dinner from off it; and it had a perfectly spotless gleaming brass letterbox. Someone had taken a lot of care to keep the outside spic and span. The small front garden was neat and tidy, the hedge clipped and the woodwork and paintwork clean and bright.

Taylor rang again. This time the front door opened and a short squat woman looked out. Her woollen-socked feet encased in brown check, pom-pom bedroom slippers seemed mismatched with the Indian print Isadora type scarf that she was wearing around her neck.

"Yes?" queried the thin reedy voice belonging to Tony's mother.

"Mrs. Clifton?"

"Yes? Who wants to know?"

"PC Taylor, Ma'am; Steelhouse Lane Police Station. I'd like to ask you a few questions, if I may?"

"What about?" she asked suspiciously.

"May I come in, Mrs. Clifton?" Taylor requested.

It was cold and it had been a long morning. Mrs. Clifton grudgingly opened the door and allowed Taylor to enter; as he did his attention was caught by a stout wooden cross on the wall above the hall door, which was surrounded by something resembling fairy lights that travelled around it, blinking on and off.

'Left over from Christmas', mused Taylor to himself.

He followed the waddling woman through a dark passage into the sitting room crowded with religious relics and dark furniture from a bygone age. Taylor had the strangest feeling overwhelm him. He felt as if he were trapped in a python's coils that were tightening and constricting his chest. He looked and felt uncomfortably hot and started to breathe heavily, tiny droplets of perspiration formed on his upper lip. He had the sensation of dizziness. He thought he was about to faint. He swayed on his feet.

"Are you all right? You don't look too well."

"Just a little warm. That's all," he explained. "Coming out of the cold into the heat, in my uniform," he added.

"I like it warm," she droned. "Can't bear to be cold. Always have a good fire." She indicated the gas fire flickering and hissing, "And my storage heaters."

Taylor looked towards the fire; Jesus' eyes followed him and stared from above the mantelpiece. He glanced at the storage heater by the frilled window almost filled to overflowing with palm crosses. A crucifix hung down by the lace curtains and the sickly smell of a sweet woody incense filled the air.

"Tell you what, I'll make us a cuppa. That'll make you feel better. Just let me finish the row I'm knitting in case I drop a stitch." She picked up the needles and click clacked at the square in garish green wool.

"Squares for a blanket," she explained. "All the ladies in the church have to do ten each. This is my sixth," she said proudly.

Taylor watched the needles prod and pull, poking their way through the yardage, looping and twisting. Taylor

156

became fascinated by the movement; his eyes followed each movement. Mrs. Clifton finished the row and replaced the knitting in her bag and retreated into the kitchen.

"Do you go to church?" she called out in her reedy tones.

"I used to," he confessed. "Don't seem to have much time now."

"You should always make time, time for the Lord."

"My mother's a keen churchgoer," he said defensively, wondering why he had a need to justify himself to this creature, "She makes things for the church bazaars; jams and marmalades, embroidered cloths, tea cosies that sort of thing."

"Does she knit squares?"

"I believe she does, yes," he replied. Taylor could hear her fiddling about in the kitchen. There was the clink of cups and saucers and the hiss of a kettle.

"Do you take sugar?"

"Two please."

The atmosphere was stifling.

"Why don't you sit down? Take the weight off your feet. I know what policemen are like. Walk everywhere, pounding the beat. Go on relax a little, I bet you deserve it."

Taylor sat down on a small easy chair with wooden arms and Draylon cushions. His eyes roamed around the room. He stared at the alcove shrine with Christ's hand raised in blessing. A scented candle flickered beneath it, accelerating the yellowing and aging of the faded print picture. The perfume from the candle mixed with the heavier spicy wood Indian joss stick that he had noticed earlier, did little to improve the air in the room. Taylor found himself having difficulty breathing. The smell was sickly.

The dead eyes of saints gazed out into the room and an artist's impression of Christ's benign face shone from each corner.

Mrs. Clifton scuttled in like a fat cockroach bearing a tray of tea and lemon cake. She laid this on the teak coffee table that stood in front of the fire. She sat opposite Taylor and grinned.

"I'll be mother," she said stretching forward to pour the

157

tea. The noise of the tea cascading into the cup sounded strangely loud in that room. Taylor felt an urge to run away from that house as the walls, with their dead watching faces, oppressively closed in on him and made his head swim.

She passed Taylor his cup and her hand touched his. It lingered ever so briefly and felt dry and scaly. Taylor was left with the impression that a lizard had crawled over his skin.

He took a gulp of his tea that was too sweet and forced a smile, "Tell me, Mrs. Clifton..."

"Oh, no questions, please. Have your tea first, then you can ask me what you like."

She took another sip and pulled back the corners of her mouth showing her yellowing teeth. Taylor tried to return her smile. He inclined his head politely and took another mouthful of tea.

"Lemon cake, Constable?" she asked. He shook his head. "Oh, go on. It's fresh. I made it this morning." She thrust the plate at him. Taylor took a slice and hesitated before biting into it. It tasted surprisingly good, crumbly and moist with plenty of flavour and not short on the sultanas. His mouth full he murmured appreciatively, "Mmm."

"Good?" she questioned, noting his pleasurable grunt. "Are you married, Constable?"

Taylor swallowed the piece he was chewing before replying, "No, no. No ideas about anything like that yet; besides, I've not even got a regular girlfriend."

"Live with your Mum do you?" He nodded, as she said approvingly, "That's a good boy."

Taylor didn't know why, but he didn't like the way she said it. She watched him as he ate and he soon finished his piece of cake.

"Do you want some more?"

"No, thank you. That was delicious."

The formalities of tea now over, Taylor wiped away the crumbs with a pristine, starched, white linen napkin with iron ridged folds and patted his mouth and chin. The gesture seemed awkward and unnatural.

She put down her cup, "Now then," she leered, "What do you want to ask me?"

"Mrs. Clifton?"

"Yes?"

"Mrs. Grace Clifton? Are you the mother of Tony Clifton, who was Head of Sales at Dempsey's?"

"Yes." Her answer was curt and monosyllabic. Her eyes never left his face.

"Tell me, Mrs. Clifton, does your son live here with you?"

"He used to, but he's recently moved in with his girlfriend."

"How recently is that?"

"Let me see. I'd have to check the diary for exact dates but round about ten weeks ago now."

"I see. Was your son living with you," he glanced at his notebook, "November 25th?"

The hooded eyes blinked once as Mrs. Clifton thought. "Yes, yes. He was with me then."

"Could you tell me whether he was at home that night?"

"That's a little more difficult, Constable. I can't remember off the top of my head. Let me think."

She moved to the sideboard drawer and took out an old RSPB bird calendar. "What date did you say?" she asked as she leafed back through the months.

"November twenty-fifth."

Her eyes narrowed, "Ah, yes. He had that night in with me. It was our scrabble night. I remember. Friday night's usually our games night. I don't see so much of him now he's living with his girlfriend," she complained. "Do you keep your mother company in the evenings?" she asked.

"Sometimes," his reply was guarded. "But, she has her own circle of friends that she entertains herself with."

There was a brief lull in the conversation as PC Taylor flicked through his notes. "What time do you go to bed on your games nights?"

"Oh, it's always late, usually one or two o'clock in the morning. We have a little bit to drink and some food, very pleasant it is."

"Do you remember what time you retired that night?" he pressed.

"Oh, Constable that's not easy for me to say. Wait a

minute... wasn't that the night that the Mason girl was killed, Tony's colleague at work?"

"That is correct."

"Then I do remember. He was in an awful state about that. Quite upset. I know he liked her."

"You said you do remember," Taylor urged.

"Yes. It was a late night that one. Much later than usual. We got to talking and didn't get to bed until about three. Tony had to be up early the next day, he had an appointment somewhere, I know he found it difficult to get up, the next morning."

"So, you were together all evening?"

"Yes."

"Can anyone else verify that?"

"No.... why? Surely you don't think we had... "

"No, no," Taylor said hurriedly.

"Then why all the questions?" she demanded, her lizard eyes unblinking.

Taylor's stomach was feeling queasy. The smell, the too sweet tea and this woman, seemingly harmless enough but with a cloying syrupiness that made him want to flee the house. She reminded him of something, he couldn't think what. He felt her eyes boring into him.

"Well, Constable?"

His mouth and lips felt dry; he hadn't heard what she had said, "Sorry?"

"I asked if we'd finished. Are you all right? You look a little pale."

Now he knew! She was like one of those slow moving chameleons with bulging eyes that swivelled independently, which then flicked out a tongue to catch its prey. That or a ...

"Would you like a glass of water?"

... A big fat bullfrog. Just sitting there, waiting for a fly. "Er ... yes, yes please."

She lumped out to the kitchen and brought back a glass of iced water, which he gulped gratefully.

"Before you go," she rasped, "Take one of these." She handed him the carved wooden box filled with scrolls.

"What are they?"

160

"Take two. One for now and take one for later. Words of comfort from the Lord to help you on your way."

PC Taylor took two. He put his notebook away and rose from the seat, pulling at his tie in the suffocating warmth. He moved hesitantly to the door, which Grace Clifton opened with a flourish and he fled from that stifling house as quickly as he could. The door banged shut behind him and he felt the need to wipe his hands down his clothes as he settled into the driver's seat of his car and tried to calm his racing heart.

He shuddered involuntarily and opened one of the tiny scrolls, which read:

'Talk no more so very proudly,
Let not arrogance come from your mouth
For the Lord is a God of knowledge
And by Him actions are weighed.'
Samuel 2 Verse 3.

*

"A voice like whispering grass," Black Lionel eulogised. It was late at the club. The customers had gone home and the musicians were having a jam session. The silver tongued black, blues singer had just torn at the heart strings with an old Bessie Smith number and Tony had persuaded Amy to sing, accompanying her on guitar.

After a hesitant start, her pure sweet voice had settled and they all had listened, enraptured by her clear tones. A tiny twinge of jealousy prickled Tony's initial pride and he broke the moment by confidently taking the microphone and launching into a medley of James Taylor songs. It was clear that he didn't like the attention taken away from him

Half an hour later they were sitting with their drinks, putting the world to rights when one of them said, "I wish I was God. I'd soon know what to do."

"That's supposing there is a God," said the drummer, Rich.

Tony downed his drink immediately and took Amy by the arm, "Time we were going." He grinned matter of factly, and picked his coat up from a chair, "See you Saturday."

Amy was surprised; they usually didn't leave until much later. What had upset him? She couldn't think. He didn't speak much on the drive back and appeared lost in his own world.

They eventually arrived home, tiptoed in quietly, so as not to disturb Amy's parents and he flopped in the rocking chair a strange look on his face.

Amy left him alone with his thoughts and went to make them both a mug of hot chocolate. She returned and passed him his drink before settling on the sofa. She slipped her lithe, well-shaped legs under her, flicked a strand of hair from out of her eyes and took a long sip from her mug.

Tony's face was serious, he sighed heavily before he asked, "Where do you think we came from?"

Amy, uncertain where this was leading asked, "Is this the chicken or the egg question?"

"What do you mean?"

"What do *you* mean?" Amy was in the mood for a good discussion.

"I'm talking about God."

Amy knew she might be on dangerous territory so she turned the question around. "What do you think?"

"I believe the Bible. Don't you?"

"I believe in some of what's in the Bible, but not all of it."

"Mum always said that everything in the Bible was true." Tony's voice was emphatic in its certainty.

Amy started to explain carefully how that couldn't possibly be correct using one and two Kings as her examples. "That's impossible. You've only got to look at One and Two Kings. Here we have two versions of the same story, each one entirely different. They can't both be true."

Tony fought to try and accept what she was saying. "What about God? You do believe in God don't you?" A note of hysteria was creeping into Tony's voice and Amy felt instinctively, whatever her feelings and beliefs that she had to answer, 'yes'.

Tony continued, "Then, do you believe in the creation? In Adam and Eve?"

"Look, let's say I believe in something very powerful and I believe that this something is known by very many names," and she paralleled Buddhism, the story of Mohammed and other comparative religions with Christianity. "Each major religion has many similarities, for example, they all have a flood. Archaeologists have proven that the event actually happened."

Tony looked extremely troubled and pressed again, "What about Adam and Eve?"

"Look, I've studied too much, not to believe in the theory of evolution but I think the story of Adam and Eve has its place." She laughed, "When I was a little girl, I used to flummox Mum and Dad by constantly asking that if God made us and the world, then who made God?"

Tony went very silent. Then, after a pause he said quietly, "I never thought of that... or I never let myself think of it."

He started to tell her more about his childhood. He told her again how he was forced to stay in on Sundays and learn passages from the Bible. He would watch his friends through the window playing in the street. He told her of the many church meetings; his mother's conversion from Catholicism to the Pentecostal church; and the laying on of hands; how he'd confessed and given his heart to Christ and the endless guilt he had suffered because he didn't conform to his mother's expectations. She had always said that one day he would be the Lord's and how, like Jonah, he had kicked against it.

The hands of the clock moved slowly around the dial and Amy began to realise what a festering wound she had opened with her words and her own beliefs on God and her recounting previous discussions she'd had with friends on existentialism. Tony's eyes were clouded with inner turmoil and she tried, for his sake, to back track on much that she had said, but it was too late.

Amy could see the mental war raging in his mind behind those stormy fear ridden eyes and again she cursed his mother for destroying the peace and stability of such a loving man.

Tony looked at her with such heartbreaking pain in those wide distracted eyes that she knew it was the first time he had ever questioned his mother's religious teachings. She did not know what that would do to him, but she was worried. His face now looked haunted and haggard.

Amy took the cups silently into the kitchen and rinsed them before going into the bathroom and preparing for bed.

Tony reached for his blue Crombie coat and as he passed the bedroom door he murmured, "I'm going for a walk. I need to think."

He went out into the early dawning, where night's sombre shadows were being evaporated by the coming of the rising sun and the waking morning.

He had to see his mother. Only she could give him the peace he craved.

*

"The police have been round," said Tony's mother suspiciously, as she passed him a cup of tea. "Checking on a statement you'd given to them that hadn't been verified."

"That's okay, isn't it?" smiled Tony.

"That depends. Of course, I couldn't remember what happened on that date but I supported your story as best I could." Her eyes flicked up and down his face. "The Mason girl, isn't that the one you told me about.... from work?" he didn't answer. She prompted, "Tony, I've looked after you all these years. Take my hand. Let us pray together."

Trustingly like a small child he put his hand in hers and a lock of his blue-black hair fell across his eyes. Her dry, pudgy fingers stroked his head and lingered on his neck. Her voice quavered as she launched into a hymn, 'He who would valiant be,' and his strong melodic voice joined with hers in the second verse. She patted his hand reassuringly and went to the wooden box. He took out a scroll, it said:

"Be strong, fear not! Behold your God will come with a vengeance with the recompense of God. He will come and save you." Isaiah thirty-five, verse four.

*

Tony fell into a fitful sleep in his mother's bed. He was confused. What was happening to him? His mind was in turmoil and his stomach twisted sickly with knots of fear. He needed to clear his head and think. The questions Amy had posed disturbed him. Had he accepted willingly everything

164

his mother had told him through the years? Did he believe in the Bible texts he'd been forced to sit at his desk and learn to recite whilst his friends played games in the street? Or had he been duped all these years? Had he been lied to? If so, by whom?

In his dreams he had flashes of memory, a woman calling his mother's name, Fluffy; a fight with death, where he felt again a fist crashing down on his nose; a line of glasses and drinks in a night club with strobe lighting and glitter balls reflecting a myriad of mocking, laughing faces and him tugging hard at a white evening scarf. He heard bones crack and a strange gurgling.

He woke with a start, his body sweating, He looked up and his mother was there. She cradled him in her arms and tenderly offered him her breast, which he suckled like a baby, before finally falling peacefully asleep.

Tony's mother sighed. The air rattled in her chest. She knew she would never completely lose her son.

*

PC Taylor was still shaken from his routine visit to check Tony Clifton's statement.

That woman had given him the creeps. Oh, she'd been pleasant enough. He'd even had a cup of tea and a slice of lemon cake. But the house, crammed full of religious artefacts with the face of Christ staring at him from every conceivable corner alarmed him.

He remembered all the seemingly normal details of the visit. He recalled how she had been in the middle of knitting squares to make a blanket for the needy when he'd rung the bell. They had chatted about her work at the church and he found that she shared many interests with his own mother. But, there was something about her, something that made him feel overwhelmingly uneasy.

However, his common sense had kicked in and he dismissed his thoughts as unreasonable and ridiculous. He concentrated on the fact that her son's statement checked out. At least, it appeared to and so he had prepared to leave but he had been unprepared for her farewell wish. He heard her thin reedy tones ringing in his ears.

"Thank you for calling, Constable. If ever you're round this way do drop in. I'm always good for a cuppa."

He had smiled in reply. Her words in that nasal twang reverberated around his head as she instructed,

"Before you go, here, take two of these." She had offered him the carved wooden box of scrolls. "Words of comfort from the Lord." He had taken two and fled. He had opened one, and now he opened the other one.

'The fear of the LORD is a fountain of life, that one may turn away from the snares of death.'

Proverbs Chapter 14 Verse 27.

He frowned, what the heck did that mean? The quotation seemed linked with his job and his own inconsistencies and struggles with his faith. David Taylor pulled himself together and completed his report, noting the time of his visit to Golden Hillock Road and confirmed that the original statement checked out. He signed and dated it and left it with Allison's secretary, Maddie for the Chief to see.

The interview had been a formality but he prayed he would never have a reason to visit the house again.

*

Amy was unnerved; her heart was thumping wildly as she stared at the pornographic magazine in front of her. Women in lewd poses pouted seductively at her. It wasn't that which shocked her but the additions; the careful biro etchings that screamed of sickness and pain; the darts that pierced the voluptuous breasts; the biro droplets of blood that sprouted from the wounds inflicted by pen and ink.

She didn't dare, she couldn't bring herself to believe that Tony had done this. She knew he had problems, problems that could be summed up in one word, 'Mother'. Gradually her anguish was replaced by anger and when she heard his car in the driveway she flung the offending piece of literature with its obscene and sadistic drawings into the centre of the coffee table, where it wouldn't be missed.

She heard him whistle cheerfully as he bounded up the stairs and walked nonchalantly into the lounge. He beamed at her and then noticed the look of utter disgust on her face.

"What's the matter, Pidge?"

"That!" She gestured to the pornographic publication, which faced him accusingly on the coffee table. It couldn't have been clearer if she had surrounded it with flashing neon lights. "That disgusting piece of filth. What sort of a sick, twisted mind could do that?" And she launched into a tirade against men who fed on and enjoyed periodicals that degraded women. "Psychotic, depraved, sick bastards who prey on women and brutalise females for their own sexual gratification are just a step away from rape and criminal assault. This sort of perverted, sadistic doodling is the first step in the making of a monster."

Tony fell silent and looked sadly at Amy, "You don't think I'd do that?" he implored.

"I don't know what to think," she retorted angrily.

Gently, he placated her. Calming her with his hands, as he placed them around her; with his lips, as he kissed away her tears, and with his voice, as he agreed with her words, agreed with her anger and agreed with her disgust. "You are so right my darling. It's foul and horrible, a complete abomination. Whoever did it is a vile creature not fit to look upon you."

"What's it doing here?" she cried, the tears still streaming down her face.

"I bought it like that. I didn't know until I got it home. And when I looked at it I resolved to return it and complain. That's why I left it out … It's probably just some kid who did it for a prank, intending to shock."

"But it's a horrible thing to do," protested Amy.

"I know, I know. Look, I'll take it away and burn it if it'll make you feel better." She nodded and turned away. Tony stroked her hair cascading over her shoulders, "Feeling better, Pidge?"

Now it was all explained, Amy did in fact feel happier. She was incredibly relieved that her Tony hadn't been responsible. Of all the things he'd confessed to her, and he certainly was sharing his problems, the imparting of his inner most feelings had lulled her into believing that she could be the cure for all his past ills. She smiled at him tenderly, blew him a kiss, and then fell into his embrace. He held her tightly with his crushingly powerful arms, and she felt safe.

Tony's eyes as he held her had turned to a dark navy blue and swam with turbulent emotions. He had to regain control of this thing inside him. Amy was the one to help him come through this. He was sure of that.

*

Allison grunted in dissatisfaction. Nothing had come back from Rebecca Mills. Men had been stationed night and day watching her practice, checking every male visitor. No one matched the description, no one who attended the clinic seemed to be remotely connected with the case.

They had managed to identify, they believed, one of the patients, whom she had been concerned about, but he was a total innocent, working as an orderly at the General Hospital and on duty, the night of the Mason murder with plenty of witnesses to verify the fact. He was in the clear.

Allison decided to call Dr. Mills and ask about her progress. "Dr. Mills? DCI Allison here. I was wondering if you were any further forward in exonerating the two men from your list that we spoke of?"

She greeted him coolly, "Inspector, it has not gone unnoticed that you have had my practice under surveillance, also that you have been harassing my patients and even intruding at their places of work. Any help I might have afforded you is now withdrawn."

She started to terminate the call but Allison's voice stopped her, "Look, I'm sorry. We were clumsy, I admit, but we are talking about women's lives here. Can you tell me anything that may eliminate the two patients you spoke of or if you have uncovered any other person who may be a likely suspect?"

Allison could hear the heavy sigh in her voice as she refrained from putting the receiver back in the cradle. She spoke slowly, "I was totally wrong about one, he has a steady job and is leading a stable life, in fact he's due to marry in June."

Allison's mind ticked like a computer. Yes, that was the male nurse. He could be crossed off his list.

"What about the other one?" He waited anxiously for her answer.

"I've not been able to get in touch with him. He is no longer at his ex-girlfriend's address and his mother tells me he has met someone new. And before you ask - No! She doesn't know where he's living. I'd say, though that you can eliminate him, too. There is no one else past or present who ticks your boxes. I don't wish to speak to you again. And, that's all I have to say." She replaced the receiver.

Allison stared at his handset thoughtfully as if it might yet yield some answer to his question. He slung it back down, flicked on his intercom and screamed his order to Maddie, "Give Taylor the transcripts of all the calls made from Dr. Mill's surgery. See if anything tallies." Allison's tone brooked no argument or dissent. In this mood he was a man to be obeyed, instantly.

"Sir!" acknowledged Maddie.

Allison didn't know it then but he had given the job to the perfect copper.

*

Amy was just putting the finishing touches to her makeup. She wore her hair up, with ringlets tumbling just in front of her ears. She looked stunning in a black evening dress with silver studs around the square neckline. She selected a black velvet choker from her jewellery box. "Tony, can you fasten this for me please?"

He came and stood behind her. Reflected in the mirror they made a handsome couple. He put his hands to her throat and stroked the wispy tendrils that curled down the nape of her neck. He kissed her soft sweet skin and drew his eyes up to her face reflected in the mirror.

For a moment, his gaze locked hers in the silvered glass. Tears of pride filled his eyes at Amy's exquisitely pretty face and the inner beauty that shone out from her. His eyes blurred and as he gazed at Amy's soft, smiling mouth the reflection seemed to liquefy and ripple, subtly changing, until her sweetly innocent mouth had become a red gaping leer. Her eyes lost their open frankness and shimmered into a hooded pair of lids shaded by black beetling brows.

He drew in his breath almost imperceptibly and his hands tightened on Amy's neck. He took in another lungful of air,

169

this time more sharply and stiffened. Amy noticed the change in his expression, "Tony, what's wrong?" His grasp was becoming tighter. Amy started to panic and cough. She cried out again trying to shock him back to reality, "Tony, please... you're hurting me."

The sound of Amy's alarmed tone brought him out of his trance. The mirror's fluid movement flowed to a standstill and Tony saw the look on his face, in his eyes, and Amy's fear. His hands left her throat as if they had been burnt, dropping swiftly to his side. Amy's black choker fell to the floor and Tony spun her around, kissing her neck, her face, and her lips.

"I'm so sorry, Pidge. So sorry," he stammered.

"What happened?" she asked her voice husky from the rough treatment.

"I don't know what came over me. I was looking at you in the mirror, so proudly. You looked so beautiful ..."

"And?"

"And it was as if someone passed a hand over my face and changed your appearance. Flashes of memory flitted past, stole your lovely face from me. I panicked. I didn't realise how tightly I was holding you... You know I would rather die than hurt you," he pleaded.

"I know, I know. It's okay. Don't worry. It's over now. It seems like you had some kind of hallucination."

"I don't know. It must be because I'm tired. It has to be."

Amy retrieved her choker from the floor and tossed it to one side and selected a small silver locket instead. She fastened it herself.

As Tony helped her on with her coat with its revere neckline, Amy reached for a long silk scarf to cover her exposed neck.

Tony froze. "Please don't wear that."

"What? Why?" she asked, puzzled.

"Don't. It reminds me of her. I don't want you ever to remind me of her."

"You mean your mother?"

Tony nodded and hung his head as Amy replaced the long Isadora type scarf with an ordinary silk square. She folded it

170

diagonally and tied it behind her neck letting the triangle fall in pleats like a cowl necked blouse.

Tony looked up at her and smiled. He was satisfied and they left for the club.

13
Identikit

"No, his chin was squarer than that." Sandra Thornton sat with the police artist, Marvin, his pad and his collection of photographs, trying to piece together a complete picture of her attacker. The artist erased the curve and angle of the face and chiselled the chin more.

"Yes, that's right." She screwed up her face and studied the developing artwork. "The eyes are wrong. They need to be bigger."

He responded immediately, "Like that?"

"Mm. That's better. I think they were blue, steel blue. It was hard to tell in the storm."

"What about the nose?"

"It's nearly correct, Marvin, but not quite. It was straight and rather like the actor, what's his name? Ian McShane. In fact, he looked very much like Ian McShane. Could have been his brother, only much more frightening." Sandra was pleased with her comparison and smiled.

The police artist continued sketching and adding detail to the eyes. He worked quickly and from Sandra's excellent description he came up with a very good likeness of her attacker's eyes.

She shrieked, "That's it! Those eyes, I'll never forget those eyes."

Spurred on by Sandra's response PC Marvin Blake matched the appropriate sections of the face she had selected from photographs, refining, shading and altering pieces until he had a complete sketch. Sandra spoke, "That's him! You've done it! Now, surely to God you'll get him?"

The police artist grinned, "You've done well. I'll get this back to head quarters and get it reproduced. If you're convinced that this is a good likeness, then someone must recognise him.'"

"I hope so, Officer. I wouldn't want anyone to go through the same horrors that I did."

"You've done well, Sandra, really well," said Marvin. "Maybe I'll see you again?"

"Maybe."

She saw the young policeman out, closed the door behind him and leaned against it, "The bastard's going to get his just desserts. And I'll be there to see it." She crashed onto the settee with a bounce. There was a change in her. Her expression was more determined; a light had come into her eyes. She was recovering from her trauma and returning to her usual feisty self.

*

Tony's head swam in the flashing lights and the artificial glare, blips and bells of the machines in the arcade. He had to keep playing. He could only find respite from the torturing voices tormenting him inside his head by channelling all his energies and concentration into winning. But winning, he was not and now other voices argued and warred inside his mind.

He knew he'd have to keep playing, get onto a winning streak to still the evil lips that whispered in his ear; and he was running out of money. He'd have to pay a visit to 'Uncle', the friendly neighbourhood pawnbroker who knew him well. His identity bracelet was always good for a hundred and fifty quid. That would keep him going until his next job and then he could redeem it. It was either that or call on his mother. He knew she usually had spare cash … but that came at a price. But, was it a price he was prepared to pay anymore?

He was trying to sever the invisible umbilical cord that bound him to her. He felt that if he didn't have to see her and he didn't have to talk to her that his safety would be assured. But, that small voice rose up to annoy him and remind him that living with Amy hadn't protected him completely. He hadn't expected to be visited by the devil girls; not only that his compulsion to gamble was becoming more difficult to control as the questions about God battled inside his head.

His forehead glistened with tiny droplets of sweat as the nudge light flashed at him. He pummelled the button with a surge of energy that blotted out all else. He was rewarded with the jangle of a number of pound coins clattering into the tray. He scraped them up and counted them into his shaking hand. There were twenty and then his eye caught a glimpse of a chromium metal plated arm clunking down then up, repeatedly.

He stared at the feminine hand that held it and looked into the bloated, cyanosed face of a middle aged woman, her head encased in a scarf, gaudy baubles around her neck and just for a second her face seemed to melt into another much younger face.

Fleetingly, in his brain, he heard the screaming kyi of a martial artiste. He passed his hands over his eyes and the image was lost. He struggled to retain its memory, which continued to elude him. It was no good. It was gone.

Tony batted at the machine with the flat of his hand, twisted his mouth in an angry sneer and pushed his way through the arcade. He strode off down the street, stopped at the corner and looked back at the arcade booth. And stared at the guy who worked there.

Mitch raised his eyes lazily from his auto magazine and caught Tony's gaze who turned and walked away. Mitch watched Tony's retreating figure. Somewhere in the back of his mind a memory stirred. He puzzled for a minute, but the effort was too great and he slipped back into the pages of the used car ads.

*

PC Taylor rubbed his head; he could feel a headache coming on as he stared at the computer printout of names. He'd been at it for hours! He sighed wearily. They were all in alphabetical order. It had taken him all morning to plough through the A's and B's. He was now half way through the C's.

He needed a cup of tea. He fished in his pocket for some money and left his desk to go to the hot drinks machine in the corridor.

"So, tell me, how's it going?" asked Sergeant Pooley sympathetically.

"Getting there," replied David Taylor, "Albeit slowly. It's a nightmare, so many names."

"Yes, it's a rum job, that's for sure. Good luck."

PC Taylor smiled affably as he slotted in his coins and made his selection. He collected his tea and took a sip. Good it was hot and instantly it made him feel better.

He weaved his way back to his desk and turned the page to the next list of names. He was now onto CL's he finger scanned the names and stopped. His jaw dropped. He felt a flutter of excitement. He read the name and address again. It tallied! There on the printout of registered owners of Ford Escorts was the name and address of that same woman he'd felt so uncomfortable with in Golden Hillock Road.

There had to be a link!

*

There was a ring at the doorbell in the Melville Road flat. Amy ran lightly down the stairs and was amazed to see Tony's mother standing there.

"I'm so sorry to bother you, but I had to see you. May I come in?" Her voice had an ingratiating whine and Amy had to suppress a shiver of revulsion and the urge to slap that reptilian face. She opened the great wooden door as wide as she could and ushered the odd, little woman in.

"Of course. Do come in. Would you like a coffee or something?"

"I don't want to be any trouble," her eyes glittered malevolently.

"Tony isn't here. He's out. I'm not sure when he'll be back," Amy said defensively hoping that the creature in front of her would change its mind and leave.

"It isn't Tony I've come to see. It's you," went on the reedy tones.

"Oh!"

The squat lump enjoyed Amy's obvious confusion. She took a fervent delight in manipulating people, exerting her will over others and here, she was sure she had another victim, in sympathetic, gentle Amy.

Amy led the way upstairs into the warm, comfortable sitting room and offered her a seat in the sage Draylon Queen Anne wingback chair.

"Coffee?"

"I'd prefer tea, if that's all right?" Her nasal voice quavered as if with hidden emotion of some terrible burden that she was about to share.

Amy went into the kitchen and switched on the kettle, puzzling as to why the woman would visit her. She knew she had tried to be as pleasant and as charitable as she could. She was sure the woman didn't suspect her dislike of her. Amy felt certain that she was a good enough actress to carry that pretence off. She prepared the tea tray and took some side plates and added the contents of the cookie jar.

Amy beamed as she entered the sitting room and placed the tray on the coffee table. She offered her a selection of biscuits as she poured out the tea from the pot.

"Thank you," Tony's mother accepted a chocolate bourbon and stared about her, "I'm sorry, Amy, you know … that I had to come…"

"That's okay," bluffed Amy.

"No, normally I wouldn't dream of intruding." She paused for the best possible effect and a pitying note crept into her voice. "I know you don't like me and I know you blame me for a lot of Tony's problems."

Amy frowned, how could she know what she was thinking?

"Believe you me, I wouldn't have come if I didn't have to; please, let me explain." She took a breath and licked those parched dry lips in a most lascivious way holding Amy's gaze as a snake might mesmerise its prey. "You think it's odd that I should have complete and utter faith in the Lord. But, since my husband died, it's all I have. It helps me to feel closer to him and to God. The church gives me a life that I wouldn't have otherwise. No!" She put her hand up to silence Amy who was about to speak, "Don't criticise me yet. I know I won't always have Tony. I know that he loves you very much and I know he has problems." She stopped again, giving her words maximum weight and that final crowning touch, "He does imagine things, you know. He used to make up the most awful stories about me to his ex-girlfriend because he liked the attention it gave him." She watched Amy's expression carefully, "I know I've been harsh in his upbringing but I brought him up to believe in God and I know that faith will save him in the end. Maybe, I was wrong to preach at him the way I did," she sighed, "But I meant well."

Amy waited. This woman certainly had a good act and the more she talked, the more Amy started to feel that perhaps she had misjudged her, that she wasn't the old witch she thought she was.

"Amy, he loves you and he needs you that's why I had to speak to you. You see Tony has a terrible problem that he inherited from his father. He gambles."

"I know. He's taken a vow never to bet on anything again."

"Yes, but the trouble is he hasn't kept it. That alone will cause him such turmoil he may break down like he did when he was sixteen."

Mrs. Clifton wiped a stray tear that escaped from her cobra hooded eye, and dabbed at it with a large, grey, man's handkerchief with quick darting movements. "You're strong. You'll need to be, he will lean on you and use your strength."

"I have been worried about him," admitted Amy, slowly warming to the revolting creature.

"Yes, I'm sure you care. But the gambling, if it's not the casinos it's the machines. It's only a matter of time before it completely rules his life again. Only you can help him."

"But he's not gambling now," insisted Amy. "I would know."

"I'm afraid he is and that's why I'm here. He's been betting secretly for the last few weeks. He's borrowed money from me to fund his habit, pretending it was for other things, but he came to me in great distress this morning because he'd pawned these." She took from her pocket a silver charm bracelet and an emerald ring, which both belonged to Amy. Amy gasped in shock.

"He pawned them locally to pay for a session at the arcade and he lost. He came to see me in tears and full of remorse for what he'd done. I had no option but to go to the pawnbrokers and retrieve them for you. I'm so sorry."

Amy looked at her with new eyes. Mrs. Clifton had done

this for her. Amy felt guilty about all the unkind thoughts she had harboured against Tony's mother. She had been wrong about her. This was just a pathetic old woman of no danger to anyone. Accepting the bracelet and ring she thanked her. "I can't thank you enough. The ring was my grandmother's. It's very special to me and the charm bracelet, well I've been collecting these since I was thirteen."

"I thought as much," said Mrs. Clifton as she slurped her tea.

"Please, Mrs. Clifton, tell me how I can help? What do you think I should do?'

And Tony's mother, eyes shining with crocodile tears, grinned. She now had Amy exactly where she wanted her.

*

Tony arrived home flourishing a big bouquet of flowers, which he thrust at Amy, "I'm sorry, Pidge. It won't happen again."

Tony's excuses and apologies were beginning to wear thin and Amy said as much as she received the blossoms. "So, you say." She pursed her lips.

"Come on, don't be cross with me. You know I can't bear it when you're cross."

"I felt such an idiot. There was me thinking you were doing so well and you couldn't confide in me that you had a relapse. I had to find out from your mum," she accused.

"I felt so ashamed and hated that I'd let you down. I couldn't help it. I'm sorry."

"And are you sorry you stole from me?"

Tony hung his head in shame, "Totally, that's why I went to mum. I had to get them back for you. Please forgive me."

"And what about the next time?"

"There won't be a next time."

"But if there is?"

"There won't be. I promise."

"Oh, Tony. How can I trust you?"

Tony flopped in despair into the rocker, "Can we stop talking about it now?" he pleaded.

Amy sighed, "I suppose so. It doesn't do either of us any good going on like this."

"No, especially when I've got some good news."

"What's that?"

"The agency has booked me a week, next week, at a club in Nottingham. Really good money I get fifteen hundred for the week."

"Less expenses. But what if you gamble?"

"I won't. Come with me and then you'll be certain."

"I can't. I'm working... but," Amy suddenly had a light bulb idea. "I have friends in Nottingham. If I arrange for you to stay with them that should help keep you on the straight and narrow, shouldn't it?"

Tony beamed that boyish smile he had and Amy's heart melted. "That would be great. Ring them now," he urged.

Amy smiled; she couldn't be cross with him forever. She picked up the phone and dialled.

*

Allison chewed thoughtfully on his Mars Bar as he mulled things over. If Taylor was right, and it certainly looked as if he was, then with a little more ferreting they should have enough to apply for a warrant.

PC David Taylor was to pay a return call to the house in Sparkbrook and ask about the Escort.

There was also the matter of a phone call from Rebecca Mill's practice to that same house. Allison had always said that he didn't believe in coincidences. He smiled grimly and hoped that they had finally got lucky and that this would be one investigation soon to be terminated.

*

Amy was downstairs with her Mum. Tony wasn't due to arrive home from the week's engagement in Nottingham until sometime on Sunday. She regretted that she couldn't go with him because of work, but had, as promised, arranged for him to stay with her friends, Ruth and Simon. Amy had tipped them off about his gambling problem, but with Tony's permission, and they had promised to keep an eye on him, not wanting him to get lost in Nottingham's notorious nightlife.

Amy's Mum was singing happily in the kitchen. Delicious aromas wafted through from the dinner she had just made.

Amy sat casually with her evening meal on her lap, in front of the fire, watching Crime Watch UK.

It was a particularly harrowing programme and featured the gruesome murders that had taken place in Birmingham. They were focusing on the attack on Sandra Thornton. Amy watched, fascinated, she had always liked true crime stories. But then, what happened next she was **not** expecting. The hairs on the back of her neck prickled with horror as an identikit picture of a man, flashed up on the screen. Her flesh itched as if caught in a web that had hatched a million tiny spiders, constantly multiplying and all running free, crawling all over her face. Apart from the hairstyle, which appeared wild and dishevelled, she could swear she was looking at a picture of Tony.

"Mum! Mum, come here. Quickly!" she screamed.

"What's the matter?" Her mother complete with tea towel, apron and serving spoon came scurrying in.

"The identikit!" Amy pointed to the screen. "Look!"

Amy's mother peered at the television, "Looks like Lovejoy."

"Who?"

"Lovejoy, on the tele. What's that actor called? It's on the tip of my tongue.... Mmm" she snapped her fingers as she recalled the name, "Ian McShane."

"Yes, but who else does he remind you of?"

"Oh, 1 don't know."

"Come on Mum, look. Tony! Doesn't it look like Tony?"

"Well, yes, it could be, except the hair's all wrong. Tony never has a hair out of place. This one's hair is all unkempt and unruly. It looks greasy or wet."

"So, you don't think it could be Tony?"

"Why ever should it be Amy? It's just someone who resembles him."

"Of course it is. It just unnerved me that's all. Seeing someone who looked so much like him," she explained.

Amy's mother retreated into the kitchen, shaking her head in a bemused fashion. Amy sat forward and listened closely. This part of the programme was about a vicious attack on a girl, some four and a half months ago. They had staged a

180

reconstruction of the victim's evening prior to the attack, using a look-alike actress in the hope of jogging someone's memory.

Amy watched the girl leave her bed-sit, post her letter, visit the arcade and munch her late supper at the chip shop. It culminated in a very realistic enactment of the attempted murder and the prompt arrival of the two medical students who had found Sandra Thornton, and saved her life.

The voice of Nick Ross was echoing in her ears. "The police wish to interview anyone who came into contact with Sandra, that evening."

A police spokesman came into vision, "Someone must know this man and is possibly protecting him. He would have suffered extreme facial injuries and bruising to his nose and under his eyes. It is only a matter of time before this man attacks again. We already believe that he is responsible for three murders in this area. If anyone knows his identity please ring now. All calls will be treated in the strictest confidence. The number to ring is 0121 - 626 - 6010."

Amy's heart was thumping so loudly, she was sure it could be heard by her mother. Her hand was trembling and a serpent of despair twisted and turned in her stomach. Amy was remembering. She remembered the scratches inside his wrist; she remembered his cut and broken nose and black bruised eyes. She remembered his hands around her throat and a cold and terrible fear gripped her heart.

The chirruping of the telephone broke into her thoughts. She set aside her dinner and went into the next room to answer it, "Hello?" Amy tried to keep her voice as light and as steady as possible.

"Hello, Amy?"

"Sheena?"

"I just tried to get you on the upstairs number. I thought you might be there."

"I was, but tonight I'm having tea with Mum."

"Have you just been watching Crime Watch UK?"

"Uh, huh." Amy hoped her words didn't betray her thoughts.

"What did you think about the attack on that girl?"

"Shocking, absolutely appalling."

181

"Come on, Amy," pressed Sheena.

"What do you mean?" Amy tried to speak evenly and normally.

"Didn't that picture remind you of anyone?'

"No?" She kept just the right amount of puzzlement in her tone, "Oh, wait a minute, Mum said he looked like Lovejoy, you know the actor Ian McShane."

"Yes, and who does Lovejoy remind you of? Come on, Amy, we've said it so many times before. Tony!"

"Yes, but you can't possibly think it was him."

"Perhaps not, but the resemblance was quite striking."

"Except for the hair."

"Yes, but it was a wild night, remember? Heavy rain and a thunder storm."

"So?"

"Maybe it's just a coincidence. But if I were you, I'd check his whereabouts that night."

"For heaven's sake Sheena, you're just being melodramatic. You've never liked him. You did your best to put me off him. All this is because I don't see you as much as I used to."

"Petty jealousies aside, Amy, I'm talking as your best friend. What about all those weird feelings you had about the guy? *Something's wrong, I can't put my finger on it*," Sheena mimicked.

"Okay, okay. I admit I had doubts, but that was because he had such an odd mother, all that religious stuff. He had a few problems. I didn't understand then but I do now. That's all." Amy tried to make herself sound convincing.

"Maybe so. I just thought I'd ring."

"Thanks, Sheena. But you've no need to be concerned."

"Well, I can't help it. You're special, Kid and I worry about you. Take care and I'll see you Tuesday."

"Right. Bye!" Amy put down the phone. Her hand was shaking and the wriggling maggot of doubt was multiplying into a seething mass that threatened to engulf her sanity. Tiny beadlets of sweat covered her downy upper lip. She felt sick in her stomach. She knew instinctively that Sheena wasn't telling her everything.

"Amy! Come and finish your dinner," called her mother.

"Can you pop it in the oven for me? I won't be a minute. I just need to fetch something."

"Hurry up! I don't want it drying up."

She hurried along the Victorian passageway to the front door and pounded up the stairs to her flat. She stopped before the lounge door, took a deep breath and went to the bureau where she kept her stationery and her diary. With trepidation she lifted out her black micro-file and turned to the previous year's diary pages, the tremor in her hand became more pronounced with every turn of the page. She looked up the date that had been cited in the programme. Her heart sank and a strange, weak, tingling pain type sensation darted through her knees. She sat down swiftly, before her legs gave way. The diary entry read:

"Tony attacked by some drunk last night. If I'd been with him, it wouldn't have happened."

A million thoughts and memories went tumbling through her mind, his hands on her throat; the defaced pornographic magazine; the many love games he played, his hands on her throat; the photographs she'd found; his confessions from the past; his hands on her throat. That memory above all others seemed to cry out to her, bludgeoning the voice that argued with those doubts, into submission. Hot salt tears coursed down her cheeks, blinding her eyes where her mascara ran into them. Her body juddered uncontrollably as Amy sobbed, sobbed in pain and anguish over her discovery, over Tony and for herself.

She picked up the phone and did the only thing she could do. She rang Tony's mother.

*

Allison looked at the mounting evidence in front of him. Now that Crabtree was out of the picture, with all the confusion he'd caused by his two slayings; he wondered at Crabtree's ingenious use of a young student's semen, which he'd collected and frozen after watching that youth's amorous adventures. Allison could now concentrate on the 'crooning killer' as Trevor Booth had dubbed him. Booth was bound to earn a tidy sum from the profits of his book on Crabtree, which was to be a sensational story in itself.

Allison had a prime suspect with a religious freak for a mother, just as Brady had predicted. She happened to own an Escort car, which her son drove, which was yet to be checked for a Flotex carpet. The car and driver were currently being sought by the West Midlands' police. There was an APB out for Tony Clifton.

That same son had worked at Dempsey's. There was the link with Janet Mason whom he had asked out, and of course there he had access to Susan Hardy's off cuts of carpet. Also, he had at one time been treated by Rebecca Mills who had believed him to be a dangerous character, although this was not openly admitted by her. The man was currently singing for his supper and so had a need to travel. It was looking better and better.

There was just one problem. How had he been given the all clear on the blood test? Allison tugged at his chin. He thought he might know.

*

Greg Allison rippled with delight as he heard the satisfying sound of ripping paper, which exposed the thick, creamy chocolate, of his cosseted Mars Bar. He lingered over the first bite and chewed contentedly and allowed his thoughts to wander.

Mark had returned to see Marie at the wine bar, to solicit the mystery singer's name, which he already was certain would be Tony Creole, judging from the calls he'd received as a result of the Crime Watch programme.

All they needed was Sandra Thornton's identification when they caught the swine.

Allison took another bite. He had enough now for a warrant to search the premises in Sparkbrook. As soon as Mark returned, they'd return to that house, with a team from Forensic and go through it with a fine toothcomb.

Calls were still coming in from the Nick Ross programme. Allison was amazed at how much help this sort of television coverage gave the police. Any other tricky cases and he determined he would use this service again.

One call in particular interested Allison. A friend of the

singer's girlfriend had rung, expressing her concern. She'd told them of an incident involving the suspect and an escort girl who had feared for her life. Allison needed to speak to her. He needed the girlfriend's name and that of the escort for future questioning. At the moment, the police didn't know where their suspect was living, but Allison was confident it would only be a matter of time. He sighed serenely and fingered the stray flakes of chocolate that had fallen onto his desk, and popped them into his mouth.

*

Mark Stringer sat at a table in Kelly's Wine Bar. He studied the escorts plying their trade. He couldn't understand why such beautiful women needed to prostitute themselves when they could so easily do something else.

A singularly attractive blonde approached his table and sat. "Hi, I'm Beth. Marie said you wanted to talk to me?"

"Yes," he extended his hand. "Mark, Mark Stringer. Detective Sergeant Mark Stringer."

Beth gasped, "You're a cop?"

"I'm afraid so."

"Oh…"

"It shouldn't change anything. We need to get the evidence to convict this guy. He's killed five women, maybe more. He needs to be put away to make the streets of Birmingham safe once more. Please. Talk to me."

Beth hesitated a moment and then spoke, haltingly at first but growing more confident as the flood gates opened and her words tumbled out. "Tony Creole." She almost spat out his name. "Mr. Good Looking, Mr. Talented and Mr. Charm, except he wasn't."

"In what way?"

"Come on, look at him. He's drop dead gorgeous. All the girls fancy him. I couldn't believe it when he turned his eyes on me."

"What happened?"

"It was late, one night. The club had closed and the guys in the band were having an impromptu jam session. They often did."

"Yes?"

185

"He'd invited me to stay behind, bought me drinks and sang to me. I felt so special."

"What happened?"

"The evening was going so well until it was time to go home." She hesitated and her hand ran involuntarily to her throat. "He offered me a lift. I was happy to accept. Saved on a taxi fare and it meant I could spend a bit more time with him. I was enchanted and thought I was the luckiest girl I the world. Not so lucky now."

She stopped and Mark pressed her gently to continue. "Go on."

Beth's eyes filled with tears, "To begin with it was fine but when I got in his car…"

"Yes?"

"It was like someone flicked a switch."

"What happened?"

"It was so utterly trivial." Beth closed her eyes as she recalled the details of that evening. "I came out of the club and got into his car. We were laughing and joking one minute and then I said something and he flipped. He went utterly ballistic."

"What did you say?"

"It was something like… I didn't want to go to heaven because all the best people went to hell and I'd meet him there." I was only being flippant and making a joke."

"Then what?"

"He grabbed me by the shoulders and said that what I said was blasphemous and I had to take it back or he'd make me." Beth paused and swallowed hard, "I told him to let me go. He took me by the throat and held me hard. He said that if I really wanted to go to hell, he'd help me on my way. And he started to squeeze my neck. I couldn't breathe." Beth stopped and Mark waited for her to continue, her voice was tremulous as she remembered. "If it hadn't been for Rich…"

"Rich?"

"The drummer. I'd left my overnight bag under the table where we'd been sitting. I usually come from my day job and change into an evening dress at the club."

"I see, go on."

Rich spotted it. He chased out after us to return it, ran up to his car and opened the door. I was so grateful I tumbled out onto the tarmac and I could hardly talk. My throat was sore. He made an excuse and said he was only playing and hadn't meant to hurt me. I went back inside the club and avoided him after that. It was so totally unexpected and bizarre. The guy is completely unpredictable."

"But you didn't report it?"

"No. It would just have been my word against his. I'm in the escort business who is going to believe me?"

"I would have, Beth. I would have," said Mark kindly. He made a mental note to track down this guy, Rich and speak to him, too. "This Rich, what's he like?"

"He's lovely. He should be in soon. He's got fair hair and will be dressed in a Tux. I'll point him out to you."

"Thanks. Let me get you a drink. What will you have?"

"Something stiff after reliving that lot. I'll have a brandy and ginger, please."

"You got it."

Mark crossed to the bar and bought a couple of drinks. He elected to have a Bacardi and coke and decided to get a cab home. He'd leave his car in the station car park. He could always bus into work the next day.

Mark walked back with the drinks and Beth took a sip, "Thanks. I needed that."

"Look, don't let me stop you working…"

"It's okay. Things don't begin to get going until after ten."

Mark changed the subject and they chatted like old friends. He found he really enjoyed her company. Still, that's what they were paid to do; make guys feel good about themselves.

"How about you? Anyone special at home?" asked Beth.

"My wife Debbie, my toddler son, Christian and a new baby, Catherine."

"That's good, a pigeon pair."

"Sorry?"

"One of each. You're lucky; not everyone can achieve that. Doesn't she mind you working late?"

"She's very good. She knows what the job entails and she married me anyway."

"I wouldn't be so understanding. If you were mine I would want to keep you close. Too many temptations in this world." She smiled at him and Mark felt himself begin to colour up. He was just wondering how he could excuse himself when she nudged his arm. "There, over there by the piano. That's Rich. He's just come in and he's talking to Steve."

Mark thanked her and picked up his drink.

"Maybe I'll see you around?" she said wistfully.

"Maybe."

Mark walked over to the small stage and addressed the two musicians, "Rich?"

"Who wants to know?"

"Beth pointed you out."

"Oh, yes. Why?"

"I need to ask you some questions."

Rich groaned and Steve patted him on the back, "Been a bad boy, then?" he laughed.

"It shouldn't take long," pressed Mark.

Rich pointed at another table. "Okay. Can we make it quick? I need to go through the running order with Steve."

Mark assured him, "It won't take long."

They crossed to the corner table and sat. "What's all this about?"

"Firstly, I just want to corroborate the details of something Beth has told me," and Mark repeated the details of the incident as Beth had described, which Rich agreed was all true. He rose to leave, but Mark stopped him.

"Was there something else?"

"Yes, I need to talk to you about the club singer."

"Tony?"

"Yes."

"What about him?" queried Rich.

"I'm sorry to say that we have mounting evidence that he is involved in the death of Annette Jury amongst others."

"Annette? No. I thought it was some maniac that was guilty." Rich looked shaken.

"We have a very strong suspicion that he may have been responsible for more than just Annette's death. I would just like to clarify a few things with you."

"Sorry, I'm just a bit stunned. I thought he had settled down now especially since he met Amy."

"Amy?"

"His girlfriend, young school teacher." He whistled under his breath. "I thought a lot of Annette. What do you need to know?"

"I just need to check some dates and facts."

"I'm not too good on dates. Don't know if I'll be able to help but I can tell you one thing …" he paused, "I've done something very stupid." Mark looked at him quizzically forcing him to continue. "It was a while ago, now and Tony asked me to do something. God what an idiot!"

"What? If it will help us catch Annette's killer…"

Rich looked into Mark's eyes, "He had an appointment to give a sample of his blood to eliminate him from some police enquiry. He didn't say what but he was afraid that the report would go through to his place of work and show that he had been using. He said he had been in trouble once before and daren't risk losing his job. He told me his newfound career was working well and he didn't want anything to blight it as bad publicity has a way of coming out. Foolishly, I offered to take the test for him. I went along and gave my blood sample and they took a DNA swab to help him get off the hook. I was stupid wasn't I?"

"You could say…"

"It means if I hadn't done that you'd have caught up with him a lot quicker. Would it have saved anyone's life?" asked Rich sheepishly and added, "What's going to happen to me?"

"I'll need to take a proper statement. Anything else will be up to my Chief. It certainly explains how he was eliminated from the enquiry."

"Oh, God. What have I done?"

"Don't panic. We have a search out for him. I'll be in touch. Just one more thing, do you know where his girlfriend Amy lives? Or indeed her second name?"

Rich screwed up his face, "I'm not sure, I think it's either

Crosby, Durning, or Latimer. No, not Durning that's the new guitarist's name. I believe that one was her friend's surname the other hers. She lives somewhere in Edgbaston."

"Edgbaston is a big place. Can you be more specific?"

"I think she said it was close to a church, I'm not sure."

"Do you know which one?"

"It's one where you can see the spire, close to the Hagley Road, I think. Sorry I can't be more helpful. If I remember anything else, I'll call you."

Mark handed him a card and finished his drink. He left the table passing Beth who was now sitting and drinking with a customer.

She gave him a wave and called, "Drop by sometime. I'll look out for you."

Mark waved back and left, he couldn't wait to tell the Chief. This was manna from heaven and just as Greg had suspected in private conversations with Mark.

*

Tony was in a bad place, a very bad place. He had left the club and wandered into one of the town centre casinos. He'd blown nearly a grand on Roulette and had only come out with some of his pay because the table had closed. He was desperate to play at something and try and win back the money he'd lost. He hadn't eaten anything. He'd walked out of Amy's friends' house unable to take their questions and constant watching him. He'd still got another spot to do at the club that's if he could remember how to get back there.

The voices were back, goading him, bullying him, and pressuring him to do something. He whimpered aloud, "I don't want to. I don't want to hurt anyone."

A young girl somewhat the worse for wear turned and asked, "What's up, cock? Something wrong?"

But lucky for her Tony didn't hear and he didn't answer. He didn't know where he was going but he needed to escape he had to find some respite somewhere. He walked on. The girl he'd spoken to, bent over and retched in the gutter emptying her stomach of the alcohol she had consumed that night, but Tony was oblivious. He meandered on to the local park but the gates were closed. He struggled through a gap in the fence and moved along the neat path bordered by miniature conifers toward a shelter past the deserted playground.

The shelter walls were covered with graffiti but Tony didn't see it. He sat on the wooden bench in one of the circular segments and lit a cigarette. It did little to help raise his spirits. He drew long, deep and hard and blew out a trail of blue grey smoke from his lungs and sighed wearily.

He didn't understand, flashes of memory were returning to plague him. These terrifying images that were haunting him were frightening and he began to sob.

The sound of a drunken voice filtered through into his mind. "Shut your rattle. I'm trying to sleep." But Tony didn't hear. He was so self absorbed all he could hear was his heart pounding and the voices whispering to him.

There was a scrambling sound coming from the adjacent segment. A down and out lurched into view. He looked like a shabby version of Dostoyevsky. His straggly hair showered his shoulders and his beard looked as if it could house a family of wrens. He staggered closer and sat with a thump next to Tony.

The smell of stale sweat and unwashed flesh and putrid clothing wafted up Tony's nose and seemed to awaken him. "What's up, Pal? Why so miserable?"

Tony turned and looked at the tramp and said simply, "I've been doubting God."

"You don't want to do that, Mate. You don't want to end up like me." His breath stunk of alcohol and cigarettes. "Have you got a fag?" he asked edging closer.

Tony obligingly offered the man one from his pack and lit it for him. The hobo sucked in hard drawing the smoke deep into his lungs and let out a satisfied "Aah!" as he breathed out. The man looked greedily at the packet. "I couldn't have one for later, could I?"

Tony passed him the packet and the man grabbed a few and stuck one behind each ear and placed another two in his top pocket. "Thanks. What's your name?"

Tony turned his head slowly toward him and looked blankly. He muttered, "I'm a Jonah."

191

"Well, Jonah, I'm Alex, at least I was the last time I looked," and he laughed. "I used to be a vicar. I expect you don't believe that." He chattered on and Tony sat silently, listening. "Got chucked out of the clergy, for my drinking. Lost my wife, family and my faith. Say, you don't have a drink do you?"

Tony shook his head.

"No matter. I ought to give up but it helps numb the pain. They told me I'd kill myself with booze but it's hard, you know. Any addiction is hard."

Tony nodded and his eyes filled with tears.

"Don't cry. I've been where you are. And I've hit rock bottom but I'm going to get better. I've made a promise to myself and to God. This night was my last bender. That's a nice coat you have on. It looks warm." Alex fingered the material of Tony's blue Crombie.

Tony removed his coat and passed it to the man who gratefully grabbed it and put it on. It did something to mask the offensive odours emanating from his person. Tony didn't appear to feel the cold.

Alex shuffled closer, "Ask me something. Ask me anything you like."

Tony turned his eyes to the tramp and said, "Who made God?"

Alex thought for a moment, "God is. He is omnipresent, almighty and all-powerful. He is always there and always has been. Everywhere you look you can see God. He touches all of us although we can't always see it."

"But who made him?"

Alex was stuck for words, "That's not a question to ask. Just accept it. He is there. I feel it and I know it. Have faith and he will be revealed to you." Alex took another long drag on his cigarette. "Jesus gave us a code to live by. Not much wrong with that. Not much wrong with the ten commandments."

"If you break them, you'll go to hell," murmured Tony.

"But what is hell? I believe hell is the suffering of being unable to love."

"Why is there so much pain and suffering in the world?

Alex thought a moment before responding, "Pain and suffering are almost inevitable for a large intelligence and a deep heart. The really great men must, I think, have great sadness on earth. I believe Dostoyevsky said that."

"You look like him."

"I wish I had his brains."

"Do you believe in love?"

"Love is our saviour. With love you can accomplish anything."

"Anything?"

"Anything. As long as you don't lie to yourself."

"I try not to."

"The man who lies to himself and listens to his own lies comes to a point that he cannot distinguish the truth within him, or around him and comes to a point that he loses all respect for himself and others. And having no respect he ceases to love." Alex recited other wise observations and Tony listened.

Tony stood up and Alex went to return his coat, "No. Keep it. You need it more than me."

Alex put his hands in the coat pocket and drew out a fistful of notes and looked amazed at Tony, "Here. This belongs to you."

Tony shook his head and waved the proffered notes away. "Keep it. Get yourself something to eat. Go back to your family. Learn to love again. I have to face up to things I have done."

"Why what have you done?"

"I don't know. I can't remember. I need to find out. I need God's help."

"God will bless you, Jonah. He will keep you as his own and I thank you for your kindness."

Tony walked away from the grubby shelter and back the way he came. He seemed to remember that he had a job to do; he had to sing again. The Lord had given him this voice and he would use it to praise him. He wandered into the town and back to the club to give his final performance. He recalled Alex's words about love. He took a pen from the Stage Door Keeper and some paper, and began to write. He

193

hummed as he wrote and penned the beginning of a song, which he found strangely liberating.

"Look back on life, see the shadows pass behind me,
Things I've seen and done, the path of love denied me,
How can I regret a feeling never in me?
Blame my foolish self, the strong self will within me.

I was offered you your heart and soul,
You promised love all secrets told.
I turned away for young adventure,
And now I realise that love'd have been better, better, better…."

Tony threw down the biro and ripped up the paper. He tossed it in the bin. The announcement came.

"Ladies and gentlemen put your hands together for Tony Creole." The applause was deafening and Tony stepped out onto the stage, picked up the mic and began to sing.

They picked Tony up at the nightclub in Nottingham. He looked bewildered and lost but he went quietly, almost relieved that it was over. Showgirls and people stared but he didn't see them. He looked through them and beyond. Amy was on his mind. She was the focus of his love and with her support he would get through this.

The memories were flooding his mind now, thick and fast. He shuddered as he thought of Natalie Blakeney and her screams that were rendered up into the wild night. He recalled the arc of blood that shot from her chest and felt the bile rise from his stomach to his throat.

Many of his atrocities he remembered, but not all. Some of them he had blanked into oblivion, and unable to cope with the enormity of his deeds he withdrew into his own silent world where no accusing fingers pointed, where no one whispered and laughed. Whilst in custody at the Nottingham Police Station he answered few questions but when he was waiting for a car to take him to Birmingham he confessed what Allison already knew that he had cleverly persuaded his musician friend, Rich to take the blood test for him. And he confirmed that he had given the drummer at his residency a story about being on drugs and not wanting the illegal substances to come to light for fear of jeopardising his newfound career.

The sad thing was that as a singer, Tony was extremely talented and fast gaining local recognition, which was spreading throughout the country. A big record company, Phonogram, were interested in offering him a contract thanks to Amy's hard work. She had sent out demo discs and tapes to various agents and companies and was in the process of organising a big concert with supporting artistes but now instead of mounting the ladder of fame, he was writing his name in the crime books alongside Peter Sutcliffe and Dennis Neilson.

Tony withdrew, and fell silent as he contemplated his future.

*

Mark Stringer had led a team of officers to Golden Hillock Road and Grace Clifton's house. He brandished a search warrant and she had no option but to admit them. She furrowed her beetling brows and watched as the police began to search her home. Nothing was kept private as they invaded her territory. She retreated to the sitting room and picked up her knitting and click clacked away at her church bazaar squares while humming a hymn, which Stringer recognised as "Bread of Heaven."

Harmon shouted down the stairs to Mark who was examining the contents of the sideboard drawers. "Sergeant, I think we've got something." Mark ran up the stairs. Harmon was holding out a pair of trousers, which were stained with a claret coloured shoe polish or so it seemed. There were also, blood spatters on the clothing. The trousers were bagged up, tagged and removed.

*

The Nottingham police towed away Tony's car from the nightclub car park to the police pound and a team of men were going over the car in a detailed search for evidence. The Flotex off cuts that he had used as floor mats and, which also lined the boot were taken away for tests. Allison had sent a message that these tests were to be done as a matter of urgency and take top priority on the workload.

Guy Eden who was the chief in the Forensic department had taken the job of the trouser stains himself whilst his team worked on the mats. Guy was pleased when the carpet fibres were identified as the same fibres on Janet Mason's clothing. Similarly, the claret stains on Tony Clifton's trousers had been made by the identical shoe polish used by Janet Mason on the night of the murder. The blood type from the spattered trousers, too, belonged to Janet Mason. This was another bonus for the police. Allison rubbed his hands in glee. He was sure that the swab taken from Tony Clifton's mouth would identify him as the attacker of Sandra Thornton and the killer of Jodie Stubbs, Lisa Shore, Annette Jury, Natalie Blakeney, and of course Janet Mason. Newcastle and Worthing police would be able to close their files on the murders on their patches.

However, they still hadn't established the address and identity of Tony's girlfriend. He had a team of men going from house to house in the Edgbaston area in the vicinity of any churches. The names Crosby and Latimer had yielded nothing but nor would they if the girlfriend had been married previously.

Allison grunted and bit into his Mars Bar he felt certain that this knowledge wouldn't be long in coming.

14
The Net Spreads Further

Now that the manhunt was concluded, Rebecca Mills was called in to examine her patient in conjunction with Brady, Dr. James Bingham, and Dr. Jeff Daniels to ascertain whether Tony would be fit to stand trial. The police had all the evidence they required and now waited for the psychiatric reports on the state of his mind.

A police van pulled up in front of the well trodden stone steps that bowed in the middle from the weight of the many feet that had for years moved in and out of this building, a secure hospital facility in Rubery on the outskirts of Birmingham.

The rear door clunked open and two uniformed coppers sprang down into the road followed by a plain clothed detective who was handcuffed to Tony. They were all closely followed by a medical looking man in a pristine white coat.

The unusual decision had been taken to release Tony from police custody into the care of the Secure Unit at Rubery Psychiatric Hospital where he was to undergo many tests to establish his suitability to stand trial in an ordinary court of law. The hospital wing at Winson Green Prison continued to be overcrowded and was deemed inappropriate for a prolonged stay.

Tony scuffed his shoes as he walked. His once proud bearing was broken, his shoulders hunched and his handsome face wore the unkempt, unshaven blue-black stubble that showed his fractured spirit and shattered personal pride. "Thank Christ the press aren't here," muttered Pooley. "I'd had enough of flash bulbs popping when we left Winson Green."

"Yep, we're lucky they've missed us," agreed Taylor. "The Chief's idea worked. Poor buggers will have a long wait at Leicester."

"But, they'll be mad when he's a no show."

"I don't expect it will take them long to work it out."

They entered the shabby brick building. Tony said nothing. His eyes once wild and haunted were veiled and numb. He listened to the policemen's chatter as the sound of their boots echoed along the polished parquet floor, scratched and pitted with scars from numerous steel tips on heels.

Tony fleetingly remembered this sound of steel tips on concrete, and a yawning chasm of emptiness cried out inside him to be filled. He just couldn't hold on to all the memories. They were as elusive as footprints in the sand when the tide was rising and edging into shore.

They took a right and followed the corridor to individual hospital cells adjoining a male schizophrenic ward. Tony obediently allowed himself to be led into a room and examined by one of the resident physicians.

The voices of those around him surged in and out like the ripples on the waves of an ebb tide. Odd words rose to a crescendo whilst others diminished into nothingness but still kept time with the pulsating rhythm inside his head. The walls around the male ward were lined with chairs and an occasional table as if set for a school dance. The pitiful collection of patients did not even turn to stare when Tony scraped in. He sat aloof and alone at a table where a plastic chess set was laid out. A frown twisted across his still handsome face. He deftly rearranged the pieces that were to him irritating; set as they were with the board the wrong way round.

A tall, smartly dressed man with glittering, searching eyes strode purposefully around the ward. He stopped at the table and the chess set and stared.

"Want a game?" asked Tony in his well modulated voice.

The man smartly stepped off once more on his marathon walk, an endless circuit of the ward. It was as if he had never heard, as if his march was the most important thing in the world and that nothing else mattered. Round and round he walked in complete isolation.

Tony's eyes followed this movement. He watched warily then let his eyes drift onto the countenances of the others in the ward. His gaze lingered briefly on the faces of the two male nurses sitting near the door to their station.

Consciously, he noted the jailer's keys on the belt of one nurse, the punch button control pad that guarded the entry to the observation room. He examined the exit, with two locks and electronic bolts top and bottom. This information was stored in his brain that was not yet without cunning.

He continued to scrutinise the faces of his fellow inmates. An elderly man, thin and bony with sparse hair and a domed head was shuffling around the room. He took small mincing steps. As he walked he seemed unable to keep his feet fitted inside his slippers, instead his heels trod down the inner sides of the shabby moccasins.

This character sported a large dewdrop on the end of his nose, which fast as it formed splashed intermittently on the wooden floor. He mumbled under his breath, swearing and cursing as he travelled around the room.

Tony didn't bother to ask him if he wanted a game.

Three chairs down sat an old benign looking gentleman. He wore a faded blue wool cardigan with the bottom button missing, who rolled his thumbs mechanically whilst peering short sightedly around.

Tony gave the old chap a nod and a half smile, but the old man didn't see well enough to acknowledge the gesture.

Minutes later the old fellow rose unsteadily to his feet. Tony could see the urine stained trousers that shouted incontinence to the rest of the ward. The gent hobbled towards Tony.

"George, George Harper," he introduced himself. "You're new aren't you?"

Tony inclined his head watching George all the while. Now that the man was closer Tony could smell the stale dried urine.

George made himself as comfortable as possible on the straight, hard backed chair with its padded seat. "Chess. Do you play?" he enquired. Tony acquiesced. "Can't see too well. Took me glasses when I came in here and I never got them back. But, I can see well enough to play," he prompted.

Tony's refined voice sounded out of place in this chamber of lost souls. "Would you like a game?" he responded.

George assented vigorously with his head, "Didn't catch your name?"

"Tony."

"Tony?"

"Just Tony."

"Tony it is then."

"Black or white?" asked Tony

"White, please."

"Your move then."

George moved Queen's Pawn to QP4. Tony mirrored the move. The game progressed quickly following the Piano Opening where each of white's moves was mimicked by black. They drifted in and out of conversation until the game became so interesting that the marathon man stopped to stare with his glittering eyes.

"Don't mind him," said George. "He can't see nor hear nothing."

"What do you mean?"

"Cut himself off from all his senses, just keeps on walking. Oh, it looks like he's interested in our game but he's not taking any of it in."

"Why's he here?" questioned Tony. 'What's wrong with him?"

"Gone over the edge?"

"Over the edge?"

"Nervous breakdown, I believe. He can't cope. He's locked in his own world. Sad really."

Tony thought for a moment how lovely that would be, to be able to cut himself off completely. Nothing could get at him then; not his mother, not anyone, not even Amy.

Amy… Her face popped into his mind, her pretty, smiling face and gentle eyes. Tony wanted to cry. And cry he did; long, shuddering, uncontrollable sobs that were wrenched from his heart. He struggled to remember why he was in this place. He couldn't. He battled with a thousand memories jumbling together making a nonsensical collage of events in his mind; his mother's face, her scarf, her pudgy hands, the violence of a storm, claret shoes and a raven haired beauty called… called… "I can't remember," he whispered.

George put out his wrinkled hand, brown with liver spots and tried to comfort his chess partner. "Just got to you has it?" he croaked, "I've been 'ere fifty-three years."

Tony's heartrending sobs were stilled.

"I know," George continued. "Shocking ain't it? Left here to rot, completely forgotten. No one can remember why I'm here now, not even me. I must have done something at sometime but my notes have gone and I'm damned if I can remember."

The images continued tumbling around Tony's mind and he took in a breath ready for the scream of anguish that was never to pass his lips. A silent scream that registered on his face and manifested itself inside his brain. Steel doors came slamming down, effectively locking and sealing those memories in that part of his brain. Tony sat hunched and still, his face a haunted mask of horror.

George leaned forward. He poked a finger at the Shuffler. "Steer clear of that one," he warned. "Oh, he looks harmless enough but he has these violent outbursts, he'll attack for no reason, just breaks out and leaves people reeling as if broken glass has been flying about. He has a habit of using anything that's sharp. He hides it and uses it. Even though there are regular searches he sometimes manages to filch something. Once it was a razor blade. Cor what a mess there was that time. One of the nurses got his face slashed. I lost the top of me finger." George held up his left hand. The top of his middle finger was missing. Tony stared, his eyes unblinking and unseeing.

George believing he had a captive audience continued, "See that young lad over there."

Tony's eyes followed the movement of that crooked finger.

"He's out of it. Just sits there all day long, does nothing. Sometimes he sits and rocks like he's doing now as if he's listening to some inner music. He can't do nothing for himself. They even have to feed him."

Tony watched the boy's rhythmic rocking, the motion seemed soothing, comforting, calming.

The nurses came rushing across, as the ward was filled

with the most terrible inhuman scream wrenched from the belly of hell itself. The agonised cry culminated in a splintering crash where the table was cleaved in two and the chess set was sent flying, swept away in the anger and hate that had been threatening to erupt and had now overflowed.

Tony stood outside himself and watched. He saw himself being physically restrained; his back bent forward and low, his arm awkwardly forced up his spine and his head pushed down as he was manoeuvred crablike at a scuttling run into a padded cell.

He saw George let go of his bladder and the trickle of urine pool together on the floor where he stood white faced and frightened with his thumb in his mouth.

The schism in Tony's mind was complete.

*

Amy was at home watching the evening news. She heard the announcement that Tony had been arrested. Unable to listen to the full report she dashed from the room and locked herself in their bedroom. She buried her head in his pillow, finding the smell of his masculinity of little comfort and she sobbed. She didn't feel sorry for herself, but was crying at her loss. This she felt was worse than death, worse than if he had died.

She had always known that there was something wrong, something aberrant in his behaviour but he had charmed her, he had loved her and she felt that there was a well of goodness in him. And for this reason, Amy felt that she couldn't turn her back on him.

She had toyed with the idea of supporting him as his mother had suggested, providing him with alibis for the dates of the different attacks. Mentally she shook herself; she knew she couldn't do that. She wasn't a liar. She truly believed that Tony's best chance was good psychiatric help and then, maybe then, he would have an opportunity of returning to normal, whatever 'normal' was.

Amy hadn't come forward; she hadn't notified the police but there and then she decided that tomorrow she would talk to the detectives in charge of the investigation. She had their number. Her mother and father had pressed her to do this as had her friend Sheena. She knew that it was the right thing to do. But first, first she would call Tony's mother and explain her decision. And Amy being Amy felt she needed to do this face to face not in a cowardly fashion on the telephone.

*

Tony's unpredictable behaviour had startled and worried the medical staff at Rubery. They wished he'd been sent to All Saints hospital instead. Violence erupting in the ward had a detrimental effect on the other patients.

The panel of the four specially selected doctors constantly observed, tested, discussed and argued. Was Tony sane enough to stand trial or not? One moment he was childlike almost to the point of naivety, sometimes he was arrogant and calculating, and at other times he could be quite pleasant and charming. More than a Doctor Jekyll and Mr. Hyde character he appeared to be three different people.

The difficulty lay in deciding whether he was genuinely suffering from multiple personality syndrome or if he was clever enough to act and pretend. If he could convince them that he had three separate and distinct personalities then he could avoid a public trial and all that would have entailed including almost definite life imprisonment. Certainly hospitalisation in a secure unit would be preferable to incarceration in a hostile and overcrowded gaol.

"Gave me a nasty shock I can tell you," grumbled George. "Frightened me half to death."

"Sorry," Tony apologised.

"Do you often go off half cocked?"

"Not usually. Things just got to me that's all."

"I can understand why. It's oppressive enough here. Pushed around, watched, questioned, tested, medicated, sedated...."

As George's voice wittered on, his tone complaining one minute, absurdly grateful the next Tony stepped outside himself. He watched and observed. He looked carefully at the two male nurses in the ward. One, always one, seemed to be there in case of an emergency. Harry was short and stocky but powerfully built with long heavy arms that seemed to hang to his knees, making him ape, even gorilla-like in stature.

Tony had seen what those hands could do. He had seen them restrain the Shuffler when the man had burst out. He had seen the bruises left by those spatulate fingers.

"Course folk out there don't realise what goes on in a place like this. How some people get their personalities taken away from them. Robbed. That's what they are. They don't know who they are."

Tony was feigning interest but continued his examination of the ward. Mentally he ran through the daily routine. The drugs trolley came round four times a day; at breakfast time, lunchtime, early evening and last thing at night. Duty staff were vigilant in the day but less so on the late night shift. The late night drug round usually found the nurses at their station and the drugs trolley manned just by the one nurse.

"I've seen people come in and forget who they are. Electric shock treatment can cause more problems than it helps," said George.

Tony appearing to be listening, he nodded his head periodically and encouraged George to keep chatting.

There were bars on the window. The fire exit he knew was the other side of the Nurses' Station and led outside to a black iron staircase that travelled down the side of the building. A punch button computer panel was on the door to this room.

"I've seen folk come and go. I've seen them stay. Shuffler, now he's been here ten or twelve years now, I can't remember exactly."

Tony looked at the doors to the entrance and more importantly the exit of the ward, again. The locks needed two different keys although he'd overheard that one of the nurses had a master key to all the doors in that wing of the building. He needed to find out whom.

"There are times when you get treated well." George lowered his voice confidentially, "Inspections and such like, get treated like royalty then. Course it doesn't last."

Tony raised an eyebrow, "How do they cope? With visitors and so on, on those occasions?"

204

"They cope," said George matter of factly, "They always do."

A wail echoed through the ward. The nurses were on their feet. Shuffler was having one of his attacks. Tony watched. He saw the man restrained and injected. The Shuffler fell limply to the floor and was dragged out into a side room. He tried to memorise the punch buttons on the pad but they were hit too quickly, but he did get the first number, it was three.

*

Mark Stringer was more relaxed. With the serial killer safely in custody, he would have more time for his family. Debbie had been having a bad time of it lately. Catherine was not sleeping properly due to a bad cold and teething. Debs had complained about feeling cut off and isolated, being at home all day with the children. She was longing for some adult conversation, not the constant chat about babies and toddlers that she got from the health visitor and other mums at the baby and toddler group. Mark resolved to book Jean to baby-sit one evening and to take Debbie out for a romantic candlelit supper. Somewhere swish, where they could enjoy being together. He wanted to revive that spark of fire, which before had been ever present in her eyes, but had now, somehow dulled with tiredness from housework and disturbed nights. The light in Debbie's eyes could penetrate his soul and arouse in him the deepest longing and love.

He temporarily ignored the sheaf of papers on his desk and enjoyed his moment of daydreaming. Now the excitement had settled down, it was back to the endless lists of burglary, car thefts and muggings.

The telephone bell shrilled him to attention, "Stringer," as Mark listened, his expression changed. He swore in exasperation, rose from his chair and grabbed his coat. He didn't wait for Allison's gruff instruction to enter, but knocked and went straight in.

Allison raised his eyebrows.

"Vencat, Chief!"

"What now?" growled Allison.

"Done a runner. He was transferring from the

overcrowded remand wing at Winson Green and bolted! Looks like it was pre-organised."

"I'm with you." Allison grunted as he hauled himself out of his chair. He slid open his top drawer, took his Mars Bar and slipped it into his jacket pocket before reaching for his coat. "You drive."

Allison's face was set in grim determination as he and Mark made their way down the corridor and out of the building.

Allison's voice drifted out into the fresh spring morning, "Preliminaries dealt with?"

"Road blocks, airport watch and the docks. He couldn't have got out of the country that quickly."

Their voices became fainter as they disappeared around the back of the building and out of sight.

*

Rebecca Mills stood coolly the other side of the two-way mirror watching Tony in interview with the prison's chief psychiatrist, Jeff Daniels. She watched Tony complete a series of visual tests. He seemed relaxed and responded to Jeff's questions with ease.

Rebecca turned to the other doctor, James Bingham, who was sitting with her and Brady on the panel to judge Tony's suitability to stand trial.

"This isn't the Tony I remember. He seems far too confident almost as if he's wiped out all memory of what he's done. He's certainly not admitting to anything."

"He's answered all Jeff's questions quite competently and his explanations to the maze problems are well reasoned and carefully thought out," said Bingham.

"Mmm," Rebecca pressed her lips together and breathed heavily through her nose. "He's being too clever by half. The Tony I knew was quite shy and in terrible turmoil. This Tony has arrogance and appears to have erased everything to do with the murders from his mind."

"What are you saying, Beccy?"

"Rebecca," she corrected icily.

"Rebecca," James Bingham affirmed apologetically.

"I wonder whether this is the proof that we're not dealing

with a severe personality disorder but definitely something more...." she hesitated slightly, "I think I agree with Brady. It's possible multiple personality syndrome. He's displaying two, possibly three distinctly different personalities. At least, that's what I feel."

"We've argued this before ... the police won't like it," said James. "They want us to attest that he's of sound mind, aware of his deeds and fit to stand trial. The press and public are demanding his blood."

"Look!" interrupted Dr Mills. "Look at him now!"

Tony's face had undergone a subtle change. Gone was the arrogant confidence, replaced by timidity. Tony's whole persona was one of childlike innocence. The two doctors watched and listened closely.

Jeff Daniels asked his question again, "I asked about your mother, Tony. What would she say?"

"Don't tell Mum. She'll be cross," he pleaded.

"Why will she be cross?"

"Please don't, I'll have to learn my Bible. Genesis, Exodus, Leviticus, Numbers, Deuteronomy, Joshua, Judges ... .Judges..." he faltered, "...Judges, Ruth, Samuel One, Samuel Two. ..."

"Why are you reciting the books of the Old Testament, Tony?"

"I have to know them all; all of them or I'll be in trouble. I'll need cleansing." Tony's face puckered. He averted his eyes and started to play with a loose thread on the sleeve of his jumper that had caught his attention.

"What do you mean, cleansing?"

"I can't tell you. It's wrong, although the priest said it was right. I feel it's wrong. God knows it's wrong. That's why I'm a Jonah. That's what mother said."

"What do you think he's up to?" whispered James Bingham as he watched the interview.

"Nothing, I think that under pressure he reverts to his real self."

"What? Evidence of multiple personality syndrome?"

"How else do you explain it? The sudden changes facially, vocally?" came the riposte.

James Bingham smirked, as was his habit when he felt uncomfortable. Rebecca Mills pounced on this. "What's so funny?" she demanded.

"Nothing, I just wonder if we're underestimating him."

"Underestimating him?"

"Yes. Have you thought that this might all be a game to him? That he might simply have everyone fooled."

Tony started to giggle, "She's a little teapot short and stout."

"Who Tony? Who's a little teapot?" probed Dr. Daniels. "Do you mean your mother?"

"Mother." The plaintive voice whimpered, his face looked crestfallen but behind his eyes he watched. He watched the roller ball pen smoothly committing his words to paper. He saw the mirror on his right that disguised the hidden observers. He rejoiced inside. This was going to be so easy, so very easy. Mother would be proud.

*

Mrs. Clifton was feverishly cleaning her house from top to bottom. An act intended to rid her of the defilement of the police invasion into her home. She felt degraded by their intrusion, as they pawed through her possessions, examining her things, her intimate things, and searching Tony's room, rummaging through his wardrobe and removing his clothing and his few remaining belongings. But she felt safe, safe that her secrets would never come to light. Oh, she had them all fooled! A poor, pathetic, misunderstood, old woman was how they viewed her.

She sang lustily as she worked, her voice cracking on the high notes of Jerusalem.

Such was the assault on her privacy that she felt a need to shower and bathe seven times, as Na'aman the Syrian had done in the famous River Jordan, to rid himself of his leprosy. She had scrubbed her skin with such force that it had bled profusely, but she needed to bleed to cleanse herself from this sacrilegious attack on her home.

Her strident voice echoed around the house, quavering through a repertoire of hymns and psalms, her eyes burning with a feral light as her lips praised the Lord.

She wiped her hands on her overall and marched ceremoniously to the carved wooden box and removed a tiny scroll.

"Your eye shall not pity;
It shall be life for life
Eye for eye, tooth for tooth,
Hand for hand, foot for foot."
Deuteronomy Chapter twenty, verse twenty-one.

She raised the scroll aloft so that Christ's eyes could bless the scripture and with a histrionic glee she offered words of comfort to herself, *"Vengeance is mine, sayeth the Lord."*

She parted her naked lips, pledged to be devoid of colour until the great wrong was righted and selected a roomy canvas bag from the cupboard at the foot of the stairs.

She strode purposefully to the dresser and opened the cutlery drawer. She spent some time deliberating over the keenness of her carving knife blades and selected a particularly wicked looking one that would be more than effective for her purpose. She sharpened it against the steel in accompaniment to 'Fight the good Fight', before she tested it lightly against the paper scroll. It cut cleanly and effortlessly and the two halves of the scroll fluttered to the floor. Satisfied she placed the knife in the canvas bag.

It was all crystal clear to her now. Tony's mission in the world was being given to her.

The phone rang three times and clicked off as the answering machine whirred into life. Tony's modulated tones reverberated in the room around her.

"Hi! Tony Clifton speaking." She pulled on her woollen hat, "I'm sorry I'm not at home right now." She buttoned her shabby coat up to the neck, "But, if you'd like to leave your name, number and or message," She tied her Isadora scarf around her throat. "I'll get back to you as soon as I can." Mrs. Clifton picked up her small case and bag.

An official voice added, "Please speak clearly after the tone."

Grace Clifton started to open the sitting room door as the tone beeped out. She looked around. The room the lights were off as was the television and radio. The incense sticks and candles were doused. Everything was switched off and secure.

"Hello, Mrs. Clifton," stuttered a voice, "It's Amy. Sorry, ...I'm just a bit unnerved hearing Tony's message. Listen, I've thought about what you said and need to speak to you. I'll be at the Ivy Bush at two o' clock this afternoon, if you could meet me. If not, call me at home. ... You've got the number. Bye."

Mrs. Clifton pulled back her lips, and sighed, Amy, dear sweet Amy. If she wouldn't be her disciple then she'd have no use for her. What a pity!

She patted her pocket housing Sandra Thornton's address that she'd so cleverly managed to get and looked around the room. It would be about a week before she was back. She looked at her watch. Ten-to-one. She had to leave. After all she'd got Tony's work to do.

Amy would be first.

Lightning Source UK Ltd.
Milton Keynes UK
UKHW04f0014130918
328781UK00001B/19/P